Butterfly

www.violetgregory.com

Butterfly

VIOLET GREGORY

First published 2013 by Grayson Magic Publishing Ltd

First edition – December 2013
Revised edition – March 2020

Grayson Magic Publishing Ltd, Waipu, New Zealand

ISBN 978-0-9922638-1-2

ACKNOWLEDGEMENTS

Thanks to Mikhail Grafik for your kind permission to use the beautiful photo on the cover of this book.

Thanks to Beth, for psycho-analyzing my characters; Morag, for your ruthless use of red pen on my first draft; Karen, for your careful and thoughtful proof-reading and editing; and Niel for always being willing to listen and offer your ideas. I love you all.

One

If you had told me when I married Hugh Fraser less than a year ago that I wouldn't know who the father of our first child was, I would never have believed you. And if you'd told me the first person I'd confide in would be my mother, I would have said you were crazy. Before my wedding, I hadn't spoken to her in fifteen years.

It was only after I got married myself that I discovered how easy it was to be seduced by a handsome stranger. And it was only then that I started to realize how wrong I'd been about my mother. In fact, I soon realized how wrong I'd been about a lot of people – including my new husband and my best friend, Willa van Krevelen.

The first thing that happened was at the opening of my Basalt Meets Pacific exhibition at the WVK Gallery in Auckland. I was hiding out in a dark corner near Willa's office, trying to avoid movement of any sort. My head spun from the roar of conversation around me – and an additional roaring noise that seemed to be coming from inside my head. It was hot. Sticky hot. I was melting just standing there. I pitied the wait staff, sweltering in their long-sleeved jackets as they squeezed their way through the crowd bearing trays of rice-paper wraps, mini bagels, polenta cakes and other delicacies. It was a pointless exercise. Most of the food was coming back uneaten, everything limp and wilted. It was too hot to eat.

I glanced at the master catalog on the sales table. There were still only three red stickers on it. I knew Willa had put a lot of effort into the opening, but I couldn't help thinking of my previous show in New York. The air conditioning had been working. Guests had pursued the wait staff enthusiastically for more of the delicious hors d'oeuvres. And all of my paintings had sold within an hour.

Suddenly, Willa was in front of me, taking my arm and pulling me out of my corner. "Georgia, you need to mingle a bit, babe," she commanded. "Come on, I'll take you around."

Willa strode ahead of me, tall and imposing. She was wearing a sateen pantsuit in a vivid moss green that matched her eyes. Her mane of strawberry-blonde curls cascaded, wild and loose, down her back, turning heads as I tagged along behind. It took all of my attention to keep up with her, hobbled as I was by my tight skirt and unfamiliarly high heels. Willa's stylist had chosen the deep violet satin evening dress and the Edwardian-style lace-up shoes. She'd done my make-up too, and my face was stiff and prickly under all that powder. I had to keep remembering not to touch my eyes and smear mascara everywhere. I'd also been attacked by Willa's hairdresser. He'd piled my dark liquorice-brown hair on top of my head in a style he called 'casual disarray' with something that resembled mangled chopsticks. I thought it looked more like a bird's nest, and it made me feel fragile and off-balance, as if the hair – and I – could come unraveled at any moment. As it turned out, that's exactly what happened.

My careful efforts to avoid getting sucked into the mass of strangers were hopelessly undone as Willa dragged me through the crowd like a stray puppy she was trying to find a home for. I hoped she wasn't expecting me to remember all these people. There was a merchant banker whose name started with A and who had large sweaty palms and a wife called Flo. Numerous gay couples with proper British-sounding names like Jeremy and Quentin, Hamish and Nigel. Jessica Tanner and Tiki Te Wai something or other, dressed in trilby hats, skinny jeans and matching tie-dyed T-shirts, were other artists represented by Willa. Helen Jennings and her mother Margaret (or was it Margaret and her mother Helen?) wafted scents of rose and lavender and invited me over to dinner with Hugh, telling me proudly that their family had been friends with the Frasers for five generations. Albert Wong from Hugh's work – balding, bespectacled and earnest – said what a shame it was that Hugh was stuck on his court case in Wellington for another week.

Every time someone mentioned Hugh, I felt a pang of desolation. If he were here, I'd be able to count on his easy manner and natural charm to do all the chatting instead of having to flounder through conversations with strangers on my own. If he were beside me, I'd have his tall, strong presence to lean on instead of having to rely on my dubious sense of balance and a pair of heels at least twice as high as I was accustomed to wearing. But, most of all, if Hugh were not stuck in Wellington, I'd have his warm, sexy body and succulent mouth to look forward to losing myself in after the opening instead of going home to spend another night alone in our dilapidated house. I grabbed a glass of wine and took a big gulp before I turned dutifully to follow Willa again, but she'd disappeared. Instead, I stumbled into a couple who'd been standing behind me. The man grabbed my elbow to steady me and I blushed furiously. It was Hugh's father, the High Court judge John Fraser.

"Sorry," I muttered as John and his wife Francesca kissed me in greeting, politely ignoring my clumsiness. I hugged them back awkwardly, trying not to smear lipstick all over them or get my hair tangled up in Fran's earrings.

"Georgia, you look lovely," gushed Fran, stepping back to examine me. "Doesn't she, Sera? Look at this lovely dress, Sera."

My heart sank when Hugh's younger sister Seraphina emerged from behind her mother. She gave me a sulky glance before replying, "Yeah, it's one of Sophie's current collection."

Damn! I knew I should have insisted the stylist choose one of Sera's designs. But the woman was so bossy – and I had to admit there was nothing in Sera's range that looked remotely as good on me as the dress I was wearing. Sera's designs and I just didn't go together.

To her credit, Francesca recognized her faux-pas and tried to correct it immediately. She turned to the paintings. "Georgia, these are wonderful," she enthused. "I'm amazed that you've captured the essence of our country so well when you've only spent such a short time here. We've been holidaying at Piha beach for nearly forty years and you've managed to paint it in an entirely new light for me ..."

"Yes, it's really ... impressive, Georgia," added John. I knew that he was trying to be kind. I could tell he wasn't used to giving his opinion on art, and he was struggling to find something appropriate to say without appearing disinterested or showing up his ignorance. It was the kind of thing my father would have done if he'd still been alive. A lump rose in my throat.

"I'd never seen the ocean before I came to New Zealand," I said quietly, changing the subject so I wouldn't cry. My mind drifted back to my honeymoon at Piha beach, an hour west of Auckland city. The sight of all that endless water, twisting and moving like a living creature under its black skin; the way it pounded and surged up the sand, sucked under, retreated, pounded, surged, again and again and again; the way the seaweed cascaded about the rocks as if it were strands of hair being tossed about. It had filled me with energy and passions I wasn't even aware I had. Then I thought of the twisting, turning, pounding, sucking and surging I had done there with Hugh on the edge of the ocean ...

Heat rose to my cheeks. I was standing in front of Hugh's parents, daydreaming about doing some very rude things with their son. I blinked and tried to focus on what Fran was saying.

"John and I can't stay long tonight, Georgia, but Sera's going out with a few friends later – perhaps you could join them, since Hugh isn't here ..."

"No!" I caught a glimpse of the savage glare Sera was aiming at her mother before she twisted her mouth into a sweet little smile. "Sorry, I meant, no, we're not going out."

"Oh?" Francesca frowned, puzzled. "I thought I heard TJ say he was taking you and some of the girls out to a club later. Never mind," she said, patting my arm. "We'll check with him when he gets back from the bar."

Sometimes I wonder what would have happened if I'd met TJ in the gallery that night, rather than a month later in very different circumstances. But, as was so often the case, Willa's intervention helped determine my fate when she appeared again at my side.

After acknowledging the Frasers with hugs and kisses, she apologized for interrupting and put her arm around my waist. "One of my clients would like to meet Georgia," she smiled. "He's bought three of her works tonight, including this one." She gestured towards one of my favorites, a triptych depicting the story of Erangi, who swam with her baby through the dangerous seas near Piha to be with her lover. A small burst of smugness overtook me as I followed Willa to the other side of the room, leaving Sera gaping open-mouthed at the twenty-thousand-dollar price tag on the triptych, then at me.

My mind drifted again to Hugh as I tottered along after Willa. I pictured him in his hotel room, freshly showered after a run along the harbor to relax after his long day in court. He'd be wearing only his underwear, or perhaps nothing at all. I imagined wrapping my arms around him; and smooching my face against his silky chest like a cat laying claim to its owner. He'd run his hands into my hair, tugging it gently, tilting my face up to his so he could kiss me ...

I was dimly aware of Willa speaking, but I was so engrossed in my daydream that I only heard the end of her introduction, "... and this is Georgia Daniels."

I looked up and was startled to find myself staring into a pair of aquamarine eyes as penetrating as they were dazzling. They belonged to a tall blond man in his forties, who gave me an appreciative smile. Still in my trance, I didn't notice at first the sensual curve of his lips, his aristocratic aquiline nose and his immaculately tailored charcoal-gray suit. He extended a long, well-manicured hand and I reached out automatically to shake it.

It was only when his fingers made contact with mine that I was jolted to attention by a current that fair sizzled through me. It was as though I was a plasma globe and his hand the conducting object that caused the filaments to rush to the edges of my sphere. If my hair hadn't been so constrained in its crazy arrangement, I wouldn't have been surprised if it had stood on end.

"I'm s–s–sorry," I stuttered. "I didn't catch your name."

"Xavier Bishop," he purred, still smiling lazily. He seemed in no hurry to release my hand, which remained in his like a scrap of metal stuck helplessly to an electromagnet. An image flashed through my mind, so fast I couldn't say what it was – like a single frame inserted into a music video to disturb the sequence. It seemed like something I wasn't supposed to see, and it made me feel distinctly ill at ease.

"So you're Hugh's wife ..." he mused, finally letting go of my hand. I pulled it back close to my body and pressed the palm against my wine glass to cool it. He contemplated me as if I were one of the paintings on display. "Very nice. Veery nice indeed. I can see now why he was in no hurry to leave New York."

I shivered. The way this man looked at me made me want to put on extra clothing. Or maybe take it off, I realized with alarm. "Er, how do you know Hugh, Mr Bishop?" I enquired, hoping he wouldn't hear the tremor in my voice.

"Call me Xavier, please." I couldn't figure out why his perfectly civil suggestion should make me feel faint and dizzy. There was that image again, vanishing before I could identify it. "Hugh and I go way back," he carried on. "Are you sure he's never told you about me?" The way he narrowed his eyes suspiciously made me squirm – even though I had nothing to hide. He didn't seem to notice that I failed to reply – he kept right on talking while I tried to focus on what he was saying through the rushing in my ears.

"What have you done with him, anyway?" he demanded. "Willa tells me the two of you have been in the country nearly two months now and I haven't seen him once." He looked at me in that way again, like he could read my thoughts and knew exactly what I'd been doing with Hugh.

I finally found my voice, although it came out an octave higher than usual and oddly formal. "Unfortunately, Hugh is stuck in Wellington on business," I said. "Shall I pass on your regards to him?"

Damn, now I was thinking of Hugh again – naked in his hotel room. I tried desperately to catch Willa's eye, hoping she would notice my distress and take over the conversation. But just as I thought she'd got the message, a portly man in a red bowtie patted her on the arm and she turned to speak to him.

Xavier's eyes were still on me, and he was still talking in his velvet voice. "Yes, please do say hello to him for me," he said. "In fact, why don't I come over for dinner one night when he gets back? Has he still got the old place in Herne Bay?"

I wasn't sure what was more alarming – the thought of cooking dinner or the idea that Xavier Bishop knew where I lived. I stood there like a deer in the headlights of a truck. The way this guy looked and talked suggested he was someone important. I racked my brains, trying to remember if I'd ever heard Hugh mention him. It wasn't as if Xavier was a common name. Nothing came to mind as I gazed, mesmerized, into the liquid crystal of his eyes – except another of those subliminal images. Was it rope? Why would Xavier Bishop make me think of rope?

"I'm sorry," I babbled. I still hadn't come up with a suitable response that didn't involve inviting Xavier

Bishop into my home or cooking for him. "Would you excuse me for a few moments? I need a bit of air."

Without waiting for an answer, I fled into the crowd and slipped out through the first doorway I came across.

TWO

I found myself in a short corridor. Willa's office was on my right. A little further along, the corridor swung off to the left. I headed down to the end and through a second door into the storeroom beyond. With two doors between me and the main gallery, the noise of the crowd had dwindled to nothing. The only sound was the quiet hum of the air conditioning system, which was working perfectly in here. I stood there taking in deep gulps of cool air until my heart stopped pounding at two hundred beats per minute.

My first thought was that Willa would be furious with me. One of her most important clients had spent over thirty thousand dollars on three of my paintings and I'd walked off and left him there. I knew I should go back out and apologize – it wasn't as though others were queuing up to buy my work. But another part of my mind told me to stay hidden here until long after Xavier Bishop had disappeared. That was the part with the 'DANGER' tape and the flashing red lights around it.

I browsed the racks of paintings and prints quietly, unable to decide what to do. The smell of paper, canvas, ink and paint felt familiar and homely to me. The storage racks were like old friends, waiting for me to sit down and have a coffee with them. I noticed work by both Jessica and Tiki, and told myself I should have made more of an effort to chat to them when Willa had introduced us. She'd been telling me I needed to make some friends in Auckland.

When my mind seemed to be functioning normally again, I hesitated by the door. I couldn't stay in here all night. But what if he was still out there? I closed my eyes and did a few of my favorite yoga breathing exercises, then slipped back out into the corridor. The noise from the gallery rose to a distant hum. Concentrating on my breathing, I walked slowly to the bend in the corridor. To my right was the gallery and the possibility of bumping into Xavier Bishop again. I knew I was procrastinating, but I turned to check my reflection in a large gilt-framed mirror that was leaning against the wall to my left.

More accustomed to seeing myself in a paint-stained T-shirt and jeans or cut-offs, the image of the poised young woman dressed in lustrous satin startled me. Wow, I thought. It was kind of Jonsu from Indica meets Lucy Honeychurch in *A Room with a View*. Maybe I should do a self-portrait like this. I rotated slowly, twisting my head to look at the back of the dress in the mirror. From behind, it could have been a vintage garment – the bodice laced with a ribbon that criss-crossed right down my back to the top of my behind, sweeping into an elegant bias-cut skirt that cascaded to the floor in a fishtail. The train at the rear swept up from the sides to reveal a tight-fitting tube of a skirt underneath, so the front of the dress appeared short when I faced the mirror again. Tiny cap sleeves skimmed my bare shoulders and the whole thing closed provocatively down the front with corset-style hooks and eyes. The top one had been left open to reveal a glimpse of cleavage I didn't know I had. Willa's stylist really had done a good job. And, despite the discomfort I'd suffered all evening, the shoes, hairstyle and make-up were a perfect match for the dress.

Before I went back into the gallery, I fingered the velvet choker around my neck. The delicate silver filigree butterfly attached to it had been a gift from Hugh, and I was glad to be wearing it that evening. I told myself it was a talisman that would prevent any harm coming to me. I couldn't have been more wrong.

While I was still standing in front of the mirror, I was aware of the door to the gallery opening. There was a flash of light and a rush of warm, sticky air wafted in. Along with it came a wave of chatter, which abated again when the door swung shut. In the dim light, I saw that a man had appeared in the mirror behind me. He was very tall, towering above me even in my heels. At first I thought I must have imagined it, like the fleeting images I hadn't managed to identify earlier. I gulped when I recognized his narrow, angular face and short white-blond hair, spiky on top. As our gazes met in the mirror, Xavier Bishop's glittering turquoise eyes froze me with an indefinable expression – was it anger?

I continued to stare, transfixed, while he moved towards me. I shut my eyes, hoping that when I opened them I'd wake up and he would be gone. I abandoned that hope when I felt the heat from his body close behind me, not quite touching me. My eyes widened in the mirror when he gently fingered a tendril of my hair. My own breathing stopped as he exhaled close to my ear, "What have we here? Hugh Fraser's wife, all alone – waiting for someone perhaps?"

I don't know if it was his warm malt breath on my ear or the faint movement of my hair against my cheek as he touched the loose curl, but at that moment my sense of reality was suspended. The scene in the mirror became a movie or a play I was watching, rather than something I was participating in. I wished I had a camera or a sketchbook. Since neither was at hand, I determined to commit the images to memory. I'd moved on from the self-portrait idea and was already imagining a series of paintings involving mirrors, figures in suits and evening dresses.

Xavier softly released the lock of my hair. He ran his finger down to the crook of my elbow and then back to my upper arm. He was barely touching my skin, but my blood charged to the surface as his finger moved along it like a magic wand. He simultaneously moved his other hand up my arm from my wrist, tracing the faintest line until both his hands were resting ever so lightly a little below my shoulders. The buzzing warmth of his touch grew into a burning sensation as he tightened his grip. He rotated me gently and moved himself so we were facing each other, the mirror on my left and the door to the gallery on my right.

He was so silent and shadowy that it was easy to believe I was a spectator and not one of the characters in this little tableau. The only thing that seemed real was the sharp, sweet scent of caramelized apples and molasses on his breath – like the cider my father used to make. I closed my eyes and inhaled deeply. There was something intrinsically warm, safe and comforting about the combination of the two smells. It lulled me into ignoring the danger signals. I was like a driver in a car chase, speeding madly through all the barriers, the warning lights and the roadworks signs designed to prevent me from plunging headlong over a cliff into the sea.

Xavier ran his hands down my front, skimming my breasts and hips. He slid his hands under the train of my dress and gripped my behind through the short, tight underskirt. He explored my buttocks as if he were handling a piece of fruit to test its succulence before consuming it. "Nice ass, Mrs Fraser," he whispered, "as

I was about to say before you disappeared so suddenly."

He stepped forward and pressed me into the wall. Out of the corner of my eye, I noticed the woman in the mirror arch backward. "Veery nice," he continued, curving the entire length of his body against mine as he leaned forward to murmur into my ear. In a trance, I turned my head to better observe what was happening in the mirror. I didn't connect the wide-eyed, wild-haired young woman who stared back at me with myself. She was simply an interesting model posing for my next painting. *Click* went the shutter behind my eyes, storing the image. I tilted my head, exposing one long side of my neck and Xavier accepted the offering, gently exploring the area from my ear to my shoulder with warm, dry lips. *Click* went my internal shutter again. *Click. Click. Click.*

When I closed my eyes, it was easy to imagine that the man nuzzling my neck and fondling my buttocks was Hugh. It reminded me of the night he had first kissed me – in a dark corner like this one, causing the buzz and chatter of the surrounding party to fade into oblivion. Hugh had kissed every exposed inch of my face, neck and arms that night at the party, and he'd explored every curve and hollow of the rest of my body in fine detail later at his apartment. In a single night, he had done something no other man had ever managed to do with me. He'd found the switch labeled WANT and turned it on. When I'd opened my eyes the next morning, it had been with the strange sensation that I was both waking from and entering into a dream.

Standing in front of the mirror with Xavier Bishop, I was in that dream once again. I glanced at the glass to observe the awakening playing out in front of me. Then I froze. Something wasn't right. We were being watched. Silhouetted in the half-open doorway that led back out to the gallery was a tall, dark-haired man, leaning casually against the door frame with his hands in his pockets. His posture looked vaguely familiar, but with the light behind him it was impossible to distinguish the features of his face. *Click*.

Xavier sensed my tension beneath his hands and followed my gaze to the doorway. *Click*. To my astonishment, rather than releasing me, he tightened his grip. *Click*. He stared brazenly at the man in the doorway and flicked open a few of the hooks at the bottom of my dress. *Click*. He ran his hand inside, above my stocking tops. *Click*. He brushed his lips languidly across the top of my breasts and up the other side of my neck as his hand burned along my bare thigh. *Click.*

My legs were suddenly weak and my heart raced madly. A warm, throbbing ache had formed deep in my belly and it was spreading to my groin. A faint thought crept into my consciousness that perhaps it was not a good idea to allow Xavier Bishop's hands and mouth such liberal access to my bare skin. Each time his molasses-flavored lips scorched a new spot on my neck, each time his long, elegant fingers ignited a trail on the exposed skin between the top of my leg and the top of my stockings, my ability to stop him ebbed further and further away. I had officially crashed through the last roadblock and was now flying off the edge of the cliff in my out-of-control car.

A shriek from the gallery slammed the door between reality and the dream. "Hugh!" It was Sera. The man in the doorway whirled and walked off into the gallery towards the sound of Sera's excited voice. It hit me like a gunshot. *Hugh? Hugh* had been watching us? But Hugh was in Wellington – wasn't he?

The door swung shut again and we were plunged into a muffled silence and semi-darkness once more. The warm pulse in my belly had turned into a bucket of ice. My skin that had moments earlier sizzled under

Xavier Bishop's caresses was numb. I struggled to escape, but he held me still. "Not so fast, Mrs Fraser," he murmured. "I haven't finished with you yet."

"Let me go!" I hissed, trying to wriggle out of his grasp. My efforts were no more effective than those of a butterfly fluttering helplessly against its captor's net. *Click. Click. Click.*

"What's the matter Mrs Fraser," he breathed in my ear. "Only fun when you have an audience?"

"What?" I gasped. "Do you really think ...?" My voice trailed off in alarm. A faint, warm pulse was returning to my paralyzed limbs and I couldn't be sure whether it was caused by his fingers continuing to trickle over my exposed thigh or the no longer subliminal images rushing through my mind as a result of his lewd suggestion.

The gallery door opened and we were center stage in a dazzle of light. "Georgia? Xavier! What the fuck is going on here?" It was Willa.

Xavier stepped away from me, withdrawing his hand casually from my dress and putting it in his pocket. I shivered as the skin on my thigh protested its absence with a wave of goose bumps. "Just getting to know the artist a little better, Willa," he smirked.

Willa gave him a hostile stare. His lips remained curled in a sly smile, but he gave a mock bow of acquiescence and skirted past Willa. "I'll leave you two ladies to it then, shall I? Don't forget that dinner invitation, Georgia," he called over his shoulder as he retreated back into the gallery, the door shutting behind him.

I stared bleakly at Willa. "Oh, Willa, tell me I was dreaming. Tell me that he didn't actually have his hand up my dress ..." Willa shook her head as I continued, "and tell me that wasn't Hugh standing in the doorway?"

"Fuck," said Willa, biting her lip and looking at me. I couldn't tell if it was anger or sympathy in her green cat's eyes.

So it had been Hugh. Oh, God. Had Sera seen it too? His parents? What had I been thinking? Nothing, obviously. I slumped to the floor, not caring that my dress was still bunched up around my thighs and my stocking tops were fully exposed. Willa was still standing in the corridor opposite me, a grim look on her face. Her silence unnerved me.

"I'm sorry if I upset your client," I muttered.

Willa flapped her hand like it didn't matter. "I'm more concerned about you at the moment. And Hugh." Her tone was icy. I cringed. "What the hell was he playing at, Georgia?"

I tried asking myself the same question. I wasn't sure what I was more upset about – how easily I had let a stranger seduce me or the fact that Hugh hadn't rescued me. I had to see Hugh, although I had no idea what I was going to say to him. But I didn't want to go back into the gallery and risk bumping into Xavier Bishop again.

I looked up at Willa, who was still frowning at me, her arms folded. "Is Hugh out there, Wills?" I whispered. "Do you think you could get him to come in here?"

Willa's expression softened. "Yeah," she sighed. "I'll go take a look for you. Don't move."

As if I could. I was numb. Legs, arms, back, brain. Even my heart. Especially my heart. I tried to imagine the state of Hugh's heart at that moment. If mine was numb, he must surely feel as if he had no heart left. I mean, I'd stood there and let another man – a man who, apparently, was an old friend – touch me in a way that was clearly and utterly inappropriate.

What was worse, the images I'd committed to memory all came flooding back into my mind. I saw my head tilting to allow Xavier access to my neck. I saw my lips part and my eyes widen as his mouth skimmed across the top of my breasts. It must have looked like I was enjoying it. *Well?* said a little voice in my head. *You were enjoying it …*

I ignored the voice, allowing indignation to shout down my guilt. *What about Hugh, then?* I let a second voice interrupt. *Why didn't he stop Xavier Bishop? Why didn't he stop you? Isn't he as much to blame?*

I sat there for what seemed like hours, running things over and over in my mind before I was blinded once more by a blur of light. The door to the gallery opened and Willa swept into view. I was almost relieved to see she was alone. I still had no answers for myself, let alone any way of explaining my behavior to Hugh.

"He's not here," announced Willa, not sharing my relief. "I checked the gallery, the bathroom and outside. He seems to have vanished. Bishop's gone, too," she added, trying to reassure me. When I didn't reply, she squatted in front of me. "Hey," she said, patting my knee. "Maybe Hugh's already at home waiting for you.

Are you OK here for half an hour until I close up? I can give you a lift back to your place."

I nodded miserably and she disappeared again. I sat in the dim, silent corridor, mulling things over once more. I had a lot to be guilty about – much more than Hugh. Yet it bothered me that Hugh had stood by impassively and watched. And if Xavier Bishop really was a friend of Hugh's, why had he followed me? Touched me? When Willa returned, I asked her if she had any idea how Xavier and Hugh knew each other.

Willa frowned in concentration, trying to remember something. When she finally spoke, she sounded a little worried. "Georgia, I'm pretty sure Hugh used to work for Xavier. I don't know quite what happened, but I do recall he left rather abruptly. It was a big shock to everyone. Apparently he was doing really well there. Maybe Xavier Bishop isn't as much of a friend to Hugh as you think."

Maybe, I thought as I sat there in the corridor, my chin on my knees and my arms around my legs, trying to hold myself together. So many maybes. I only hoped her 'Maybe Hugh's already at home waiting for you' turned out to be true.

Three

I had overheard neighborhood children calling our place 'the haunted house' as they walked past it on their way to school. I'd never taken much notice before, but that's exactly what it looked like when Willa and I pulled up outside it in her VW shortly after 9:30 pm. Unlike the other homes in our street, which were all impeccably cared for by a host of painters, cleaners, gardeners and security companies whose signwritten vehicles announced their presence daily, our home looked like it hadn't been lived in for a century. The weatherboards were almost devoid of paint and two downstairs windows had been boarded up. Overgrown bushes in the front yard formed strange, shadowy figures with distorted, oversized hands and heads. Stuffing and springs poked out of an old sofa on the veranda, making it look like it might come alive at any moment. The only light came from the waning moon, recently risen above the harbor behind the house.

I looked at the dark, empty windows in despair, although I was hardly surprised. I still had my phone in my hand, and I felt around on the floor of the car for my bag so I could put it away. After leaving him five voice messages and about twenty texts, it was obvious that Hugh didn't want to talk to me. Willa had even contacted Sera, who said the last she'd seen of him he'd been heading back to the gallery after walking her to her car. At least she hadn't seen what had happened, I thought.

When we got inside, Willa sat me down in the dining area and busied herself making coffee. "Jesus, Georgia – you really ought to do something about this kitchen," she muttered. A cupboard door had nearly fallen off its hinges as she hunted about for coffee beans and now she was standing there looking at a drawer handle that had come off in her hand.

I glanced up at her miserably. How could she be hassling me about my kitchen at a time like this?

"Sorry," she said, noting my abject disinterest. "At least you have a decent coffee machine." She filled the machine with water and set it running, then leaned forward to look at me over the bench. Her tone was businesslike. "Right. Now, do you know anyone else who might know where Hugh is?"

I shook my head. I was sitting slumped at the kitchen table, listlessly tracing patterns in the old 1950s Formica with my finger. I didn't really know any of Hugh's friends yet. We'd arrived in the country a week before Christmas and, since we hadn't had a honeymoon when we'd married in July, had opted to spend our first month out at Piha beach. It had been bliss, but I'd been so absorbed in my painting and Hugh that I hadn't wanted any other company. And since Hugh had been back at work, he'd been out of town a lot and I'd been painting seven days a week in preparation for my show. Both of us had found the little free time we had together too precious to share with others.

"You're the only person I know apart from Hugh," I started saying to Willa, realizing how pathetic that made me sound. Then I trailed off, distracted by the light blinking on and off on the phone which sat on the corner of the kitchen counter. On. Off. On. Off. On ...

"Willa, the phone – there's a message!" I leapt up so abruptly that Willa nearly dropped the milk she had pulled out of the refrigerator. I grabbed the phone from its cradle. My fingers shook as I punched in the code to retrieve the message. Please, let it be Hugh, I muttered silently over and over to myself as I waited for the recording to play. I stood the phone on the table and set it to speaker so Willa could hear it too.

It was Madeleine Knight, Hugh's PA. "I'm trying to get hold of Hugh with some important information for the court session tomorrow. He's not answering his cell phone and I can't reach him at his hotel. So, I'm sorry to bother you, but I know he often, er, Skypes you in the evenings. So if you're talking to him, could you please ask him to call me urgently on my mobile. The number is ..."

I blushed when I heard Madeleine's pause before she mentioned the Skype calling. I didn't like the idea of his PA knowing – or even speculating – about the content of those calls.

"Great," said Willa, interrupting my thoughts. "Call her."

I hesitated. It was nearly ten o'clock. I wished I'd put a bit more effort into meeting Hugh's colleagues. It wasn't like he hadn't asked me enough times to go in and have lunch with him so he could introduce me to everyone. But when it came to a choice between staying at home and painting or meeting a bunch of strangers, the painting always won out. Madeleine only knew me as a voice on the phone, asking for Hugh or checking when he would be home from work. I always felt awkward when I spoke to her, like I was interrupting something important. And she always called me Mrs Fraser, too, which seemed weird – especially as I knew she was only a year or two younger than me.

As if she could read my mind, Willa sighed. "Look, Georgia, I know it's late and you don't know her all that well, but she's the only contact you have. That message was left just before six this evening – maybe she saw Hugh at the opening and knows where he went."

I stared at Willa. "Madeleine was at the gallery?" I whispered. It occurred to me that Madeleine would have had the advantage in recognizing me from the photo Hugh kept on his desk. I, on the other hand, had no idea what Madeleine looked like. I winced. "Did she ... did she see what happened?"

Willa thought for a moment. "I don't know," she said. "I only saw her briefly early on. At the moment, though, she's the only option you have for finding Hugh. Talk to her," she instructed, dialing the number. She handed me the receiver just as Madeleine picked up the phone. I fumbled and dropped it on the tabletop, pulling a face at Willa. She frowned and shoved the phone back into my hand. "Talk!" she mouthed.

"Hello? Hello?" a female voice snapped. "Who is this?"

"Oh. Um ... sorry. Hello? Is that Madeleine?" I began timidly.

"Yes. Who is this?"

I cringed at her irritated tone. "Er, it's Georgia Dan— Georgia Fraser," I said, feeling like I was about ten years old and in trouble with my teacher. "I'm, um, wondering if you've heard from Hugh this evening ..."

During the long pause that followed, I picked up a small padded bag that my latest book purchase from Amazon had arrived in that morning. One by one I squeezed each bubble until it burst. When she finally answered, her tone was almost accusatory. "No. Has he not contacted you yet tonight?"

"Er, I've only just got home." At least that bit was true, I thought as I paced up and down, trying to ignore Willa's mimed instructions, which I couldn't understand anyway. "I, um, thought I saw him at my exhibition opening. I guess he wanted to surprise me. But there were so many people. It's so stupid," I tried to laugh casually. "I kind of got distracted and lost sight of him." Her silence was unnerving. "I just thought ... maybe you'd know if he had a late flight back or ... what his plans were," I babbled.

After another long pause, during which I viciously popped more of the bubbles, Madeleine replied. Her voice was cold, as if I'd said something to offend her. "I didn't know Hugh was intending to be in Auckland tonight, Mrs Fraser. I didn't book any travel for him. I assumed he was in Wellington, as planned. I've got no idea where he is, sorry."

I was dumbfounded. Hugh never booked his own travel. Was Madeleine lying to me? But why would she do that? And why was she being so ... unfriendly? Then I heard a man's voice in the background and I felt so dense. I was obviously intruding at an inappropriate moment. "Uh, OK – thanks Madeleine," I stammered. "I hear you have company so I'll ... let you go." I dropped the phone onto the couch and flung a cushion over it.

"What?" asked Willa anxiously. "He's not there, is he?"

"No!" I reacted automatically, but the moment I said it, I wondered if I'd spoken too quickly. Surely I would have recognized Hugh's voice if it was him in the background ... wouldn't I? It would make sense though – it would explain why she had been so strange on the phone. I sank down onto the couch, suddenly cold although the temperature in the room was still like a sauna. The terrible thing was, I would only have myself to blame if Hugh was with her. Tears that had been threatening since I'd left the gallery with Willa now streamed down my cheeks and I heard a strange animal wail coming from my mouth.

Willa put the coffee on the low table in front of us. She sat down beside me and pulled my head onto her lap. She stroked my hair as I howled noisily, dripping mascara all over her elegant green trousers. She slowly unraveled my crazy hairstyle and combed out the knots with her fingers. When she had removed the last of the sticks and the worst of the tangles, she began lightly massaging my temples and tracing soothing patterns over my head. Under her touch, my weeping gradually abated. I decided to tell her something I'd never told anyone, not even Hugh. "Willa?" I sniffed. "You know how when we met in Colorado I told you I'd never had a boyfriend?"

"Mm-hmm," replied Willa, "and I set you up with that Australian guy we were working with in Jimmy's Bar. He was hot. What was his name again? Peter?"

"Yeah, I think so," I mumbled, trying not to think about my disastrous first attempt at sex. "The thing is, it wasn't quite true. That I'd never had a boyfriend. Something happened in high school that really put me off guys. I thought I'd gotten over it when I met Hugh, but now ...," my voice choked into a thin squeak, "now it's like it's happening all over again."

Willa's hand stopped massaging my scalp for a moment. She had asked me not long after we met if there was anything in my past that could explain my almost pathological fear of dating. And she'd continued to probe every time she tried and failed to set me up with some guy she claimed would be 'the one' for me. "Tell me, babe," she said soothingly as she resumed her gentle, calming touch.

I remembered it like it was yesterday as I poured the whole story out to Willa. I was fifteen and crazy about skiing. Ryan McGregor was new in town and had started school at the beginning of the winter term. Every girl in the school had a crush on him, including my best friend Ashleigh. I'd gotten to know him in the holidays because my father knew his parents from their time together as professional skiers. I showed him all the out-of-the-way spots you'd only find if you were local, and we had a blast trying to out-ski each other on increasingly more remote and difficult trails. But when school went back, I kept away from him. I was sure he wouldn't be interested in me when he had the pick of all those other girls who were prettier, richer and more outgoing than me.

No one was surprised when the school ski team was picked and Ryan was on it. And everyone knew I would be as well. At ski camp, Ryan constantly complained to our coach, Ms Schaefer, if he wasn't paired with me. That's when I started to think he might like me. When he tried to kiss me on the chairlift, I confided in Ashleigh. And when he told me he was going to come and see me in our dorm one night, I told Ashleigh that too. I didn't really believe him, but I was afraid of getting into trouble and I asked her to protect me if he did show up.

When I woke up and found him in my bunk, kissing me, telling me how pretty I was – one hand up inside my pajama top and the other down my pants – it had felt so surreal, so unexpected, I thought I must be dreaming. It was exactly the same sensation that had come over me tonight, staring at myself in the mirror with Xavier Bishop – like my brain had been switched off and my body was on autopilot. Rather than keeping me safely on course, though, my version of autopilot caused me to veer completely out of control – with no thought for the consequences of my actions or the feelings of anyone who might be hurt by them.

Afterwards, when the lights came on and Ashleigh was standing there beside Ms Schaefer with a smug grin on her face; when I had to explain to my father why he had been called to come and collect me in the middle of the night; when I was kicked off the ski team; when Ashleigh told everyone at school I was a slut – I decided I couldn't be trusted with boys, so I'd better keep away from them.

I dyed my hair and dressed in black. I shut myself in my room. I listened to Marilyn Manson and Nine Inch Nails. I drew bugs and demons and skulls. I made myself distant and scary so boys wouldn't like me. I was determined not to be like my mother.

I looked up at Willa. She spread my hair out over the arm of the couch, making tiny circles along my hairline with her fingers.

"I've always felt so … safe with Hugh, Willa. Since we've been together I haven't needed to worry about trusting myself. I've trusted him with everything. I think tonight was the first time since we met that I've been anywhere without him. I can't believe how badly I've messed up," I whispered, tears falling again.

I wanted Willa to deny it; to say no, don't worry honey, you haven't messed up, everything will be fine. But she didn't. She just sat there, staring out into the dark room. The gentle rhythm of her hands on my head gradually slowed until they stopped altogether, coming to rest lightly on my crown.

Four

When Willa finally spoke, I was almost asleep. I'd thought she was, too. "Georgia?" She arched her back and sat me up beside her. "Why don't you try calling Hugh again? It's 11:30 now. Maybe he didn't hear his phone before."

She dug the phone out from under the cushion I had thrown over it and handed it to me. When I took it, I saw that the *Talk* button was still lit up from my previous call to Madeleine. "Oh, shoot," I groaned. "We forgot to hang up last time." What if Hugh had been trying to call me? I checked the phone, but there were no new messages. I got up and retrieved my bag from beside the front door. I rummaged around in it for my cell phone. There were two missed calls – both from a number I didn't recognize.

I sat down again, shaking. I handed my cell phone to Willa with the number on the display. "You ring," I said.

I sat perfectly still and silent, listening to the faint brrr brrr coming from my phone as Willa held it to her ear. It rang five, six, seven ... eight times, and I'd resigned myself to there being no answer. Then I heard a click and there was a voice on the other end. I drew breath sharply. Willa frowned and motioned me to stay still as she listened intently. After a few more moments, I slumped back against the couch, disappointed when her continued silence told me it was a recorded message.

Eventually Willa hung up and sighed. "I think it might have been a wrong number. A bit hard to tell if it was a man or a woman. Foreign, I'd say – DJ? TJ, maybe? Couldn't pick the accent. Sound familiar?" I shook my head, wishing again that I'd made more of an effort to meet Hugh's friends.

Willa was still on a roll, like a detective determined to solve a case. "Let's try Hugh again then," she said, flicking through the contacts on my phone. She pulled up Hugh's cell phone number and pressed *Call*, then handed the phone to me.

"Hello? Hello?" There was a lot of background noise, but it was definitely a woman's voice. "Hel–lo?"

I felt like I had been slapped. My body reeled in shock, and tears smarted my eyes. I pressed *End* and dropped the phone on the couch between us. I drew my knees up under my chin and hid my face – like I wanted to hide myself.

I was dimly aware of Willa picking up the phone and trying Hugh's number again. When the woman answered a second time, she took a deep breath. "Who is this please?" she asked firmly. I think she thought I wasn't listening, but I could hear enough. A screech of laughter followed by muffled giggles greeted her enquiry. "Who are *you*?" the voice said. "Wassup?"

"I'm looking for Hugh, and I believe this is his phone you are talking to me on. Can I speak to him please?"

"Hee-yoo-oo!" shouted the voice. Obviously intended for whoever was at her end, it was so loud that Willa had to move the phone away from her ear.

Now the conversation was clearly audible to me. "Hew-wy, it's your Muuum-meee ..."

Scuffles and more giggles followed, and then another female voice came on to the line. "Sorry," it said in a husky voice, "Hugh's busy right now. He'll have to call you back." There were shrieks of laughter in the background, and then the phone went dead.

"Fuck!" hissed Willa as she threw the phone back down between us. The look on her face reminded me of how she'd looked that night in New York, a couple of months after she'd first introduced me to Hugh.

Having appointed herself my own personal Cupid while we were working together in Aspen, Willa had remained resolutely undaunted by her lack of success over the years we'd known each other. Apart from the fiasco with the Australian, I'd never made it to a second date with any of the men she'd set me up with. I'd only had one other boyfriend since, and that had only lasted a couple of months. Oddly enough, Hugh was probably the only guy she hadn't deliberately set me up with – which was just one of the reasons I made the assumptions I did about him and let him slip past my scary black security fence.

I still remembered Willa's reaction when I'd told her I was sure Hugh was gay. She spluttered coffee all over her favorite white T-shirt and looked at me like I'd told her I thought the pope was a Buddhist. "Not where I'm from, he isn't," she assured me emphatically, right before telling me equally emphatically that I shouldn't get involved with him. But later that night, she'd done a complete about face.

We were sitting in a diner, where we'd just finished eating before heading out to a party at Willa's friend Macy's loft. Hugh and I were on one side of the booth and Willa and her latest girlfriend were on the other. Or it may have been a boyfriend; it was always hard to keep track of Willa's love affairs. Hugh and I had been laughing like crazy about some stupid joke he'd told, when Willa rolled her eyes at whoever she was with and then sat back in her seat and groaned. "Stop it!" she snapped abruptly, freezing us both mid chortle. Then she shook her head, as if trying to decide whether to say something or not. I giggled, wondering why Willa looked so serious all of a sudden.

"She's not gay," she blurted at Hugh, transforming my giggle into a gasp. Hugh stared at her in astonishment. Willa sighed impatiently. "Just because she wears Doc Martens and hangs out with a bunch of tattooed lesbians, does not mean she's gay. You egg." She shook her head hopelessly at the stupid grin spreading across Hugh's face, but frowned when he looked around at me with an altogether different expression. Even I, with my paltry experience with men, recognized it: raw, hungry desire. For one excruciating, delicious second, I had thought he was going to kiss me right then and there, in the middle of the diner – until Willa called him back to attention sharply. "Hugh ..." I was surprised at the sudden note of menace in her voice. "Be nice."

Hugh shrugged innocently, as if he had no idea what she was talking about, but Willa persisted.

"You know what I mean," she growled. "Don't make me regret this."

The look on her face I'd seen then – one of foreboding, like there was no way this could possibly turn out well – I saw that look again now. And as we sat there in the dark with my phone between us I wondered, not for the first time, why she had felt the need to issue that warning to Hugh. What did she know about him that I didn't?

I heard the antique grandfather clock in the hall striking midnight. The sound reverberated grimly through the big, empty house, mirroring the dull, empty ache that grew in my heart with each discordant chime. Willa stood up beside me. "Bedtime?" she suggested, holding out her hand. I took it numbly and followed her upstairs to the bathroom.

Willa flicked the switch by the door and the old fluorescent tube flickered and buzzed momentarily before illuminating the room. While she rummaged around in drawers for cleanser and wipes, I turned to face the mirror. I blinked. I looked like a vampire. Not a pretty one. My mascara and eyeliner had melted into ghoulish rings around my eyes. Black tear marks dripped down my pale cheeks. The remains of my deep blood-red lipstick was smeared around my mouth. My hair was a wild mass of confused tendrils that snaked around my face. *Click.* I couldn't believe I wanted to commit that image to memory, but it seemed my brain was on autopilot once more.

"Turn around, babe," said Willa softly and I did as I was told. Deeply buried memories of my mother unexpectedly flooded my thoughts as Willa tenderly wiped the mess off my face with soft tissues. My mother, picking me up after I'd face-planted in the snow, carefully brushing the icy crystals away from my eyes with her suede gloves. My mother, taking me in her arms and dropping soft, fluttering kisses on my cheeks and forehead until the hurt was all better. My mother, before she became the source of my hurt. The pain was sharp, searing and, coupled with the hollow ache I felt for Hugh's absence, left no room for anything except more tears.

"Come on," sighed Willa as she led me shaking and sobbing to the bedroom. When we got there I fumbled with the front of my dress, but my fingers were thick and clumsy, like they were wearing padded gloves, and I couldn't separate the hooks and eyes. I glanced helplessly at Willa. She sighed again and moved forward to help, although she seemed irritated. In three deft moves she had undone the dress, leaving me shivering in my shoes, stockings and panties. Before I could say a word, she was in the dressing room, opening drawers and rummaging through shelves. "What do you wear to bed?" she asked, her back to me. Her voice was strained, as if she was rapidly losing patience with me.

"Um, one of Hugh's T-shirts will do. Third drawer," I said shakily. I sat down on the bed and managed to pull off my shoes before she flung a soft cotton bundle at me. I pulled on the T-shirt and curled up in a fetal position on the bed, not even attempting to remove the suspender belt and stockings. I closed my eyes, although I knew I wouldn't be able to sleep.

Willa's hands brushed my waist, then the tightness of the suspender belt relaxed and the belt and the stockings were peeled off my legs. A duvet was laid gently over me and the edge of the bed sank a little as Willa sat down beside me. "I'll, um ... see you then," she said quietly, her hand on my shoulder.

It hadn't occurred to me until that moment that Willa planned to leave. The idea of being left alone with a gaping Hugh-shaped hole in my bed brought a fresh wave of tears flooding into my eyes. I grabbed her hand and looked up at her. "Stay," I whimpered. "You can sleep here." I gestured vaguely at the empty side of the bed.

She sighed. "Georgia, I really ..."

"Please," I begged, before she could say any more. "I know you have to get up early, but ... can you stay just a bit longer? Maybe Hugh will come back."

Willa sighed again. The expression on her face told me she thought there as much hope of Hugh showing up as there was of the Queen of England walking through the door. "All right," she said reluctantly. "But I have to leave at 5 am, regardless of whether he's here or not. I've got a 6:30 Skype call to New York." She stood up. "I need to take a shower, OK?"

I lay in the bed, shivering despite the still oppressive heat and the warm duvet tucked around me. Willa seemed to be taking a very long time in the shower. It was only when she slipped under the covers beside me and wrapped her arm around me that I finally dozed off. I wasn't sure if it was minutes or hours later, or if I was still dreaming, but the next thing I was aware of was sound: Willa's footsteps as she padded around the room gathering her clothes; the click of the front door as it closed shut behind her. After she had gone, there was still a presence in the bed next to me. I rolled over and opened my eyes.

Five

Hugh was leaning up on one elbow beside me – the perfect line of his jaw the only feature of his beautiful face clearly discernible in the dim pre-dawn light. His deep sapphire blue eyes gazed at me, their expression unreadable. Every fiber of my being wanted to touch him, be embraced by him. It seemed the only way to make things right between us. But I was sure that, the second I reached out to him, he would evaporate again and all I'd be left with was a half-empty bed and a falling-down house. Even though it was obvious he was an apparition, I decided to speak to him. Maybe talking to this ghost would give me some kind of absolution.

"I'm sorry," I whispered. "I am so sorry about what happened in the gallery. That guy, he just ..."

"Shhh," he murmured back. The sound was lighter than a breeze, wafting through my barely conscious mind. I was definitely dreaming, I thought. It was only when he reached out to touch me that I began to believe he was real, that he had come back. He tangled his free hand in my hair and kissed me gently down my forehead and nose until he was speaking into my mouth. "Hush, baby G. You don't have to explain anything. You haven't done anything wrong."

I extended a hand and tentatively stroked his hair. It was damp. He must have just got out of the shower. He smelled delicious – like grapefruit and honey. I put my other hand on his chest and I was amazed that his heart thudded so ... humanly under the fine silky hair. Waves of relief and desire coursed through me when he rolled on top of me, pinning me to the bed. I could have cried for joy when the crush of his weight descended on me, and I knew for sure it was really him. I didn't care that I could hardly breathe.

There was a faint sense of unease in the back of my mind about his assertion that I'd done nothing wrong. And the issue of where he'd been all night lurked uncomfortably beside it. But both my need to explain and my need for explanation were swiftly overtaken by my need for Hugh. I submitted to his lips, his hands, his firm, lean body pressing into mine the way a piece of soft malleable clay might give itself up to the workings of a master sculptor. I wanted him to recreate me – to recreate us both – in a way that was as beautiful and perfect as we had been before.

He inhaled the scent of my skin and hair like a man who had been deprived of fresh air. His lips were a thousand honeybees, seeking the nectar of my eyes, ears, neck and breasts with delicate, stinging kisses. His hands molded me tightly against him. As they kneaded their way down and around my body, I opened beneath him, swelling like molten glass at the tip of a glassblower's pipe. He pulled off the T-shirt I was wearing with an impatience that belied his tenderness. And then his mouth found the sweet, sticky honey between my thighs that invited him to explore more deeply.

The sensation of being tasted, consumed, sent fire racing through my blood, but what I wanted more than anything was him inside of me. I ran my fingers into his hair and pulled, hard. He slid, half eagerly, half reluctantly back up my body, nipping and sucking, dropping tiny pools of melted heat on my crazed skin as he moved. When his lips reached mine, it was as if someone had poured a jug of warm syrup onto my mouth and its liquid heat spread like a delta throughout my body.

I twined my arms tightly around him. I felt an electric jolt as his cock leapt against the honeyed slit between my thighs. He knew what I wanted without me having to say a word. I gasped as he separated my legs with his in a practiced move. Then I felt his full length on me, in me, around me. It was as if both of us had been plunged into a furnace and we were now shaping ourselves against each other – white hot metal melding frantically against liquid glass. It took me back to the beginning; to the first night we'd spent together in New York. The only difference now was that Hugh knew my body much more intimately, and it seemed only minutes before I was ready to explode.

"Stop," I cried, wanting it to last longer, but it was too late. I pulled Hugh in to me and wrapped my legs tightly around him as I burst against him, sobbing with pleasure and relief as I let go. Hugh stopped before he came, too – his body tense and twitching with the effort of holding back, lying perfectly still with his weight and bulk enveloping me. The pulse in my neck seemed to be connected to his lips as he kissed and nuzzled me back to consciousness. When at last I managed to focus my eyes, he grinned at me in triumph, then immediately shifted his weight to increase the pressure of his pelvis against my soft, tender mound.

"Ready again?" he whispered. I moaned and he started grinding into me without waiting for an answer. This time, the connection between us was even more intense. My first orgasm had sensitized my body so that I felt every hair on his arms, legs and chest as they glanced against me, every shift in the air around us as we joined and separated and joined again, over and over. "Oh, Georgie, Georgie girl," moaned Hugh. His lips hungered for my mouth and his hands on my breasts delivered violent shocks of pleasure to unseen parts of my body. He moved to roll over and pull me on top of him, but I resisted.

"Let's ... stay like this," I said softly. I still didn't trust myself. I wanted him in control. I wanted to give myself over to him completely, so we would both be sure that the incident in the gallery had been an aberration. I moaned as he plunged back into me, filling me to the hilt. He pulsed hard and deep, bringing us both to the edge of orgasm, then easing off moments before we tumbled in. Like the surge and ebb of the ocean waves, he built the pressure again and again until I could take no more. "Please," I begged finally. I pushed up against him and he reciprocated with faster, more forceful thrusts until the rushing filled my ears, my eyes, my body, my brain and I was powerless to stop. Moments after my orgasm began, Hugh lost control too. With a deep guttural moan, he surged and melted into me like the tide, and finally we were whole and perfect again.

After a few minutes, Hugh slid his weight off me and pulled my head onto his chest, twining one of his legs between mine. His light, sweet breath fanned my face as our heartbeats progressively slowed and we dozed in the cool before the sun rose. Gradually, I became aware of the hum of the motorway traffic growing louder in the distance and the sound of birdsong reaching a crescendo. Hugh twisted underneath me to check the time on the clock beside us. I glanced up too. The shadowy masses of the furniture in our room had begun to take on more distinct forms, and a wash of pale color had replaced the grays of the early dawn. It was 6:21.

"Crap!" he exclaimed. He disentangled himself gently but swiftly from our embrace and slipped out of bed, leaving a void of chilly air in his place. "I've got an 8am flight to catch – there's a taxi arriving in ten minutes." I shivered and pulled the duvet closer in an attempt to close the wound left by his abrupt exit. When he returned from the bathroom a few minutes later, I studied him intently as he donned underwear and shirt, pulled on dark trousers, shrugged on the matching jacket and knotted his tie in quick, graceful movements.

I wanted to savor every second of the remaining minutes he would be near me. A lump caught in my throat when I thought about the next three nights I'd be spending without him; wishing we'd had more time together this morning; wondering if I should have insisted we talk first.

I sat up, swaddling myself in the duvet. "Hugh," I said, "About last night. I need to explain … about the thing you saw. And … where did you go?"

Hugh stopped midway through putting on his second sock. Something about the way he looked at me – cautious, guarded – made the lump in my throat grow bigger and stick harder. "Actually, where I was is a bit of a long story, babe, and … I really need to be on this plane." He finished putting on his shoes as he continued, his eyes towards the floor. "I know it's not ideal, but it's going to have to wait."

Now fully dressed, he came to sit on the edge of the bed and pulled me close to him. I could hardly feel him through my cocoon of bedding. I struggled to get my arms out so I could put them around him, but he held me fast. "As to you explaining, I ... know Xavier Bishop. I know what I saw would have been initiated by him. So don't worry about that." He kissed my forehead in a benign, cursory way that I knew was meant to reassure me. It had the opposite effect.

We both started at the sound of a car horn in the driveway. The taxi. Hugh tensed, about to stand up, then paused. He glanced at the clock, then back at me. He grabbed my shoulders through the duvet and spoke to me quietly, urgently. "Georgia, there are some things you should know about Xavier and ... other stuff in my past," he said. "I probably should have told you in New York, but ..." there was that guilty, guarded look again, "it didn't seem important, then."

"What?" I asked, feeling slightly nauseous. I was shivering again, even though I was still bound inside the bulky feather duvet.

There was a loud knock on the door downstairs. "Taxi!" called a voice.

Hugh stood up. "Be right there!" he shouted.

He looked at the clock again and turned back to me in mild panic. "Fuck. I really need to go now, Georgie girl. Can we Skype tonight?" Without waiting for an answer, he bent down to kiss my cheek – another chaste, unsatisfying brush of his lips. "Love you," he whispered. Then he was gone – out the bedroom door, down the stairs and into the taxi waiting outside.

I sank back into the pillows, my mind whirring. It's a long story? It's not ideal? Don't worry about it? There are things you should know? *Love you*? It was like I'd been speaking to three different men. And none of them were the man who'd crept into my bed at 5 am and knew exactly what to do to ... divert me. For me, our lovemaking had been a precious opportunity to reconnect and close the gap that Xavier Bishop's unwanted attentions had created between us. But perhaps for Hugh it had simply been a pleasant diversion that by happy coincidence had also kept me from asking awkward questions. What secret involving Xavier Bishop could be so terrible he had kept it from me all this time? And where the hell had he been until five in the morning? I huddled back into the duvet and closed my eyes – shutting out not only the morning sunlight, but also the questions and disturbing possibilities that intruded on my hazy mind. Eventually I drifted back into an uneasy sleep.

Six

The sun was high when I woke again hours later. I squinted, trying to adjust to the dazzling light coming in through the bare windows. A fine trail of Hugh's milky essence trickled down the inside of my thigh. I stretched luxuriantly and smiled to myself. There was a sudden fluttering between my legs as I recalled Hugh's weight pinning me to the bed and the way our bodies had collided in waves of early morning desire. Then I remembered the conversation we'd had before he left to go back to Wellington. As if a cloud had drifted over the morning sun, a shadow of doubt and uncertainty descended over me. Is that what a one-night stand felt like, I wondered. The sweet fullness of love hollowed out by some unseen, unforeseen plague of burrowing insects? A bitter aftertaste of anxiety and unanswered questions? The night after I first slept with Hugh I'd half expected it – despite what he'd told me beforehand. Now, after I'd known him nearly a year and been married to him for more than half of that time, I'd grown used to being able to trust Hugh and depend on him to be constant and true.

Notwithstanding the dead chill in my heart as I lay in our bed that morning, I was stifling hot – and desperate to pee. I threw the covers aside and headed for the bathroom. After washing my hands and splashing my face with cold water, I padded back into the bedroom and flung open the French doors. A cool sea breeze wafted into the overheated room. When the tide was in, the view of the Waitemata harbor from the back of our house was stunning – glittering turquoise at the edges where dozens of sandy bays were chomped into the tree-covered cliffs; and shimmering navy blue in the center channel. It was always dotted with boats of every kind – huge cargo ships and passenger liners heading for the port; ferries that served the many islands in the gulf; and many smaller craft – yachts big and small, kayaks, windsurfers and the dinghies of fishermen. Usually I found it calming to sit and watch the ever-changing scene on the sparkling water. But today, the tide was out and long fingers of brown and gray estuarine mud were exposed – a dark underbelly that sucked the intensity from the normally brilliant blues and greens of full tide. I turned abruptly back inside, seeking something more reassuring.

I looked around our bedroom. Tan carpet with a faint lilac paisley pattern. Victorian sofa covered in grape-colored cut velvet, patterned in black and dark brown and orange with phoenixes emerging from flaming urns. Rumpled bed with Egyptian cotton bedding the same color as the huge lump of amethyst on the wrought-iron bedside table. On the other table, a tall bronze art nouveau vase, converted to a lamp and containing seven fairy-light tulips in a deep shade of indigo. They were still lit up, their stems casting vague sinewy shadows on the white painted wall behind them. Above the king-size bed and on the wall beside the door were two large works of art – one a collage of three fantastic sea creatures engaged in some sort of battle; the other an oil painting of two shadowy brown figures emerging from a violet-black background, like dancers in a forest. Everything in the room had been chosen by Hugh long before we met, and even though there were some things I liked about it, I longed to restore this room and the rest of the house to its original Victorian-period style.

The problem was, we were prevented from doing anything at all to the house because it didn't belong to Hugh. It had been left to him and his three brothers by their uncle Don – the elder brother of their biological mother, Catherine. Hugh's brothers wanted to sell the house, but for ten years Hugh had stubbornly insisted on retaining it and living there – and equally stubbornly refused to spend money fixing up a place he didn't own outright. Our bedroom and my studio were the only rooms that had been touched since the 1970s.

Although I shared Hugh's love of old architecture and furniture, I didn't really understand why he was so attached to this particular house. I'd asked him why he didn't simply buy his brothers out. But, even allowing no value for the house in its current state, the large plot, right on the harbor's edge and just a half hour's walk from the central city, was worth millions of dollars. Despite his six-figure salary, Hugh would never be able to get a big enough loan to buy his brothers' shares. And every time I tried to talk to him about moving, he changed the subject. So I'd resigned myself to living in the house the way it was – flaking paint and broken windows on the outside; peeling 1970s wallpaper, faded psychedelic print curtains and threadbare shag-pile carpet on the inside.

I wandered into the hallway and leaned against the pull-down stairs leading up to the attic. Hugh had had it converted into a studio for me before our arrival in New Zealand. The sloping ceilings and walls were all painted white, with recycled timber floors running the length of the room. A long stainless-steel bench and two sinks had been installed at the eastern end, and shelves for all my art materials and books lined the south wall. Three large dormer windows faced the harbor to the north, meaning the room was flooded with warmth and natural light from early morning until late in the day.

As I stood there, I indulged in one of my frequent daydreams about what I'd like to do with the house if it were ours. Sometimes I imagined myself appearing in a glossy home magazine a few years into the future – a well-known artist welcoming guests to my beautifully renovated historic mansion. The entire house would be a treasure trove of antique and classic retro furniture, sculpture and art – my paintings and the work of other artists. Our collections would be funded with the proceeds of my wildly successful exhibitions, supplemented with Hugh's bountiful salary.

This morning, though, everything felt so uncertain. I hardly dared to imagine myself living there in a month, let alone a few years. I sighed and trailed listlessly back into the bedroom. At one end of the room, two doors opened into a second, smaller room. It had been a sun porch before all the windows were blacked out with heavy drapes, and it now served as our wardrobe and dressing room. The left-hand wall was filled with Hugh's clothes – neatly arranged on kitset racks and in two large wooden chests of drawers. The wall on the right was taken up with more kitset shelving, which was newly erected and empty save for a dozen items that I'd brought over with me in December. The rest of my clothes were still in boxes and suitcases on the floor. They had arrived from New York by ship a month ago, and I hadn't gotten around to putting them away yet. I dug about in one of the boxes and extracted a battered silk kimono. Wrapping the pink and orange dragons protectively around myself, I headed downstairs to the kitchen for coffee.

While I was waiting for the coffee to brew, I wandered into the garden. It was mostly overgrown with long grass, which had gone dry and spiky over the hot summer. There were a few ancient fruit trees growing at the bottom of the garden, near where it dropped down to the sea, and I noticed some of the apples were ripe. I found it weird that apple season started in mid-February in this half of the world. We'd had a small orchard out the back of my home in Basalt, Colorado, and I'd continued to associate August with apple picking and honey harvesting – even once I was living in New York.

I picked a dark red apple and took a bite, but spat it out immediately. The core was brown from some kind of moth that had burrowed in there to lay its eggs. I remembered my father teaching me as a child how to set traps for those moths, reminding me how important it was to regularly nurture and care for the trees in order for the fruit to be healthy and sweet. I thought of the bitter, empty pang that had spoiled my awakening this morning, and felt a sudden stab of hatred for Xavier Bishop. He was like a piece of brown rot that had surreptitiously entered my relationship with Hugh, and I wanted to spit him out. If only I could have last night over again ...

Then I remembered something I'd discussed with Willa a couple of weeks back, when I found out Hugh would be in Wellington on the night of my exhibition opening. Maybe I *could* reinvent the evening for both of us in a way that would cut Xavier Bishop right out of the picture. All I needed was a bit of help from Willa. I threw the apple far over the edge of the cliff and hurried back into the house. It was almost midday. Hopefully not too late. I ran upstairs to the bedroom to find my phone and text her.

Need 2 discuss Friday with u. R u free 4 lunch?

Yes good idea. When?

1 pm? Need 2 shower & dress. Only just got up

Lazy trollop. Obviously made up with H ;-) CU soon

I didn't bother to correct her assumption. I wasn't quite sure if I had made up with Hugh or not. Hopefully Willa would be able to help me make sense of his strange behavior, I thought, as I caught the bus into the city.

Seven

Willa was busy with a client when I arrived at the gallery, and she waved me into her office to wait. There were a couple of magazines on the coffee table and I picked one up. When I came across an article about a vintage textile fair coming up, my eyes lit up. New York had been full of retro clothing and textile stores and flea markets, and I'd had a big calendar of antique fashion and textile fairs permanently taped to my refrigerator door so I wouldn't miss any. I had already picked over everything on offer at the half dozen vintage boutiques in Auckland and I was suffering major withdrawal symptoms. I glanced around on Willa's desk for a scrap of paper so I could write down the web address. Her laptop was on, and I wondered if she'd mind if I went online to check out the website. I looked through the slats of the venetian blinds into the gallery. She was still chatting animatedly to her client. I sat down at the keyboard.

The internet browser was already open on the screen and I couldn't help but notice the URL in the address bar – www.willowyblonde.com. Before opening a new tab, I scanned the open page out of curiosity; Willa was always a great source of interesting websites. It seemed to be a blog. As I read the first few lines of text, my jaw dropped.

I've always carried a bit of a torch for my good friend Sasha. Sadly, since she recently married the brother of my old school friend, all the fun we've had in the past has come to an end. Get this though – last night she has a tiff with her husband – he goes AWOL and I end up sleeping over at her place. I try my hardest to behave, but when she asks me to undress her, I can't help myself.

After I've undone her dress and she's standing in front of me in her g-string and stockings, I reach out and take her breast in my hand. I love how her nipples are so neat and brown – how they pucker instantly under my fingers into little hard nuts. She steps into my touch and I wrap my arms around her. I've just spent the last two hours stroking her hair and massaging her scalp and I've been dying to hold her properly. She's so small and delicate next to me. I pull her hair gently and lean down to kiss her. Her lips are so soft. I slip my hand down her belly, into the front of her panties. I feel the tremor as she gasps. My fingers slide easily against her wet ...

My skin prickled. Was this something Willa had written? I thought back to last night. Her hands on my head, gently untangling my hair. The way she'd moved away from me so quickly after she'd helped me with my dress. How she'd deliberately stood with her back to me until I was dressed again in Hugh's T-shirt. How she'd seemed reluctant when I asked her to stay. Was this what had been going through her mind?

I peeked through the blind again. Willa was still deep in conversation. I reached for the mouse and scrolled down the page. I gulped in disbelief.

It's a shame I'm leaving when her husband finally comes home. He's just got out of the shower and we surprise each other in the bathroom when I go in to brush my teeth. He asks me if I want to stay and watch them making up. I'm not sure if he's joking but I can't anyway as I have an early morning meeting. I ask him to tell me what he's going to do to her. I take his cock in my mouth. It's satiny smooth, honey scented. He tells me he's going to lick her pussy like I'm licking his cock. I run my tongue along it. It grows to fill my mouth. He tells me how he's going to slide it deep inside her ... make her come ... make her beg for more. I slide my hand down. I do with my hand what he's going to do to her. I only intend to make him hard and then send him in to her, but as I come, he shoots into my mouth ...

A cold sweat broke out on the back of my neck. My throat constricted and my breathing came in short, shallow gasps. Could this be true? I thought about how Hugh had been this morning. He'd wanted me. Badly. Badly enough not to be interested in my explanations about Xavier. He'd been very hard. And he'd come a lot. Not like he'd just had a blow job in the bathroom. But then again, it wasn't as if Hugh had trouble getting a second or third erection in quick succession ...

My heart had frozen mid-beat at what I'd read. Now, thinking about Hugh – hard, wanting me, coming in me – it raced again at double speed. There was a familiar ache at the top of my thighs and a tiny pulse throbbed in my groin. I felt hot and dizzy.

I was in such a state of confusion I didn't hear Willa saying goodbye to her client. It was only when I registered the sound of her heels clicking purposefully across the gallery floor that I realized I was still sitting at her desk, goggle-eyed, with the blog open in front of me. My hand was shaking so much I could hardly control the mouse. Instead of scrolling back to the top of the page I accidentally closed the browser altogether. *Damn!* I hoped she wouldn't notice. I picked up the magazine again and dived onto the couch in the corner seconds before she opened the door. "Hey, babe," she said, walking over to me with her arms out. "Sorry about the wait."

I couldn't meet her eyes as I stumbled back to my feet. I could barely endure her customary warm hug and three kisses on alternate cheeks. I hoped she wouldn't notice the color of my face or my shaking hands.

"Uh, that's OK," I muttered, glancing involuntarily at her laptop. *Shit.*

To my relief, she reached over and shut it down without looking at it. "How was Mr Big?" she asked as she dug under her desk for her bag.

Normally I would have laughed at Willa's goofy reference to the *Sex and the City* character. For most of my first five years in New York, I'd explained away my lack of a boyfriend by telling her all the good-looking guys were gay. So when I'd finally got together with Hugh, Willa had jokingly called him Mr Big. Now, I wondered if there was another reason Willa referred to him by that name. I also wondered if perhaps I hadn't been so far off the mark after all when I'd started calling her Samantha in response to her Mr Big jokes. I'd always reassured her she was nowhere near slutty enough to be like the TV character. Perhaps I'd been wrong.

My vision had gone blurry around the edges and Willa's face was distorted, like I was seeing it in a fairground mirror.

"Georgia, what's wrong?"

I couldn't believe she could stand there looking so innocent. Whether she *had* sucked Hugh off in my bathroom or whether she'd only thought about it ... written about it. Had she no shame? I opened my mouth to demand the truth and tell her exactly what I thought of her. Then I remembered that it was me who'd used her laptop without permission. And also, I had a big favor to ask her. I shut my mouth again. "He was fine," I muttered finally, ducking my head so she couldn't see my eyes.

"Fine?" Willa's raised voice made me look up again. "That's all you're giving me? The guy comes home at five in the morning with blood all over his shirt and you tell me he was 'fine'?"

"What?" I gasped, the blog momentarily forgotten. "What do you mean?"

"Well, he looked like he'd been in a fight or something. Didn't you notice?"

I was tempted to say, 'No, but you obviously did because you were giving him a blow job in our bathroom.' I held my tongue. Perhaps if I let her talk, she would let slip what had really happened.

Even so, I frowned as we made our way to the door of the gallery and Willa called to her assistant, Guy, that she'd be out for an hour. I'd been so bewitched by Hugh's touch that I'd hardly looked at him this morning. What sort of wife wouldn't notice if her husband came home covered in blood?

"He'd had a shower when he came to bed," I told Willa, scanning her face carefully to see how she would react. "I didn't see his clothes."

"Oh, that's right," said Willa. "I saw him in the bathroom as I was leaving." She seemed perfectly relaxed about telling me she'd seen Hugh in the bathroom. Surely if anything had happened, she would be more secretive?

"But he never said anything to you about the blood?" she asked curiously.

"No," I muttered as we headed for Willa's favorite lunch place, the Sushi Factory.

"Did he say anything about Xavier?" Willa continued questioning me, giving no sign that she was trying to hide anything at all.

I tried to act normally myself. I started to tell her what Hugh had said – that he knew Xavier and needed to tell me something about him. Then I stopped and stared at Willa. "Maybe that's why Hugh was covered in blood," I said. "Maybe they had a fight."

A picture of Hugh and Xavier Bishop engaged in a violent confrontation sprang to mind. To my horror, rather than finding it distressing, it stirred up an unnamed emotion somewhere deep within me that disturbed me. Like the fleeting images that had flashed into my thoughts the night before.

Willa gave me a dubious look. "I'm not sure Dr Bishop's the brawling type," she said dryly.

Willa was right. It didn't make sense. I'd never known Hugh to resort to violence either. "Hugh did say he knew him, though," I told her. "That guy Bishop. But he … we … ran out of time to discuss it." When I saw Willa smirk in response I wished I hadn't told her that last bit. And I wished I hadn't read her stupid blog. I'd been counting on her to help me process Hugh's confusing behavior. Now I couldn't tell her anything.

Willa was mixing wasabi in with her soy sauce. "So, did Hugh say where he was, then? Before he finally came home?" she asked.

I shook my head, scanning her eyes again for any sign that she might know more than she was letting on about where Hugh had been before he'd appeared in our bed.

"Oh?" she said. It really did seem as if she didn't know. It was also obvious she thought it was the first thing I should have found out when I'd seen him.

Which is what I would have done, I thought crossly, if he hadn't come to bed all hot and hard ...

My cheeks were growing warm and there was a faint buzzing at the top of my thighs. In an effort to stop thinking about Hugh and what he'd done to me that morning, I tried to focus on Willa. She picked up a piece of sushi with her chopsticks and dipped it in the soy sauce the way she'd learned in Japan, careful that the rice didn't make contact with the sauce. She held her napkin fastidiously under the roll as she brought it to her mouth to ensure there was no chance of anything spilling on her immaculate silk shirt. Her lipstick was the exact same shade of plum as the silk. Her hair cascaded in sexy waves around her face, seemingly immune to the humidity that was causing everyone else's hair to frizz or flatten. She looked so cool. So perfect.

Sitting opposite her, I felt decidedly scruffy. I'd been in such a rush after texting her that I'd decided not to wash my hair before heading out. I'd tried to plait it, but it was so knotted and full of product that I'd given up after three or four twists, leaving large matted tufts at the end of each braid. I hadn't bothered with make-up either, but my eyes were still outlined with the remains of eyeliner from the night before. My red corduroy pinafore had a splash of paint down one side of it, and I hadn't been able to find a clean T-shirt to wear under it, so I'd worn it on its own. It was nice and cool, but as I sat there I was aware that the armholes gaped and my bra was probably visible underneath. And even though I liked my knee-length stripy socks and black Mary Jane Doc Martens, I could see a few of the well-dressed people around us looking at my feet slightly oddly.

Willa was staring back at me, obviously waiting for me to elaborate on what little information I had managed to elicit from Hugh. "He said it was a long story," I muttered. "We're Skyping tonight."

I knew what was coming next.

"He must have told you *something*. I mean, you didn't just ...?" It was obvious from her tone and her raised eyebrows that the idea of me falling into Hugh's arms without requiring some sort of explanation for his absence was outrageous. Was she deliberately teasing me when she knew very well what had happened? Or was she trying to find out so she could put that on her blog as well?

I squirmed. There was no way I was giving her any more fodder for her licentious blog. "There wasn't much time," I mumbled. I could see another smirk building on her face. "He didn't stay very long," I blustered. I was sure my face was the same shade of scarlet as my dress. "He had an early flight ..."

Willa raised her eyebrows again, not bothering to hide her lascivious grin. "Yeah, right," she said. "I know what time he came in. I'm sure he was there long enough."

I knew my face was as pink as the salmon she was popping delicately into her mouth. I gulped. It was infuriating not knowing what she was thinking as she slowly and deliberately wrapped her lips around the soft, pink flesh. I wondered if I'd ever be able to have lunch with Willa again without feeling completely paranoid. Even so, when I looked at her wicked grin and thought of Hugh in my bed I couldn't help smiling shyly back at her. "Just ... shut up already," I muttered.

To my surprise, Willa did stop her teasing. That strange foreboding look crossed her face again, and she looked as though she were about to say something important. Then she stopped and shook her head.

"What?" I asked, still feeling paranoid.

"Nothing." She gave me a brief smile that didn't quite reach her eyes. "I'm glad Hugh came home. I'm glad you made up."

I chose to ignore the slight hesitation in Willa's voice. I was still mad that she'd written that stuff about me – about Hugh. Half of me wanted to have it out with her about the blog. But the thought of asking her if she'd been fantasizing about me was enough to make me blush right down to my stripy socks. And I didn't want to accuse her of doing anything with Hugh unless I was certain it was true. What if she hadn't written it? I decided to keep my mouth shut until I was sure of my facts. Plus, I really needed this favor from her on Friday night.

"Thanks," I muttered, "And thanks too, for, you know, taking care of me."

As soon as I said, it, I realized that was something else I didn't want to think about – Willa 'taking care of me' by taking all my clothes off and getting into my bed. Even though I had asked her to. I tried to think of a topic that wouldn't remind me of the blog. I knew there was one thing that could be guaranteed to hold Willa's interest at least as much as sex. Money. "How were sales in the end last night?" I asked, finally able to look her in the eye.

"Not bad," she said. "Eight were sold last night, another by phone this morning, and that guy I was talking to when you came in asked me to put the big Whatipu painting aside for him. He's going to pick it up next month."

"So, another twenty not sold," I mused, half to myself, thinking back again to my sell-out shows in New York.

"Hey," said Willa, slightly defensively, "that's actually pretty good, you know, for someone who's relatively unknown here. You need to understand that the market's a lot smaller here. There's less cash around for discretionary things like art.

"I did have a thought, though," she added, seeing my glum expression. "I sent some photos off to Dennis first thing this morning. He said he thinks these paintings would go down really well in The Isles and he wants me to send ten of them over asap." Dennis owned several galleries in New York, and Willa often supplied him with work for The Isles, which specialized in Pacific art.

"Great," I mumbled, suddenly missing Dennis and all my friends in New York. I reminded myself to ask

Willa for Jessica and Tiki's phone numbers when we got back to the gallery.

"Yeah, it's perfect," continued Willa, "And I've got space in a container leaving for the US next week. The only thing is ...," she hesitated, "... to get them packed and down at the wharf by midday Monday, I'll have to take half the exhibition down this week instead of at the end of the month." In my distracted state I still hadn't spotted the problem.

"It's fine with me," she carried on. "I've got plenty of other work I can put up, but ... I know we talked about Friday night. You wanted to bring Hugh in here? I'm assuming that's not necessary now, since he saw the show last night?"

I had initially told Willa I wanted to bring Hugh to the gallery because he hadn't even seen some of my paintings yet. He'd been away nearly three out of the past four weeks. However my plan had morphed into something more ambitious. I wanted us to spend the night in the gallery. I'd been inspired by a scene in *The Dreamers* – a movie I'd watched recently during one of Hugh's many absences. I'd planned to construct a romantic 'tent' in the middle of the room and string up some old silk saris to create a canopy over a pile of soft pillows. I'd imagined us wandering through the gallery as if through an enchanted forest, then snuggling in our 'camp' for the night, surrounded by fairy lights. I'd imagined us making love there until the small hours of the morning – making up for all the nights he'd been in Wellington since our honeymoon had ended.

I'd been looking forward to telling Willa all about my plan – and getting some help from her to implement it. That was before I discovered it might end up on her dreaded blog.

"No!" I exclaimed, much louder than I'd intended. "I mean, yes. It's absolutely necessary," I reduced my voice to a whisper when several people turned to stare at us.

Willa was mildly alarmed at my reaction. "Calm down, I'm sure we can work something out," she said. "Maybe I can get a couple of my students in to help me take the paintings down after you've been in on Friday night. What time is Hugh getting back from Wellington?"

"About 6:30, I think. But we probably wouldn't get here much before eight. Maybe 7:30 if everything goes a hundred percent smoothly."

"We can probably work around that," said Willa cheerfully after thinking for a moment. "I'll just get the guys to come in at 8:30 or nine, after you've had a look around."

My heart sank. Half an hour was nowhere near long enough for what I had in mind. "Er, we might need a bit longer," I said without thinking. "Midnight?"

"I can't have students working that late," she exclaimed. "What do you need that long for anyway ..." Her voice trailed away and her mouth fell open. "Jeepers creepers, Georgia," she dropped her voice. "Are you going to ...?" A salacious grin spread over her face. "In *my* gallery?"

Merely thinking about it made me blush again. I glanced around furtively to check that no one had overheard her. My face glowed as if I'd eaten a whole dish of wasabi. Who knew what she was going to say about me in her next blog post? I stammered in protest, trying to convince her it was only a contingency in case Hugh's flight was late, but she shook her head, her green eyes sparkling with a mixture of amusement and mischief.

"I never thought I'd say this, but I might owe Hugh an apology," she smirked.

"What do you mean?" I asked defensively, wondering for one terrible moment if she was about to tell me that the blog was true – that she and Hugh were having some sort of affair.

"Maybe being married to him is good for you after all," she mused, smiling. Then her face clouded like it had before; her expression became serious, thoughtful. "Just make sure you find out where he was last night, OK?"

Even though it was on the tip of my tongue to tell Willa she was a fine one to be casting aspersions on Hugh's integrity, I knew what she was getting at. I'd been worried about the same thing. The most obvious explanation for Hugh's absence was that he'd been somewhere – or with someone – he shouldn't have been. It was the one thing I'd really wanted to talk to Willa about – before I'd read her blog and discovered she'd been having fantasies about him – if that's all they were. And in any case, we were out of time. After promising to give Hugh and me the run of the gallery until ten on Friday night, Willa gave me a swift peck on the cheek and dashed back to the gallery for a two o'clock appointment.

As she left, I knew I should be grateful to Willa. She was really putting herself out for me. She normally had Sundays and Mondays off. Since she was working all day Saturday, she was going to have to come in on

Sunday to finish packing the paintings *and* get up at the crack of dawn on Monday to get them on a boat to the US – all because I wanted to use her gallery as my own private boudoir. With a huge effort, I pulled a bright, cheery smile onto my face as I waved her goodbye – even though I felt sick inside at the thought that everything she knew about my plans might appear, twisted and warped, on her blog.

Eight

The tiny fluffy clouds that had dotted the horizon in the morning had spread and stretched to form a thin gray skin over the entire sky. Rather than providing relief from the mid-afternoon sun, the cloud cover served only to contain and magnify its heat. Trudging home, I was still trying to figure out what I should do about Willa's blog. My thoughts danced uncertainly in my head like the blur of figures and vehicles that rose ahead of me in the sweltering haze from the roads and pavements.

Normally, I found walking a great way to process information and resolve problems – whether it was a painting I was working on, or a person I was having trouble with. Today, after only two blocks I was exhausted. I couldn't think beyond the same three images that kept going around and around in my head. Me in the mirror with Xavier Bishop. Hugh whirling away from the doorway. And Willa in my bathroom with Hugh.

Despite the fact that it seemed to take me forever to walk home, it was only three o'clock when I got in the door. I was dripping with perspiration and my legs ached as a result of the climb up the hill from the city. I felt better after I had a cool shower, washed my hair and changed into an old Victorian cotton slip, but the hours until my Skype call with Hugh yawned ahead of me like a chasm. I decided to kill some time getting things organized for Friday night. The kitchen was the coolest place in the house in the afternoon, so I took my laptop downstairs, turned on the big old ceiling fan and settled myself at the green Formica-topped table.

First, the food. Not my specialty. I googled 'sexy food' and wrote up a list of things that smelled good and wouldn't be too messy to eat. It looked pretty simple and for a moment I wondered if I should tackle it myself. Things like the almonds and strawberries and chocolate just needed arranging on a plate. And surely I could manage to steam some asparagus and slice up a bit of watermelon and avocado without any major disasters? Then I remembered the slimy, lumpy mess I'd created recently when I tried to make a chicken and roast vegetable salad, and decided not to risk it. I called Willa's caterers and gave them Hugh's credit card number, hoping he wouldn't mind. I wondered how long it would be before Willa paid me for the paintings I'd sold last night. I hated being so dependent on Hugh for everything.

Next was the music. This would be easier. I wandered over to the boxes of CDs that were still waiting to be unpacked in the corner of the snug. After he was forced to close his ski school, my father found work as a DJ at a local radio station in Basalt. He and I had always listened to music together – it was one of our rituals. Every afternoon when I got home from school he'd put on one of the latest CDs that had come in. We'd rate it out of ten, and if it didn't score highly enough, he'd pull out some of his favorite old vinyls – mostly English bands like Cream, Pink Floyd, Deep Purple and Black Sabbath. Or I would beg for something more 'modern' and put Pearl Jam or Nirvana in the CD player. That was before I started hiding in my room and listening to Marilyn Manson and Nine Inch Nails.

Hugh didn't like the same music as me at all. He said it was unnatural for a girl to enjoy the sort of music I listened to. I laughed and told him his taste in music was much too girly – even for a girl. We'd tried shopping together for CDs, to see if we could find anything we both liked, but without much success. Now, as I sat on the floor with hundreds of albums scattered around me – the sum of my collection and Hugh's, plus some of my father's – nothing seemed right.

I sighed. Sweat was trickling down my neck again. The sun had found a sudden gap in the clouds and was now blazing directly into where I was sitting. I decided to open one more box and then give it up as a lost cause. If there was nothing acceptable in this one, we'd just have to go through the gallery in silence.

And there it was, right on top. Finally, a CD we both loved.

Neither of us had known what a theorbo was – we'd been attracted to the album cover, which featured the fingerboard of a seventeenth-century lute-like instrument inlaid with stylized flowers, vines and leaves. I slid the disk into my laptop and pressed play. It was perfect. Both joyful and sensual; even the pauses seemed erotic, capturing the light breathing of the musician like the sighs of lovers between bouts of passion. It reminded me of the time in New York when Hugh and I had first become lovers. When we'd been drunk on each other's touch. When we'd spent hours – entire days, sometimes – in bed together, drifting helplessly between sex and sleep and back again. My whole body pulsed unexpectedly just thinking about it. I set my laptop to copy the album onto my MP3 player and resolved that, whatever Hugh told me tonight, I would try to recreate that feeling for us this weekend, beginning on Friday night.

Since we weren't going to be sleeping in the gallery now, my job organizing Friday night was done. It was only 4:15 pm – still three hours and forty-five minutes until our Skype call. I wondered what Hugh was going to tell me. And I wondered how I should approach him about what I'd read on Willa's blog.

It was still stinking hot, despite the fact that the sun had disappeared again behind clouds that gathered ominously at the horizon – the steely gray and black of an army readying its machine guns for an assault. The air was thick and tense, and everything seemed unnaturally still. All I wanted was for the storm to be over, to have the conversation with Hugh and to be able to breathe again. My questions hung in the air all around me, hot, humid, sucking every ounce of energy from me. I barely had the strength to swat away a lazy fly that buzzed clumsily around my head. I stared at my laptop still open in front of me. Even as I was doing it, I knew it was probably a bad idea, but I couldn't seem to stop myself. I typed www.willowyblonde.com into the search bar on my internet browser and pressed Enter.

The first thing I did when the page opened was reread the latest post, to check that I hadn't imagined what I'd seen in the morning. It was so embarrassingly much more explicit than I'd thought. Was it really Willa who'd written this, or was it nothing more than a very bizarre coincidence? I trawled through previous posts, hoping to find it was the latter. But the more I read, the more certain I became that it was Willa's blog. The countries and cities mentioned matched up perfectly with places I knew she'd visited on her two years travelling around the world – and even some of the characters seemed similar to people she'd told me about.

I hunted for entries from the time we met in Colorado. The first one that caught my attention was dated a week after she'd started a casual position in Jimmy's Bar, where I had worked since finishing high school the previous year. I gasped.

I've just finished wiping down the bar and putting the last of the clean glasses away. When I turn around, India is standing in the doorway with her coat on, looking at me. I freeze. I've been trying to get a moment alone with her since I started working here a week ago, but she always gets a lift with Carmel, the Irish girl who works with us – or her dad picks her up. I'm shaking as I grab my coat and move towards her. I ask if I can take her home. She looks kind of alarmed that I've spoken to her. Her big brown eyes are like a doe's – so wide and soft and startled. She shakes her head and tells me her dad is picking her up in ten minutes. Her voice is like her eyes – soft and startled.

Once I know I have ten minutes I take my chance. There's no one else left in the bar – the owner has left India to lock up. I step closer to her and take her hand. She lifts her head in surprise to look at me. I can tell she's not expecting it and I hope she won't freak out. With my other hand I hold the back of her head and then I kiss her. At first she just stands there and lets me. She doesn't freak out, but she doesn't exactly reciprocate either. When I stop and look at her though, she gulps and slowly puts her arms around me. I can't believe it – she's actually pulling me towards her, wanting me to kiss her again ...

There was another post, a day later ...

Tonight when we finish work, India tells me her dad's going to be fifteen minutes late picking her up. She doesn't have her coat on. She lets me put my hands inside her top and feel her breasts as we kiss. Her skin is heavenly – soft and warm and velvety and she reminds me again of a timid female deer ...

And another, a week after that ...

I can't believe I've had to wait another week before being alone with India again. But it's worth the wait. She tells me early in the evening her dad can't pick her up and asks if I can give her a lift. Of course I say yes. I can hardly concentrate on work all night, waiting for closing time. When she finally finishes locking up and we get to my car, I ask her if she wants to go to my place first. She nods ...

There were spots in front of my eyes. I could hardly see any more, but I couldn't stop staring at the screen. Even though my 'name' was different from the one in her most recent post, everything else added up. I recalled Willa teasing me, calling me 'little doe' when we had worked together, and there had been an Irish girl who'd often given me a lift back to Basalt – although her name was Eileen, not Carmel. None of the other stuff was true, though. Willa had never kissed me. I had never been to her place in Aspen. She'd lived in a backpackers' hostel, and she didn't have a car back then. And what she described next I had certainly never done with her.

I covered my face with my hand and peeked through shaking fingers as I scrolled down to the next posts. I was hoping to find something that would prove to me it wasn't Willa. But when I read her description of a dark red velvet dress that 'India' had worn, I recognized it as one of mine. I knew Willa had written this and I knew 'India' was supposed to be me. I clicked through page after page describing an intense lesbian relationship between Willa and 'India'. My head was spinning and I felt dizzy; I realized it was because I wasn't breathing. I took a huge shuddering gasp of air.

It made no sense. Why would Willa have written all this stuff that wasn't true? I went back to the archive and found the oldest post. It dated back twelve years. I did some quick math in my head. Assuming the blog was written by Willa, that would make her about sixteen when she started it. I didn't think blogging had even existed that long ago.

The very earliest entry I could find was about an incident that had happened between Willa and the older brother of a good friend.

> *When I decide to pass the final frontier out of virginity, I choose carefully. I want it to be with someone I like. But not someone I love – not someone who's going to break my heart. My friend Talia's brother Ash seems perfect. Until he tells Talia what we did – and that he's in love with me. Then Talia tells her parents and they tell my parents and none of us are allowed to see each other any more. And Talia goes around school telling everyone I'm a slut. It sucks ...*

My first thought when I read this was that it sounded strangely similar to my own experience. Then I wondered if the friend could be Sera – and, if so, was the brother Hugh? Surely Willa and Hugh would have told me if there was a history between them?

Especially one that important. Or perhaps both of them had conspired to keep it a secret ...

But, like the rest of the blog, there were things that didn't add up. I thought about how warmly Hugh's parents had greeted Willa in the gallery on Monday night. Willa and Sera were as thick as thieves. There was no hint of animosity between any of them.

I should have stopped there. I already had enough evidence to be convinced it was Willa writing the blog, even if everything in it wasn't true. But, like a masochist, I picked another date from the files. It was the day after that fateful night in the diner in New York, when Willa had virtually invited Hugh to seduce me – and then threatened him if he did.

I have finally succeeded in getting my friend Virginia laid – by a man. But I can't decide if I'm pleased about it or not. After my years of plotting and introducing her to dozens of perfectly lovely guys, she's gone and fallen for my old friend's brother Lawrence, who has recently moved to NY.

Virginia? Lawrence? I grimaced at her choice of alternative names for Hugh and me. However, I soon had much worse things to be upset about.

I mean, he's sexy, smart and incredibly charming –
but he had a serious bad-boy reputation back home
…

My mouth fell open. Hugh? Bad-boy reputation? Was that why Willa had warned me off him – warned him to be nice? I thought back to what Hugh had told me after we'd left the diner that night and gone on to Macy's party. It was a very different story. The whole scene was etched into my mind, along with other turning points in my life – The day my mother left. Getting the letter saying I'd been accepted into art school in New York. Leaving Daddy for the first time at the airport. My first sell-out exhibition.

As soon as we'd arrived at Macy's place, Hugh had grabbed me by the hand, hauled me off into one of the bedrooms and shut the door. At first I'd thought he was going to undress me right then and there, but he didn't. He just leaned against the door looking at me – a blazing blue gaze that made me feel like he *had* undressed me. It was like someone had taken a blowtorch to both of us and set us on fire. All the oxygen had been sucked from the room and there was nothing between us but heat.

"Come here," he said finally, softly, into the haze. It wasn't an order. It wasn't a request. It was inevitable. I stepped forward in a trance. When his fingers tangled in my hair, tugging me in slow motion right into the innermost circle of his personal space, I was sure there must have been a shift in the universe. When our lips touched, it was as if all the planets instantly realigned in my favor. The noise of the party receded into the distance, only to be replaced by the wild thumping of our hearts. Hugh's hands, sliding under my top and over my bare skin, were like flames licking me into life, and the gasped whispers of breath we drew were fuel to the fire. Every second his mouth touched mine he was feeding me – pouring power and energy into every cell of my body, creating a new universe around me. I was finally alive.

I almost couldn't bear it when he paused for a moment. I thought I was going to die when he stared at me and shook his head. "Jesus," he breathed. Time stood still. Then, like a prayer, like an incantation of magic, he spoke again and I was thrown back into orbit, spinning so fast it was dizzying. "God, I want to fuck you," he moaned, releasing his words into my mouth as if we were already connected. Dark liquid flames raced through my limbs. I didn't think anything could have made me want him more. Except what he said next.

"I've never done this before," he whispered. "But ..." he pulled his head back again slightly so he could look into my eyes. "I love you, Georgia. This is not some ... one-night stand."

I found it hard to believe that this beautiful, sexy, perfect man who was at that moment causing every cell in my body to go weak with desire had never done this before. And a few hours later, in his apartment, I wondered again whether I'd understood him correctly. My first orgasm had been just inside the doorway, when he'd slid his fingers down the front of my panties because he said he couldn't wait any longer to touch me. The second and third had been on the couch as a result of something he did with his mouth. And the rest had happened sometime between when he tumbled me into his big soft bed and when I woke up there the next morning.

When I opened my eyes, it was like all my molecules had been rearranged and I was levitating above the surface of the bed. The shape and weight of my body seemed to have changed. I was soft ... light ... transparent. Under Hugh's touch, I had been transformed into the person I was always meant to be.

It was well into Sunday evening before Hugh finally delivered me back to my own apartment with the promise of returning as soon as he finished work the next day. I hadn't wanted to leave him – partly because, after just one night, I was already completely addicted to him. But I'd also dreaded the inevitable inquisition from Willa, who was still staying at my place. After I'd been on a date, she normally wouldn't rest until she'd wrung every last detail out of me. And what had happened between Hugh and me was so private, so new – so infinitely precious to me – that I was afraid to share it, in case it disappeared in a puff of smoke before I figured out what it was.

However, Willa had been surprisingly reticent on my return. I wasn't sure if she simply noticed my state of advanced euphoria and decided there was no point in asking me anything; or whether I'd done something wrong, but she'd seemed almost unhappy about the fact that I'd been with Hugh.

Now, I stared at Willa's blog. *'Bad-boy reputation.'* What did it mean? How bad could it be? Was it something to do with what had happened to Willa as a sixteen-year-old? Or was there something else? When I'd pressed Hugh for details of past lovers, he just told me the past didn't matter and he wasn't one to kiss and tell. And I loved him all the more for it.

Now, I was more desperate than ever to talk to him. I glanced at the clock: 5:23. Less than three hours until our Skype call.

Nine

I was halfway through reading another post – where Willa had apparently been sitting on my balcony in New York while Hugh and I got naked on the couch on the other side of the glass – when the phone rang. I jumped at the shrill intrusion into the silent kitchen and leapt up guiltily to answer the call. It was Madeleine.

"Mrs Fraser?" She sounded unusually pleased to be speaking to me, which put me immediately on edge.

"Thank goodness – I've been trying to get hold of you since lunchtime. Have you been out?"

"Uh, yeah," I replied, wondering what business it was of hers where I'd been.

"Oh, well, great that I've caught you before I leave for the day," she continued. "Hugh's asked me to give you a couple of messages."

I frowned. Why couldn't Hugh give me his own messages? Why couldn't he have texted me like he usually did? Why didn't he tell me tonight? I sat down at the table again, distracted by Willa's blog, imagining Hugh bending me over the couch like she'd written. Madeleine was still yabbering, but I wasn't really listening.

"... lost his cell phone last night, so he won't be able to pick up any texts or calls on it for the rest of the week ..."

"Lost?" I echoed, checking I'd heard her correctly.

"Yes. It must have fallen out of his pocket when he was chasing the mugger."

"Mugger?" I stood up and walked away from the laptop, tearing my thoughts away from the blog at last.

Madeleine paused before replying. "Did Hugh not tell you what happened?" There was a note of surprise in her voice.

"No?" My skin prickled in sudden panic. Hugh had been mugged? Even though I'd seen him myself this morning, I couldn't help worrying if he was all right. What was Madeleine saying?

"Well, he only gave me very sketchy details, but it seems he witnessed a mugging as he was walking home. He chased the assailant and brought him down. He's quite the hero apparently – we've had the victim's family and the media contact us today trying to get in touch with him."

"Oh." I sank down onto the couch. Now that I knew Hugh definitely wasn't hurt, I wondered why he'd been walking home – or somewhere. Was it because of what he'd seen at the gallery?

"His phone was handed in to the police station this morning," Madeleine was still gabbling away merrily, full of importance at being the one to tell me the news. "Some girls picked it up off the side of the road, which was lucky. It's a bit scratched so he'll probably need a new one. It seems to still work, though, and at least he hasn't lost his SIM card. I went down to the station and picked it up for him, but I was thinking ... as he won't be back until Friday night, I should probably get it back to you. Will you be home for me to courier it to you? Or perhaps you could pick it up from the office if you're coming into town ..."

Last night seemed so long ago. I finally collected my thoughts enough to remember the screeching, giggling women who had answered Hugh's phone. Maybe there was a logical explanation for everything that had happened, after all. I still couldn't figure out why Hugh would have only arrived home at five in the morning, though – mugging or no mugging. Something about Madeleine's uncharacteristically friendly chatter was bothering me, and I thought back to my phone call with her the previous night – the man's voice in the background and Willa saying, 'He's not there, is he?' Was she trying to cover something up? I made a split-second decision.

"I'll come in and pick up the phone, thanks," I told Madeleine. "Maybe I can take you out for a coffee if you're not too busy. Is tomorrow morning good?"

There was dead silence on the other end of the line. "Uh, yeah, sure ... fine," she finally stuttered. It sounded like she *was* trying to hide something from me. Now that I'd arranged to meet her, I wasn't at all sure I wanted to find out what it was she was hiding. I was about to tell her I'd remembered another appointment when she spoke to me again.

"Oh – I nearly forgot. There's another message for you, too. Hugh says he can't Skype you tonight, but he'll contact you tomorrow at the same time."

I imagined her smiling as she gave me this news. Since last night, I'd felt like a climber who'd fallen off the edge of a cliff. The rope I'd managed to grab hold of had been slowly fraying – snapping strand by strand. My Skype call with Hugh had been the final thread still intact. With that gone, I was now in freefall, with no way of knowing what would happen when I hit the bottom. I found it hard to keep my voice steady as I thanked Madeleine for cutting off my lifeline and said goodbye.

Without looking at it again, I shut down the browser on my laptop and flipped the lid down. I plodded into the kitchen, looking for something to ease the painful yawning in my stomach. I wished now I'd eaten my sushi at lunchtime – which started me fretting about Willa again. The refrigerator was empty – I'd already used up all the leftovers three days ago. The fruit in the bowl was inedible – blackened bananas and wrinkled plums spotted with mold had spoiled in the heat and lay in a pool of brown liquid dotted with fruit flies. I rummaged desperately in the back of the pantry and found a can of tuna and some crackers. I made a mental note to pick up some food the next day on my way home from seeing Madeleine. That was another reason I missed Hugh – he always did the grocery shopping.

I used the crackers to scoop the fish straight out of the can and munched half-heartedly as I sat on the patio and watched the water in the harbor change color and the light gradually fade from the sky. I wondered what Hugh was doing. Why hadn't he been able to Skype me like he'd promised? Did he really have to work, or was he avoiding me? For one irrational moment I wondered if he was seeing someone else. He had been spending a lot of time in Wellington lately. The thoughts drifted through my mind, changing direction and intensity like the evening sky – melting from turquoise to cobalt, to orange, to gold, to indigo and finally to an inky, impenetrable black. I sat there until long after dark, waiting for the moon to rise. Eventually, when it was already high in the sky, I went inside. I took another shower and climbed into bed, exhausted by my thoughts and the long walk in the heat. Despite my fatigue, when I lay down I couldn't sleep. I tried reading, but when I found myself starting the same page three times, I put the book down and turned on the television.

After flicking through dozens of channels that all seemed to be playing the same rugby highlights or endless variations on the elimination contest theme – cooking, fashion design, modeling, home improvement, survival on a desert island – I came across an old 1980s documentary about New York artists. There was something comforting about seeing all the familiar places I'd left behind only a couple of months ago. There were quite a few names and faces I recognized, including Dennis, looking young and slim, with back-combed peroxide blond hair and eyeliner. He had just opened his first gallery. I shut my eyes, wondering if I should tell Hugh I wanted to go back to New York. Maybe it had been a mistake to come here, where I didn't know anyone and everything was so different to what I'd expected. Even Hugh was different here. In New York, our apartment building had been the nicest one in the street. He never went out of town for work. His PA had been a middle-aged woman. And I'd never felt the need to question his past.

Hours later I woke to find the television still going. The documentary had finished and there was a movie playing. Groggily, I grabbed the remote control to switch it off, but a piece of furniture in the scene caught my eye and I sat up to watch for a moment.

The movie was set in Paris in the early twentieth century. A woman and a man were in bed together, and it seemed the man was having some sort of performance anxiety. The woman dressed and went out into the street, where a carnival was in full force. People were variously naked, masked, painted from head to foot, dressed in exotic and outrageous costumes. Wild drums played and the woman was carried along by the crowd. A masked man in a gold loincloth – the rest of his body painted entirely in blue – appeared to be following her. She ducked down a side alley, and still he followed. A growing feeling of panic came over the woman when she reached a pair of locked gates, which formed a dead end. Drummers and acrobats cavorted on the other side of the gates, but the noise of the carnival was so loud they were deaf to her cries as the masked man dragged her away and raped her. She was terrified yet aroused and, against her will, she responded to the man. When they were both sated, the man spoke and she realized it was her husband, Hugo.

The experience appeared to reignite the passion in the woman's marriage, although she seemed to be also continuing an affair with Henry – the man from the hotel. The woman and her husband visited a brothel, where they watched two prostitutes making love. One was tall and blonde; the other was smaller and dark-haired, like the woman watching – like me. Later still, the couple went out dancing. While her husband took a turn on the drums, the woman took a man she seemed to barely know into the backstage area and made love to him urgently, to the sound of her husband's drumming on the other side of the curtain.

The woman had erotic dreams about the prostitutes. She dreamed she was in the scene in place of the shy, reluctant, dark-haired woman, and she kept seeing the face of another, different blonde woman in place of the blonde prostitute. The man she took backstage reappeared, telling her, 'Be careful Anaïs. Abnormal pleasures kill the taste for normal ones.' From this, I figured out that the film was about the erotic writer Anaïs Nin, her husband Hugo, her lover Henry Miller and his wife June. Having missed the beginning, still woozy with sleep and confused about how all the characters related to each other, I flicked off the television with the remote and drifted back to sleep.

But the scenes from the film had become superimposed on my own restless thoughts, invading my dreams with disturbing images. Xavier Bishop was fondling me before the mirror; when I looked at the mirror, it was Hugh touching me. I was tempting a man into the back of Willa's gallery, thinking it was Hugh; when I turned to face him, he was a stranger. I was the dark-haired prostitute being watched by Anaïs Nin; and as the blonde woman went to kiss me, I realized it was Willa. A foreign voice said, '*Be careful, Georgia,*' as I walked naked through a crowd of masked and costumed people, all laughing and talking. Beyond the crowd, Hugh was making love to me under a bridge; but when he removed his mask, it was Xavier. Hugh was somewhere far in the distance with a blonde woman, who was kneeling to undo his trousers.

Ten

I woke up just before dawn. It was Wednesday, but I didn't think about what day it was, or the fact that I'd promised to meet Madeleine that morning. My mind was still crowded with dreams – confused and disturbing. Willa, kissing me. Hugh, being undressed by a blonde woman. Xavier Bishop, with his hands all over me. Me, naked in a crowd of masked men. Voices, saying '*Be careful, Georgia.*'

I didn't try to sleep any longer. I did what I always did in times of crisis. Not bothering to change out of the cotton briefs and tank top I'd slept in, I headed up to my studio. Turning on the speakers and plugging in my MP3 player, I searched for Marilyn Manson and set it to play – loud.

I pulled out half a dozen of the biggest canvases I had. I could hardly reach from one edge to the other with my arms stretched out. I staggered as I carried them across the room, laying them on the floor in a grid, like oversized pavers, with just enough space for me to move between them. I took tubes of acrylic paint and squirted them over the clean, white surfaces. Working quickly, I blended dark, murky backgrounds in indigo and sepia tones, interrupted by violent slashes of teal, scarlet and fiery orange where I left some of the paint unmixed.

At first glance, it may have appeared haphazard and random. But as I worked, distinct shapes emerged on each canvas: two faces about to kiss, with a streak of scarlet both joining and separating their lips; a pair of tall silhouettes gracefully curving into each other, with a third separated from them by a stark white space. One entire canvas was filled with a row of elongated figures in teal and indigo; the shapes of their hips, breasts and necks delicately highlighted in bronze. Another canvas simply contained a man's profile facing a large letter X.

By the time I had covered all six canvases, the paint on the first was already dry. The sun had fully risen and the light in my studio was clear and intense, mirroring the transition of my previously muddy thoughts. Still fueled by the ticking, syncopated beat of the music, I pulled out calligraphy pens and ink and began drawing a series of minute, detailed figures on top of the dry paint. Many were hidden in the shadowy depths of the paint. Some were more exposed, standing out on the negative white spaces like tattoos on skin that had never seen the sun. From a distance, I knew the figures would blur to become part of the texture of the work, but up close they created multiple layers of sub-text underneath the more obvious story told by the paint. I didn't think about what I was drawing. I never did. I just drew – images from my head flooding out through the pens and onto the canvas like a machine on autopilot. Except, unlike Monday night, this time my autopilot was set to Create instead of Destroy.

I'd worked solidly for several hours when I became aware that the music had finished and the only sound in the room was my breathing and the quiet shuffling of my bare feet on the floorboards. I stood, arching my back and circling my shoulders one after the other to relieve the tension in my neck and spine. My whole body ached from the physical exertion of squatting and bending and moving constantly around my work. But the first canvas was complete. I dragged it over to the wall and stood it up so I could keep looking at it as I continued stretching my muscles.

What I saw startled me. I had painted an orgy. There was no other word I could think of to describe the writhing mass of figures: male and female; clothed and naked – dancing among trees, vines, flowers and ferns which formed a sort of winding river that connected them all. Their limbs intertwined sensually – hands on each other's faces, breasts, legs, genitals; slipping inside clothing. Heads and bodies tilted back, offering sensitive, exposed flesh on necks, arms, between thighs for the kisses and caresses of their companions. Eyes were closed and lips curved in ecstasy, forming a thrilling catalog of love and lust.

Usually, what flowed from my pen when I was working came from sources I could identify. All the works in my recent exhibition had been based on the native Maori legends and histories of the Piha area. But this was like nothing I had ever seen or imagined. I closed my eyes, trying to recall where the ideas might have come from. I pictured myself in the scene – walking naked through a crowd of people, all reaching out to touch me. To my horror, Xavier Bishop's face appeared before my closed eyes.

A dizzy sensation came over me as I was reminded of Monday night – his hand slipping inside my skirt and Hugh standing in the doorway watching. I opened my eyes. For a moment I thought I was going to black out. When my stomach growled audibly, I realized it wasn't only my thoughts that were making my head spin. I checked the time on my MP3 player. It had just gone ten o'clock. I'd been up since dawn and I hadn't eaten yet. I left the canvas leaning against the wall and headed downstairs to the kitchen.

It was only once I'd gulped down a huge glass of water and set the coffee on to brew that I remembered my sad lack of food supplies. The fruit in the bowl was in an even worse state than it had been the night before. There was also no cereal or milk left. I wandered into the overgrown orchard at the end of the garden, hoping to find something to eat there. I managed to scrounge an apple and a couple of misshapen nectarines, which I took inside to cut up and eat at the kitchen bench. Then I poured myself a black coffee and went back outside to bask in the morning sunshine while I drank it.

Lazing on the sun lounger, I closed my eyes to the delicious warmth that penetrated my body and stretched languidly. As I did so, I noticed the crotch of my briefs was decidedly damp. Squirming, I ran my hand down to the top of my thighs. I squeezed, then squirmed again at the electric pulse that shot through me as a result. I opened my eyes and glanced around the garden, wondering if it was private enough to put my fingers inside my pants. It probably was, but what I really wanted was Hugh. The three days until I would see him again seemed like months. Even the Skype call he'd postponed until this evening felt like it was still an eternity away. I wondered if I dared send him a text, even though I knew he would be in court by now.

Text. Phone. Fuck. I leapt up in alarm, knocking over my coffee as I remembered. Hugh didn't have his phone with him. I was supposed to be picking it up off Madeleine. I'd told her I would come by mid-morning and I wasn't even dressed. I dashed inside, flung my coffee cup into the sink and charged upstairs to get ready.

After a two-minute shower, I stood in the middle of our dressing room, wondering what to wear. Most of my clothes were still squashed into the cases that had arrived a month ago from New York, and the rest needed washing. I'd been far too busy preparing my exhibition to even think about unpacking or doing laundry. I dug around in the largest of the suitcases, searching for something that didn't look too crumpled. Settling on an above-the-knee sundress in a pale vintage floral print, I tugged it on and rummaged in another case for shoes. I knew I'd packed them in pairs, but it was as if gremlins had gotten in and gleefully separated them all during the journey. Finally, having found a pair of cream leather Doc Martens with lilac butterflies embroidered up the sides, I threw my bag across my shoulder and bolted down the stairs, out the front door and up the road.

I got to the top of our street to see the bus pulling away from the stop 50 feet away and cursed. The next one wasn't due for another half an hour. Flopping onto the seat in the bus shelter, I pulled out my phone. Eleven o'clock. It was already a stretch to call that mid-morning. I pulled up my list of contacts and dialed Hugh's work number, so I could let Madeleine know I was running late. When she didn't answer after three attempts, I sighed. A heat haze shimmered above the pavement and I was already sticky from my dash up the hill to the bus stop. If I started walking now, I could be there in 30 minutes. It would be a drag in the heat, but at least it would still be morning. If I waited for the next bus, I wouldn't get there until midday and Madeleine might have gone to lunch. I shoved my phone back in my bag and got to my feet, telling myself I really did need to learn to drive.

I'd never felt disadvantaged before by my lack of a driver's license. In Basalt, I was so anti-social I'd hardly gone out anyway. And Daddy had been happy to drive me anywhere I couldn't get to on my bike. In New York, it was easy to walk or take the subway. And there had been a grocery store three steps from my apartment building. In Auckland, everything was so spread out. Even a trip to the supermarket in the next suburb required major planning and at least half a day to accomplish without a car.

As I half walked, half ran down the road, I contemplated the logistics of learning to drive. There was no way I'd dare get behind the wheel of Hugh's big black Audi, so I'd need a car of my own. I had no idea how to go about choosing a car – or even how much one might cost. I didn't know how much driving lessons were either. I tried to calculate in my head the amount Willa would be paying me at the end of the month for my paintings once her commission was taken off, wondering if it would be enough to cover both. And if it was, whether there would be any money left over to re-stock my supplies of paint and canvases. I wasn't that comfortable using Hugh's credit card to pay for living expenses, but I drew the line at letting him fund my painting materials.

I was so busy thinking about cars and driving and money that I didn't notice the black clouds gathering overhead, or the sudden chill in the air as the pressure plummeted. It was only when the first drops of rain smacked heavily onto my bare arms that I looked up.

'*Damn*,' I muttered to myself. It was one of those brief, heavy thunder showers that, even after two months in Auckland, I still hadn't learned to anticipate. Within seconds of the first drops hissing one by one onto the hot pavement around me, I was standing in the middle of a torrential downpour. Although I was just minutes away from the city, the steep street I was climbing bordered a fenced off car rental yard on one side and a demolition site on the other. There was no shelter anywhere. I started to run, but by the time I reached the canopy of the shops, I was soaked to the skin – and the sun was beating down again. I trudged the rest of the way up the sharp incline and down into Queen Street with my dress clinging to my thighs and water trickling from my legs into the tops of my boots, telling myself things couldn't get any worse. As usual, I was wrong.

Eleven

Hugh's office was on the 25th floor of the IAG building, halfway up Queen Street. The slender, stepped facade of bronze mirror glass glittered in the now dazzling sunlight. It screamed wealth and class and I slunk into the marble foyer feeling like a vagrant in my disheveled state. Exactly how disheveled I was only became apparent as I stood in the elevator, with mirrors on three sides of me. My face was sweaty and blotchy from the exertion of walking the last part of my journey uphill in the heat. My hair hung in wet, knotted clumps about my face. My dress was still damp and the outline of my underwear was visible through the light cotton fabric. I tried to wring out my skirt, but all I succeeded in doing was wringing in a whole bunch of creases and making a small puddle on the floor of the lift. I was still trying to blot it into the carpet with my boot when the doors opened to the 22nd floor reception area and I came face to face with Hugh's colleague, Albert Wong.

He greeted me in surprise, making a point of standing aside to let me out before getting into the lift with two women in their 30s, both dressed in dark suits. As one of the women pushed the button, I noticed the other one eying me curiously and murmuring surreptitiously to Albert – obviously asking him who I was. When he replied, I saw her peek at me out of the corner of my eye, although she was evidently unaware that I'd seen her – or that I could hear her as she spoke to Albert again more loudly. "Hugh Fraser's wife?" I heard her ask Albert disbelievingly. "I thought ..."

The lift closed before she finished her sentence. I could have shrugged it off as unimportant. After all, it was logical they were surprised to see me there, given that Hugh was in Wellington. But as I hovered uncertainly outside the elevators, a wave of paranoia overtook me. Several other people had peered over when first Albert, then the woman, had spoken, and I was sure they were all staring at me. Like Albert and his two companions, they were all immaculately dressed in dark suits – there was not a hair out of place or a bare leg or a floral print to be seen. I hurried over to the reception desk, hoping no-one would notice my wet boot prints on the gleaming parquet floor.

The receptionist was on the phone when I approached. After a cursory glance at me, she mouthed '*Be right with you*,' and continued with what sounded suspiciously like a personal call. Standing there awkwardly with my hair dripping onto the front of my dress, I contemplated trying to find a bathroom so I could dry myself off. A quick scan of the area revealed no sign of one. I searched more desperately for a way to escape my embarrassing situation, but the more I looked around, the more my discomfort grew. It wasn't only my bedraggled condition – there was something about the atmosphere of the place that weighed on me and prickled like a dusty old woolen blanket.

The foyer could have been transported into the present straight from 1932, the date on the bronze plaque attached to the massive dark oak reception desk. The two enormous leather Chesterfield sofas which flanked the desk were an almost identical shade of deep chocolate brown, as were a pair of highly polished low wooden tables in front of them. Even the portraits of the firm's founders, Mr Angus and Mr MacTaggart, were in the same somber hues, their heavy, gilded frames hardly making an impact against the dark wood paneled walls. In stark contrast to the exterior of the building, it was as if time had stood still within the walls of the firm, and the decor of this foyer, which might once have represented the height of fashionable luxury, now gave the impression of an old sepia photograph – stuffy, conservative and belonging to another generation. It wasn't at all the sort of place I'd imagined when I pictured Hugh at work.

I was just wondering if the people who worked with Hugh were as conservative as the environment when a gray-haired man in a dark brown suit marched up to the reception desk, confirming my theory. The receptionist was still merrily chatting away on the phone, but she hung up immediately when he approached, so he was obviously someone important. Although he barely noticed me, I smiled at him, inwardly thanking him for rescuing me from my predicament. After he had instructed the receptionist, whose name I discovered was Helen, to order him a taxi and get some documents on an urgent courier, the man headed for the elevators and Helen turned to me with a benign smile.

"So sorry to keep you waiting – how can I help?"

"Er, I'm here to see Madeleine Knight," I said.

With a seashell pink fingernail poised above her PABX system, ready to dial Madeleine's extension number, she looked me up and down. I wasn't quite sure, but she might have wrinkled her nose at me. "Can I let her know your name and what it's regarding?" she asked in a bored voice, clearly more interested in who was coming out of the lift, which I heard ping open behind me.

"Georgia Daniels," I muttered quietly, hoping that no-one would hear – or if they did, that they wouldn't recognize my name. Helen looked blank. Her hand was still hovering above the keypad, as if she required further explanation before she was willing to trouble Hugh's secretary with my presence. "I'm Hugh Fraser's wife," I added, still more quietly. I glanced around surreptitiously, checking that no-one was within earshot. I still had an irrational feeling that people were staring at me, and decided the less attention I drew to myself, the better it would be.

When I turned back to Helen, I saw that her fingers still hadn't moved. What more could she want to know? "I'm here to pick up his phone," I tried. Then I stopped. Her eyes had widened into saucers and her cheeks were scarlet under her carefully applied foundation. I looked around anxiously. "Is there something wrong?" I asked, willing her to call Madeleine so I could get out of there as quickly as possible. People had noticed that she was upset about something.

Her voice was abruptly loud, cutting through the library-like hush like a bell chiming in the somber silence of a churchyard. "No, no, nothing, Mrs, er ... Miss ... Ms ... Fraser," I cringed as she almost shouted the name, but she misinterpreted the cause of my distress. "I mean Daniels," she blurted out, louder than ever. "It's just I wasn't ... we weren't ... expecting you. Mr ... Dr ... Fraser isn't here," she finished lamely.

After I'd explained the purpose of my visit to Helen again, and she had finally dialed Madeleine's number, I was even more painfully conscious of the people loitering around the reception area waiting for the lift. It was clear some of them had overheard our conversation, and several of the women were now definitely glancing in my direction and whispering to each other.

Too nervous to sit, I picked up a magazine off one of the low tables and tried to nonchalantly thumb through it while Helen announced my arrival to Madeleine. Inside, I was churning. Why were all these women staring at me and talking about me? Did they know something about me? or about Hugh? Memories of the school gossip grapevine and Ryan McGregor come flooding back and I wondered if, somehow, all these people were party to the incident with Xavier on Monday night. I wanted to leave the building right then, but before I had a chance to do anything, the lift arrived. A small blonde woman a couple of years younger than me, with a neatly styled bob and wearing a dove gray crepe suit over a white blouse stepped out, and the waiting group disappeared into the lift.

The blonde woman approached me cautiously and extended a hand. "Mrs Fraser?" she enquired uncertainly. "I'm Madeleine Knight."

I dropped the magazine as I fumbled to shake Madeleine's hand. "Hi, nice to meet you in person at last. Call me Georgia, please," I said. She seemed as cold and superior in the flesh as she always sounded on the phone. I tried desperately to think of a way to break the ice. "Er, thanks for coming to my exhibition opening. I hope you enjoyed yourself."

"Yes, it was ... great," she said stiffly. "I'm sorry I couldn't stay longer. My brother was in town and I had to go and pick him up from the airport."

"Oh, that's OK," I replied. Relief surged through me. Madeleine's early departure meant there was no chance she would have seen Xavier follow me into the storeroom – or worse. "I felt bad I hardly knew anyone," I grimaced apologetically at Madeleine, "I've been ... tucked away a little. I always prefer solitude when I'm preparing work for a show. I hope people here don't think I've been rude – not showing my face yet."

"Don't worry about it," said Madeleine bluntly. "Hugh's usually pretty busy when he's in the office. He doesn't really like distractions." She looked pointedly at my short dress and bare legs.

I felt a tiny stab of irritation at her thinly veiled criticism of my appearance. I also fought to suppress a smirk. Some of the texts I sent Hugh during work hours – and his replies – would definitely class as distractions. A slight 'ahem' from Madeleine brought me back to the present. I blushed, hoping she hadn't read my thoughts.

"Uh, I'm sorry I'm so late," I said to her. "I was on a roll with some painting and lost track of time. I guess you've already taken your coffee break." I added, remembering my offer on the phone. Then, to my horror, I found myself inviting her to lunch instead. I barely knew what to say to her for the next five minutes, let alone for an hour over lunch. But I had a sudden urge to find out why Madeleine was always so unfriendly to me. It was as if she was trying to hide something, or I'd offended her in some way.

"Oh," Madeleine looked as alarmed at being invited as I was having asked her. "I've actually got a couple of emails I need to send before lunchtime ..."

"That's OK, I don't mind waiting," I insisted. The more she seemed to want to avoid me, the more determined I was to find out what was behind her apparent hostility. "In fact, I'd love to see where Hugh works. Maybe I could wait in his office?"

Madeleine agreed, although obviously reluctantly, and there was an awkward silence between us as we stepped into the lift and she swiped her security card to give us access to the upper floors.

When Madeleine showed me into Hugh's office, I declined her offer of coffee or tea and strolled over to the window. Despite the density of buildings surrounding us, there was a magnificent view of the harbor from the 25th floor. I sat on the edge of the desk, enjoying the sight of boats and cranes, trucks and men all working in unison to create a sort of industrial ballet against the sparkling backdrop of turquoise water. It occurred to me that Hugh must be reasonably senior within his firm to have this spacious office with such a lovely view – and not for the first time I wondered with something akin to guilt whether I really knew Hugh at all. He rarely talked about his work, and I never really asked. In fact, I wasn't entirely sure what sort of lawyer he was – something to do with human rights, I thought. Or maybe international relations. Or both.

I stepped away from the desk behind me and turned to look into the room. Filled with many of Hugh's own possessions, there was a sense of light and color in this space that filled me with relief after the oppressiveness of the reception area. The wall opposite the window was mostly taken up with a large painting of a New York streetscape, which I'd given him for his birthday a few months before we left the USA. Another wall featured a number of smaller works which together formed a montage representing Hugh's favorite artists and styles. Below these paintings was a small sideboard and a Victorian-style chaise upholstered in acid green ruched velvet – a welcome burst of vibrancy in this studious, formal environment.

On the opposite side of the room, behind the desk, were dark oak bookshelves stuffed full of encyclopedic looking volumes. Several small abstract pieces of sculpture among the books relieved their stiff lines, as did the perfectly proportioned desk in front of them. I'd been with Hugh the day he bought it in New York – a classic 1930s L-shaped piece with a thick figured maple top curving off at one end to form a vertical plane that cascaded down to the floor.

I glanced toward the door. Madeleine still seemed busy at her computer. I slipped into Hugh's chair and leaned back. Putting my feet on the desk, I closed my eyes and inhaled deeply, trying to pick up his scent. As I quietly absorbed Hugh's essence, I imagined him coming into the office and finding me ... approaching me from behind and slipping his arms down my bare shoulders and onto my breasts ... squeezing them, tilting my head back and kissing me until I was breathless and hungry for more. I sighed deeply and arched further back into the chair. I pointed my toes and then curled them, picturing Hugh leading me over to the chaise, loosening his tie ...

A quiet shuffle of shoes on the carpet made me open my eyes. Madeleine was in the doorway. There was a look of alarm on her face at the sight of me sprawled in her boss's chair with my boots on his desk. I hastily swung my legs down, stood up and grabbed my bag from the floor beside me, once again hoping she couldn't read my mind. "Sorry, must have dozed off. I was up early this morning," I explained to Madeleine, deliberately ignoring her shocked expression. "Are you ready to go?"

Madeleine nodded and, as we headed to the lifts together, I asked her about Hugh's favorite places to eat. "Well, he's usually quite busy, so I often go out and get him something from the Sushi Factory or a sandwich from Big Al's. If he's taking a client to lunch he goes to Vivace or Kitchen. If it's a friend, Kushi for Japanese or Rakinos for a burger. It's a bit ... arty there though." Madeleine pulled a face, then stopped, recognizing the implications of her last comment. "But I guess that's why he likes it," she finished awkwardly.

I felt another prickle of irritation. She was so conservative. Something about the way she'd screwed up her face when she said 'arty' made me think again of all the girls I'd been at high school with, who'd made judgments about my black clothing and choice of music without knowing anything about me. Yet there was also a twinge of something else – a kind of defensiveness – around the fact that Madeleine seemed to be so intimately acquainted with Hugh's habits. I was tempted to insist on going to Rakinos, just to push her out of her comfort zone, but I convinced myself that being familiar with Hugh's favorite eating places was simply part of the role of a good P.A.. I let Madeleine choose and we ended up at the Japanese place, Kushi. After we had each ordered a lunch box, Madeleine started opening her purse in order to pay.

"I'll get this," I said, pulling out Hugh's credit card and extending a hand to indicate Madeleine should put her purse away. As I did so, I noticed a photo of Madeleine and a man in the clear plastic photo sleeve of the purse. I inclined my head slightly to get a better look. Our conversation had already dried up – perhaps I could show an interest in her boyfriend to keep things going. However, when I focused on the photo, I gasped in shock and dropped my credit card. The man beside her in the photo looked like Hugh. It *was* Hugh, I was sure of it. He had his arm over her shoulder and they were smiling at the camera, holding champagne glasses aloft as if celebrating something. I glanced sharply at Madeleine's face, but she wasn't looking at me. Apparently oblivious to my scowl, she closed her purse and swooped down to pick up my card. When she handed it back to me, she laughed nervously, although she gave no other sign to indicate she thought anything was amiss.

My legs shook. It was all I could do to make it to the table with my meal. Everything was painfully clear all of a sudden. That's why everyone had been staring at me, whispering about me. That's why she was always so unfriendly to me on the phone; why she'd been so reluctant to come to lunch. She was having an affair with Hugh, and everyone at the office knew about it.

Bitch, I thought as I stared at her blithely squeezing a couple of edamame beans out of their pods. I couldn't believe she had the audacity to laugh when she gave me back Hugh's card so I could pay for our lunch. How many times had *he* bought her lunch? What else had he bought her? Did she have a card with his name on it, too?

Even more painful was the realization that Hugh had been deceiving me. He'd clearly gone to her place after he left the gallery on Monday night, and had been there when I phoned her. Willa knew it too – that's why she asked if he was there after I'd spoken to Madeleine. No wonder Hugh had been so quick to dismiss the whole fiasco with Xavier Bishop when he finally came home. My whole body throbbed with humiliation and fury. It took me a while to become conscious of Madeleine speaking to me. "Pardon?" I said, my voice sounding oddly loud through the vacuum of anger in my ears.

"I was saying you must be really proud of Hugh – catching that mugger and everything. Apparently the guy nearly wet his pants when Hugh got hold of him. But you know what Hugh's like – he would never resort to violence. It was a bit of a nuisance that he lost his phone though, especially as he's away this week. It's amazing that it still works, given the damage. Look." Madeleine fished about in her bag and pulled out Hugh's iPhone, which looked seriously worse for wear.

In a daze, I took it from her. I stared at the cracked screen, then back at Madeleine. Did she honestly think I was going to believe her ridiculous story about a mugger? She must have deliberately trashed his phone in order to create an alibi for their tryst. Was Hugh aware of what she'd done?

"I hope you got to spend a bit of time with Hugh before he flew back to Wellington," Madeleine was still chatting away. "I understand it was quite late by the time he finished at the police station. I guess it must have been a bit disappointing for you, after he made a special effort to be there. Still, I suppose he's already seen the paintings anyway ..."

My hands were shaking so much I could hardly undo the zipper on my bag to put Hugh's phone away. What kind of a fool did Madeleine take me for? Did she really think I hadn't seen the photo? Hadn't heard Hugh's voice in the background when I was speaking to her?

"Mrs Fraser ... Georgia ... are you alright?" Madeleine touched my arm. I shrank away from her, resisting the urge to scream.

I glared at her. "No, I'm not," I snapped. I stood up. "I can't stay for lunch after all – I think you know why." Without waiting for a reply, I stumbled out of the dining room and into the street – first walking, then running – as quickly as I could away from her astounded face.

Twelve

When I stopped running, I was standing beside a fountain tucked into the corner of a small courtyard; a narrow slope of grass and several large Phoenix palm trees above it. I recognized it as Freyburg Place, around the corner from the WVK Gallery. My first instinct was to run into the gallery and pour my heart out to Willa. Then I remembered she was out of town until Thursday night. And even if she was there, how could I trust her after reading her blog? The stories about me might not be true, but I still had no idea whether there was any truth in the one she'd written about Hugh.

I sank onto a park bench near the fountain. A couple in matching his'n'hers pin striped suits leaned back to back on the seat nearest me, reading in companionable silence while they absently munched on gourmet sandwiches. Pigeons loitered nearby in the hope of a crumb or two falling in their direction. Another pair of lovers sat on the grass, designer jackets neatly folded beside them, exchanging spoonfuls of ice cream from waxed tubs marked 'Giapo'. Everywhere I looked, I saw couples – hand in hand; arm in arm; stealing kisses – all dressed as if they could actually afford the clothes in the nearby shops, with hairstyles and shoes to match. I thought of Madeleine, with her gray skirt and tailored jacket, pristine white blouse and carefully groomed hair. And of Hugh, as he'd looked yesterday when he left for Wellington in his dark suit and tie. I stared down at my wrinkled dress and Doc Martens. What had I been thinking of, marrying Hugh? Why had he even asked me?

I knew the answer to that, of course. A week after I took Hugh home to meet my father, Daddy told me he was dying. They'd given him 6-12 months. Not long after that, Hugh told me his work Visa was expiring. He said he'd been planning to ask me if I'd come back to New Zealand with him, but with Daddy sick he knew I wouldn't want to go. He asked me to marry him so he could stay with me and support me through what we all knew was going to be a tough time. And he had. The knowledge that Hugh had promised to love me in good times and in bad, and that he would be there for me after Daddy was gone, sustained my father and me both through those terrible months. Why would he have done that if he didn't love me? He could have simply gone back to New Zealand and forgotten all about me.

My thoughts were interrupted by the sound of laughter coming from a balcony opposite where I was sitting. I glanced up and saw the name – Rakinos – in large metal letters across the front of the building. The 'arty' place. I looked around at all the tailored suits and designer dresses walking past me. Making a split-second decision, I picked up my bag and walked purposefully across the road, into the cool gloom of the arcade and up the tiled stairs.

As soon as I walked through the heavy glazed doors, I felt at home. The stained concrete floors and walls covered in graffiti art reminded me of my old New York haunts. A group of people at the bar were talking about their piercings and tattoos. A DJ was mixing cool jazz grooves with some lazy drum and bass. A couple of guys in black T-shirts and faded jeans were playing on an old Pinball machine in the corner. A girl in a long semi-transparent floral skirt sat in the wide windowsill, soaking up the sun and sipping her drink, looking for all the world like a 1970s Coke ad. The seating was a mixture of battered leather sofas and utilitarian plywood chairs, arranged haphazardly around simple wooden tables.

After ordering a steak sandwich, I found a table in a corner behind an oversized palm. A newspaper was lying on one of the sofas nearby and I picked it up. Even though it was yesterday's, I leafed through it idly while I waited for my sandwich to arrive. Somewhere in the middle pages, a narrow column of text and a photo of a man's face caught my eye. I blinked in surprise, then read the headline – *'Lawyer makes Citizen's Arrest'*. I checked the photo again. I wasn't mistaken – it was Hugh. The story explained that Hugh was being hailed as a hero after apprehending a man who assaulted a Japanese tourist and attempted to steal his backpack. It was all exactly as Madeleine had described, and a flood of conflicting emotions poured through me. Pride, that my husband had done something so selfless and brave. Concern, that he'd put himself in danger and possibly been hurt. Relief, that Madeleine hadn't been lying after all. And acute embarrassment at the way I'd behaved to her. She must have thought I was insane, walking out like that for no apparent reason.

It still didn't explain why she had a photo of Hugh in her purse, though – nor why he hadn't come home until nearly 5am on Tuesday morning. Surely it couldn't have taken that long at the police station? I wished I could call Hugh or Skype him right there and then, so he could explain everything to me and put my mind at rest.

I was still brooding about Hugh and where he'd been on Monday night when my meal arrived. I glanced up to thank the waitress and got another surprise. It was Jessica Tanner, one of the artists Willa had introduced me to on Monday night.

"Oh, hi," I said, pleased to see a familiar face. "What are you doing here?"

Jessica grinned ruefully at me. "Just paying the bills. You know how it gets sometimes."

"Uh, yeah," I muttered, instantly regretting asking such a stupid question. The reality was, I'd never struggled to pay my rent. My father's income as a small town DJ had been modest, but, as I discovered after he died, he'd borrowed heavily against our family home to put me through five years of Art School and continue paying me an allowance until I'd established a career as an artist. When we got married, Hugh insisted I keep all the money I earned from my painting, adamant that his salary was easily enough to support us both. The only reason I was so broke now was that all my savings had gone to pay for Daddy's hospital bills and funeral, which had been more than I'd got from selling his house after the bank loan had been repaid. Even so, Hugh did take care of providing a roof over our heads and food in the cupboards – and, although I tried not to use it at all, he repeatedly urged me to spend whatever I liked on his credit card. Jessica's comment made me painfully aware of how much I depended on Hugh, and how lost I would be without him if I had to try and make my own way.

Jessica hovered at my table for a moment, as if she wanted to say something. I hesitated, too. I had intended to call her and ask her to have a coffee with me, but now I felt unsure. Maybe she couldn't afford to go out for coffee. And maybe she would be insulted if I offered to pay. Or she'd think I was some sort of spoilt sugar baby with a rich husband. Maybe I had no more in common with her than I did with Madeleine. Finally, she just said, "Enjoy your meal," and walked off looking slightly sheepish. When I left, I couldn't decide whether to add a big tip to the credit card charge or put a few coins in the jar on the counter. In my quandary, I did neither, which made me feel like even more of a fraud as I wandered forlornly down High Street.

It was only after I saw big pink and red hearts in the fourth store window I looked into that I remembered what day it was. February 14th. I'd been looking forward to my first Valentine's day with Hugh – in fact, my first Valentine's day with anyone who could remotely be classed a Valentine. With everything that had happened in the last couple of days, though, I'd completely forgotten about it, and it seemed Hugh had too. He hadn't phoned me this morning. He hadn't left me anything on Tuesday before he rushed off in such a hurry. I wondered if he was the sort of guy who got his secretary to buy his wife presents and send her flowers. I hoped not – it seemed so impersonal. Whether he was or not, Madeleine hadn't mentioned it, so he obviously hadn't asked her to send me anything today.

I focused with difficulty on the window of the store I was standing in front of. It was a small lingerie boutique. There was a gorgeous inky blue satin slip in the display. I had Hugh's credit card in my purse. Since he hadn't bothered, I decided, I may as well go ahead and buy myself a Valentine's day gift. I walked up to the door and pushed it open.

Once the assistant had found the slip in my size, I accepted her offer to put it in one of the fitting rooms while I looked through the rest of the store. After I had bypassed rows of pretty bras and panties similar to plenty I already owned, courtesy of weekend shopping trips with Hugh; and a selection of way too sensible silk pajamas; I decided there was nothing else that took my fancy. I was about to head into the fitting room when I noticed one more rack right at the back of the store.

It was a little difficult to tell what some of the items on it were; they were so insubstantial. I pulled out one of the more identifiable garments – a sheer black mesh chemise with lovely lace detailing around the top – and laid it on top of the rack for consideration. Hugh would probably like it, I thought. It reminded me of the outfits worn by the prostitutes in the film I'd woken up to last night. I wasn't sure if that was a good thing. As I continued browsing, I caught a glimpse of some similarly antique looking lace on another hanger and pulled that out, too. I held it up, trying to work out how the collection of scraps fitted together. The panties had a deep slit in the front, which rendered them somewhat ineffective as underwear; and the bikini-style halter top was so tiny the triangles were barely wider than a couple of my fingers. They came with a set of matching lace cuffs and a choker, which were all joined together with delicate silver chains. I'd just figured it out and was deciding it wasn't my thing when I was startled by a low murmur in my ear.

"A difficult choice, I agree. Myself, I prefer the collar and chains, but I think Hugh will like the other one better."

I whirled around and was shocked to find myself face to face with Xavier Bishop. His pale blue eyes glinted at me audaciously. He was close enough to … kiss me, I realized I was thinking. He smelt good. Too good. Like apples and cinnamon. The scent wafted over me, dragging me into its comforting haze like an opiate. I held my breath, using all my willpower to avoid falling under its spell. *This is not a dream. This is not a dream. This is not a dream,* I repeated silently to myself. I stepped backwards warily, the pounding of my heart abating only slightly when he didn't move to follow me. I opened my mouth to respond with some witty, carefree remark, but the simple effort of stepping away from him had sapped me of energy and no sound came out.

Xavier's eyes flicked over my body – the same way they had on Monday night. The same shiver of sensation ran through me, and my thin cotton dress felt like it offered inadequate protection against the power of his gaze. Once again I was frozen, like a deer staring into the headlights of an oncoming truck – unable to move in the face of impending disaster. When I didn't speak, he shrugged and gave me a wolfish grin. "Of course, you could always take both," he suggested. His tone was full of innuendo, although I couldn't figure out exactly what he meant. Before I could ask him, he nodded politely in farewell and left.

"Would you like me to put those in the fitting room for you, too?" I don't know how long I had been standing there, one hand on the chemise and the other clutching the chain outfit, when the assistant's hesitant enquiry startled me back to reality.

"Er, Yes. No. Sorry – I'll ... I'll take both of these – and the slip," I heard myself saying, wondering as I did so why I didn't simply leave all of them. I didn't need underwear. And I definitely didn't need any of this ... non-underwear.

The girl looked surprised. "Wouldn't you like to try them on first?" she prompted gently. "It's just, we don't take returns." She referred me to a discreet sign on the counter.

"No." I assured her as I handed Hugh's credit card over and signed off the transaction. "They'll be fine." Xavier Bishop's presence seemed to have flicked the autopilot switch in my brain again, and for some reason I didn't understand, it was vitally important that I buy all three items and leave the store immediately.

As soon as I got home, I flung the stylish little carry bag onto one of the empty shelves in the dressing room and retreated to my studio. I was desperate for something else to occupy my thoughts until the evening – something that didn't involve Xavier Bishop. Still on autopilot, I turned on the music, grabbed pens and inks and began working on the next of the canvases lying on the floor. I worked blindly, intuitively, letting each tiny figure flow from my pen in a kind of catharsis. Hours later, finally purged of the disturbance Xavier Bishop had created in my thoughts, I stood up to review the work as a whole. Once again, I was troubled by what I saw.

The canvas I had unwittingly chosen was the one with the man's profile on one side and the X on the other. Unlike the painting I'd worked on in the morning, there was little love in the couplings of the figures inked so delicately in and around the paint. The exchanges were savage – morphing in places into murder, torture, cannibalism, rape. Many of the figures were masked or bound; cruelly constrained by Victorian corsetry; their naked flesh cut with ropes, whips and chains that connected them and wound through the spaces between them like snakes. Their torturers were scaly, reptilian looking humanoids; tiny nymph-like creatures with evil eyes and sharp pointy teeth; grotesque giants and monsters with oversized genitals.

It was as if my second encounter with Xavier Bishop had opened the door to the subliminal images that had been fluttering through my mind since Monday night, releasing them to fly like demons from the shadows and come alarmingly to life on my canvas. I thought about Xavier Bishop. There was definitely something dark and dangerous about him. Yet there was also something comforting. I felt calm ... loved, even ... when I was near him. I'd sensed it again in the lingerie store. Like I could trust him. But these images didn't look at all comforting – or like something I should trust or be drawn to.

They reminded me of Eve and her tattooed friends – the subjects of my first sell-out exhibition in New York. My paintings had focused on their glamorous clothing and hairstyles, and the brilliant colors of the birds, butterflies, flowers and nymphs that adorned their skin. Critics had raved about the way I'd left the dark undercurrents of their culture carefully hidden, deliberately unexplored – although I knew privately it had been fear as much as deliberate intent that had prevented me from delving more deeply into their world of pain and submission.

Now, as I surveyed the stark black and white catalog of agonies in front of me, I had an urge to take more paint and fill the tiny macabre figures with brilliant pinks, oranges, greens, scarlet and turquoise. But there was something about it that refused color, lured me instead to embrace its darkness – more powerfully than Eve and her friends ever had. I shivered. I wondered if I should paint over it. I couldn't do that either. I recognized good work when I saw it. And it was nearly eight o'clock – time for my Skype call with Hugh. I hauled the huge canvas across the room and leaned it into a corner facing the wall before heading down to the bedroom.

Thirteen

Lying on the bed with my iPad, my stomach tightened in an unwelcome attack of nerves. Hugh and I didn't normally talk much on our Skype calls – most of them were spent simply watching each other – stripping, masturbating, coming. I was craving such an exchange, but I was also determined to put my mind at rest about all the things that were worrying me – Xavier Bishop, Madeleine, Willa's blog, where Hugh had been on Monday night. I tried to rehearse our conversation in my head – me asking calm, reasonable questions and

Hugh reassuring me with soothing, logical explanations. As eight o'clock came and went with no sign of him, though, anxiety rapidly displaced my forced calm. By the time Hugh finally checked in at ten past eight, the knot in my stomach was a hard, cold mass of dread.

"Hey, baby G," he said softly, putting out a finger as if to tap my nose. There were no apologies – just his usual playful grin. He had his shirt off, so he was obviously expecting this call to progress much the same as any other.

"Hi," I muttered, then faltered, my carefully rehearsed questions escaping me. I tried to avoid looking at his broad, muscled chest and the patch of dark, silky hair that trailed from it to a spot somewhere below the camera. I had to focus on getting some answers.

"Happy Valentine's day," he said unexpectedly, catching me off guard.

I should have been pleased that he'd remembered. And I was, kind of. But it also made me ashamed for thinking he'd forgotten, and for forgetting about it myself. "Uh, yeah, happy Valentine's day," I muttered uncomfortably.

Hugh frowned. "What's wrong, baby? Didn't you like my present?"

"Present?" I replied. "What present?" Hugh had sent me a present? Now I really felt bad. I hadn't gotten him anything. And I'd spent over $500 on his credit card.

Hugh looked crestfallen. "I put it on an urgent courier yesterday. It should have arrived this morning."

I thought about my early start to the day. "I was painting," I mumbled, feeling like I owed him some sort of explanation for why I hadn't taken delivery of the package. "I couldn't sleep, so I got up early. I had the music up loud. I guess I didn't hear the door."

"Oh," said Hugh, still disappointed, but with a tinge of relief in his voice. "I was kind of wondering where you were. I tried to phone you as well." He gave me a wistful smile. "Ah, well. It's not the end of the world. I guess the courier will come back tomorrow. So." He raised his eyebrows flirtatiously. "Did you get me anything?"

"Uh," I stammered, trying to think of a way I could say yes without lying. "Well, kind of. I thought I'd give it to you when you get back on Friday."

Hugh smirked. "That's OK. I can think of something you can give me now." He narrowed his eyes and pursed his lips meaningfully. "You're a little ... overdressed, though."

I squirmed. Part of me wanted to go along with his game and start undoing my buttons. Another part reminded me of what Willa had said on Tuesday – make sure you find out where he was on Monday night. I took a deep breath.

"Can I ask you something first?"

"Only if you take off your dress," he murmured seductively, running a hand lewdly over his chest, down his stomach and below the edge of the frame.

"Stop it," I reprimanded him. "I'm serious. You told me we were going to talk. And ... put your hands where I can see them."

Hugh's grin faded a little. "Alright, then," he sighed, folding his arms like a naughty schoolboy.

"Madeleine told me about the mugger. I picked up your phone," I began. I thought of his shirt, covered in blood. "Are you OK?" I asked, feeling remiss for not trying to find out sooner. "I saw your shirt."

Hugh shrugged, laughing off my concern. "Yeah, I'm fine," he reassured me. "It wasn't my blood." I was momentarily distracted by the image of Hugh wrestling someone to the ground and immobilizing them while they struggled helplessly and bled all over his shirt. "Georgia?" said Hugh. "What's wrong?"

"Nothing," I said hastily, returning my focus to our conversation, embarrassed at the strange direction of my thoughts. "Um, it's … good that you're not hurt. The thing is, where did you go? On Monday night?"

"I walked Sera to her car. She came with a friend, but he had to leave early and I didn't want her wandering around there alone at night. I was on my way back to the gallery when it happened."

"What happened?" I asked, thinking I was at last going to find out where he'd been.

Hugh frowned. "The mugger … thing, of course. That's what we're talking about, isn't it?"

Was it? It seemed that was only part of it. "But, after that," I said, frowning back at him. "What happened after that? Where did you go? Why didn't you come home?"

Hugh glanced away, silent for a moment. It seemed too long before he answered. "It took a while at the police station," he said finally.

"Till five in the morning? Come on, Hugh." I hated sounding so suspicious and mistrustful, but Hugh was clearly blowing me off.

Hugh grimaced. "Look. After I'd finished at the station they offered to give me a lift home, but things were pretty busy there, so I told them I'd walk. I bumped into an old friend on Ponsonby Road and we went for a drink. I lost track of time." He was trying to sound calm, bored, even, as if what had happened was so dull it wasn't worth discussing. Yet there was an edge to his voice – something that made me think he wasn't giving me the full story. And why was he being so evasive if what he'd told me was true? I mean, what was so bad about bumping into an old friend? Except ...

"Hugh, nothing in this whole city is open until five in the morning on a Monday," I pointed out. "Just tell me the truth. Where were you? Why didn't you at least call me?" I could hear the pitch of my voice rising. I didn't want to hear his answer any more than he apparently wanted to give it. But not knowing was even worse. To my frustration, he continued with the story about his old friend.

"My friend was staying out of town. He was ... in a bit of a state when we left the bar and I didn't want him to drive. I walked back into the city with him and checked him into a hotel. I tried to call you earlier in the night from his phone to tell you I was OK, but our home number was engaged and you didn't answer your cell."

I was about to tell him outright to stop lying when I recalled the phone left off the hook and the missed call to my mobile on Monday night. I hadn't mentioned any of that to Hugh. What had Willa said about the accent on the voicemail when she'd called the number back – it sounded foreign? "Where's your friend from? Is he a New Zealander?" I demanded.

"No, he's not. Why?"

My tension dropped a notch. Hugh wasn't aware Willa had called the number. He had no way of knowing that I knew his friend had a foreign accent. He still sounded defensive, though, like he was hiding something. Willa had said something else, too – about the name – sounded like DJ?

"What's his name?" I asked.

Hugh's jaw twitched. "What is this, twenty questions?"

"Just answer me, Hugh," I snapped. I didn't care any more whether he thought I didn't trust him. If he wanted me to trust him, he could be a bit more forthcoming with his information.

"TJ," he replied at last. "Now, will you ..."

The fear that had been pumping through my heart subsided like a balloon deflating, only to be replaced with confusion. "The guy Sera's dating?" I interrupted, remembering that Fran had suggested I go out with Sera and someone called TJ after the opening.

Hugh looked surprised. "Yeah. They're not exactly ... dating," he muttered.

"Whatever," I said impatiently. "From what your mother said, I thought they were at the exhibition together." I wasn't interested in the status of Sera's relationship with this guy. It was the status of my relationship with Hugh that I cared about.

"Yeah," said Hugh, misinterpreting my impatience. "It's kind of complicated." He winced and rolled his eyes. "You don't want to know."

From the little I knew of Sera, I could just imagine her getting into a huff with some guy and leaving Hugh to deal with the mess. I rolled my eyes back at him to confirm he was right. I didn't want to know. There was still something I couldn't understand. "But, why all the secrecy? If you were just out with this ... TJ guy?"

Hugh took a deep breath and looked away, frowning. When he turned back to the camera, he had a slightly sheepish grin on his face. "I just thought you'd be mad with me, baby. For going out drinking instead of coming straight home." He gave me a beseeching look. "I'm sorry."

I stared at the screen intently, scrutinizing his expression. I had no choice but to believe him. In fact, I told myself, I was the one who should be apologizing. I'd been sitting there giving him the third degree about what he'd been up to when it was my behavior that had been so clearly reprehensible on Monday night. I bit my lip and stared back at him. "I wasn't mad with you," I said, full of contrition. "I was really scared." My voice shook, remembering how I thought he'd gone for good. "I was scared you were mad with me. About what you saw ..."

"I already told you not to worry about that," he interrupted. "Really. Let's forget about Xavier Bishop. Let's make this about us." His voice was a low, seductive purr. His eyes sparkled with mischief. He licked his lips, his mouth curving into a smile that turned my knees to jelly. A pang of longing tore through me. I reached up and undid a couple of buttons on my dress. Hugh's mouth twitched. He unfolded his arms and leaned in to the camera. But I couldn't do it. Even though I was relieved to avoid any further discussion of Xavier Bishop, there were so many other questions I needed answers to – about Willa, Madeleine, why he hadn't called last night. Questions that wrapped themselves around my pang of longing like a net – trapping my desire and twisting it into a hard knot of fear.

"O-kay," I said slowly, agreeing to his offer to forget about Xavier. "Just ... before we carry on ... what else were you going to tell me? About your deep dark past?" I tried to keep my voice light, flirtatious, as if we both knew already it would turn out to be some silly misunderstanding – like the one about the mugger, and him being out with TJ. Something we could have a laugh about and then get on with our usual Skype activities.

To my disappointment, Hugh arched back in his chair, rubbing his hands over his face and tilting his chin up so I couldn't see him properly. "You know, I thought about that stuff, too," he replied. "I decided it's not something we should discuss on a Skype call. I'll tell you about it on Friday, OK?"

The knot tightened. "Hugh," I protested, still trying to sound lighthearted. "You promised."

Hugh brought his face back to the webcam. "Georgia, I assure you it will be the first thing I do when I get in the door on Friday. Before I lay a finger on you." The idea of his fingers on me made me desperately inclined to continue unbuttoning my dress. It took all my willpower not to.

"Come on," I insisted. "Surely it can't be anything that terrible." I stopped when I saw the black expression on Hugh's face. The sparkle in his eyes had flattened off into deep, unreadable pools.

"It's not terrible, G," he tried to reassure me, although everything about the way he said it made me think it must be worse even than I was imagining. "It's just ... well, it might shock you a little. I want to be with you, so we can talk about it properly."

I stared at Hugh. Was he playing some sort of game? The relief I'd experienced a few minutes earlier, when he'd given me a logical explanation about where he'd been on Monday night, evaporated. "Well, that's great," I retorted sarcastically. "You have something so shocking to tell me that I have to wait another two days to hear it? Do you want me to sleep *at all* for the next two nights?"

Hugh shook his head. "I'm sorry baby, I know it's not ideal, but ..."

"Not *ideal*?" I was shouting, now. "Damn right it's not ideal. Just tell me."

Hugh kept his voice smooth, even. "Georgie girl ..."

"Don't call me that!" I snapped. "And stop doing that ... lawyer thing." His calmness infuriated me more than anything. He'd told me once it was one of the techniques he used for winning arguments. Well, if he wouldn't tell me, I'd have to use some lawyer techniques on him. Cross examination, for a start. His earlier explanation seemed to have eliminated Madeleine from my list of key suspects, so I went straight on to the next most likely option.

"Is it about Willa? Do you two have some sort of ... history together? Have you slept with her?" I demanded.

"Willa?" Hugh looked genuinely bewildered. "Fuck, no. What makes you think that?"

I opened my mouth, then closed it again. I couldn't tell Hugh what made me think that without telling him about Willa's blog – and, despite how shocked I still was about it, I wanted to discuss it with her before saying anything to Hugh. "I don't know," I mumbled, "She's very attractive, and she's a friend of your sister's. It's not such an impossibility."

Hugh rolled his eyes. "I've generally avoided screwing my sister's friends," he drawled. "Made things too complicated if it didn't work out … "

I scowled. I didn't like the way he said 'screwing' so casually – like that's how he'd been used to interacting with women. Also, what did he mean by 'generally'? Were there exceptions? I thought about the 'bad-boy reputation' thing on Willa's blog.

"Are you seeing someone in Wellington, then?" I blurted out. "Where were you last night? Why couldn't you Skype me?"

"I was working!" he exclaimed impatiently. "I didn't get in until 2am. What the …"

"Is it someone at work?" I interrupted. It was as if the demons from my painting had possessed me and were flying about in my brain, taking every tiny worry I'd had since Monday night, adding fuel and setting them alight, creating a series of raging, out of control bonfires.

"Is what someone at work?"

"Are you ... screwing someone at work?" I thought about the women staring at me and whispering as I'd waited by the reception desk at his office.

"What?" He ran his hand through his hair in exasperation.

"Is it Madeleine?" I persisted. Even though what he'd told me before made it seem unlikely, there was still the issue of the photo in her purse.

"Don't be bloody stupid."

"Stupid, am I?" I retorted icily. "If I'm so stupid, would you mind explaining to me why she's got a photo of you in her purse?"

"Ahhhrrrr!" Hugh slammed his hand on the desk. I jumped. He got up and walked away, out of shot of the webcam. When he returned, his face was dark with fury. "Georgia, I'm not ... screwing Madeleine," he growled. "My relationship with her is strictly professional. The same goes for Willa. I am not fucking anyone here. Or at work. The only woman I want to fuck is you. Now, can we please end this conversation?"

I stared at Hugh. I'd never seen him lose his temper like this. And I'd never shouted at him like that either. Tears pricked my eyes. I took a deep, shuddering breath, making a real effort to maintain control. "You tell me, Hugh," I whispered. "We can end this conversation any time you like. Just as soon as you tell me what the hell is going on."

Hugh put his head in his hands, tearing his hair. He looked up at me. I noticed his eyes were bloodshot. "It's not that simple, Georgie. It's not only that I want to tell you in person. What I have to say involves other people. I owe them the courtesy of ensuring the conversation isn't ... recorded or ... stored somewhere."

"Xavier Bishop?" I asked, my mind whirring. Why did everything always come back to him? And what sort of secret could be so awful that Hugh was worried about information leaks?

"No comment," he replied stiffly.

"I saw him today," I said, carefully watching Hugh's reaction. Maybe a different tactic would work. Maybe if he thought Xavier was going to tell me something – had already told me – he would open up to me.

Hugh sat up, alarmed. "What did he say to you?"

"He gave me his opinion on some lingerie I was looking at, actually." I straightened my back and eyeballed Hugh. "I ignored him of course," I lied. "Although now I'm thinking I should have taken the opportunity to consult him on some other matters. Since you are being so annoyingly reticent. Perhaps I'll call him tomorrow." I stared at him defiantly. I had no intention of calling Xavier Bishop – I wanted to keep as far away from him as possible. I didn't even have his number. But Hugh didn't need to know that.

Hugh paled and I could see his jaw tense, even on the small screen. "Don't do that, baby."

"Why not?" I challenged him. "If you're so worried about what he'll say, why don't you tell me yourself?"

"He won't tell you anything," said Hugh, speaking again in that irritatingly calm voice. "You'll only make a fool of yourself. I know it's killing you, and I know you think I'm being an ass, but it's only two days. You'll understand when I tell you. Will you just ... trust me?"

I wanted to scream with frustration, even though I knew it was a lost cause. Hugh was an expert at getting his way – he did it for a living, after all. "I don't have a choice, do I?" I said flatly.

"No," said Hugh with an air of absolute finality. "You don't." He looked away for a moment, and then coyly back at the camera. "Um, you do have a choice about something else, though ..."

I stared at him, incredulous. "You don't seriously think I'm going to get naked for you? After this?"

"Why not?" he shrugged. "Might make us both feel better."

"The only thing that's going to make me feel better right now is information."

"You sure about that?" he smirked. "I bet if I licked your pussy for you, I could put a smile on your face."

"Shut up," I hissed, trying not to let him see me squirm.

"Come on, baby, show me how you like it," he coaxed. He unfolded his arms and shifted his right hand down below the edge of the screen. "Undo your buttons ..."

I had to stop this. If I listened to him for one more minute, I would be doing what he asked. "Fuck off," I snapped. "Go ... watch some porn!" Before I could change my mind, I reached out and clicked the little red X at the top of the Skype window.

It was a hollow victory. I knew it as soon as Hugh's stunned expression vanished into a dot before my eyes. He was right. I'd wanted what came after our pointless conversation as much as he did. Even so, I stubbornly shut down the Skype window again when it reappeared several times, finally succeeding in logging out of the insidious program properly. I ignored my cell phone when it rang, and our landline after that as I logged on to Pornhub. I'd never dreamed of watching porn before I met Hugh. Or touching myself. Let alone doing it while he watched. Had being around him impaired my judgment? Or was it normal to do those things? I had no benchmark for what was normal in a relationship. All I knew was that, as long as Hugh was with me, everything was perfect and everything we did together felt right.

At that moment, though, knowing that he was probably jerking off to the sight of some other woman's body, it didn't seem perfect. It seemed all wrong. I gave up on the video clip I'd selected before the actors or whatever they were had even taken off their clothes and shut down my iPad. I pulled the covers over me, not bothering to change out of my dress.

It was a long time before I finally fell asleep, and when I did I was once again haunted by strange dreams. I was in the fitting room of the lingerie boutique. I tried on the sheer chemise and looked in the mirror. There, instead of my reflection, I saw Hugh, naked in a chair, his cock erect in his hand, masturbating. The assistant came in to check on me and began fondling my breasts, kissing my neck and sneaking her fingers under the hem of the chemise. When I whirled around in shock, I saw that it was Willa. She pulled the chemise off and helped me into the chain ensemble while Hugh continued watching us intently from the mirror. He told me he was close to coming. But before he did, Willa took me out of the fitting room into the store, where Xavier was waiting. He nodded approvingly as Willa handed me over to him by the neck chain. Then he led me out into the street, where a carnival was in progress. Men and women turned to stare hungrily at me as Xavier led me through the crowd like a sacrificial animal.

Fourteen

The next day was hot and cloudless. I woke early again and went straight to work in my studio. I painted in silence this time, so I would hear the door if the courier called, although it was early afternoon before he finally arrived. Once I'd signed for the package, I took it into the kitchen and set it on the table, trying to decide if I should delay opening it with a trip to buy food. I cursed Xavier Bishop for making me forget about the grocery shopping I'd intended to do on my way home yesterday. The last thing I'd eaten was the steak sandwich in Rakinos.

The nearest convenience store that accepted credit cards was about 20 minutes' walk away. I was shaking so much, I didn't know if I would even get that far before I passed out. A more thorough search of the refrigerator uncovered half a pack of frozen peas iced over in the back of the freezer and in the pantry I found an almost empty jar of peanut butter, which I managed to scrape a couple of spoonfuls out of. The icy coating on the peas helped to compensate for the dryness of the peanut butter, so I wolfed them down together, then turned to Hugh's package.

Inside the plastic courier bag was a gift-wrapped box and a separate envelope containing a card. I opened the card first.

Dear G

Since we're missing our first Valentine's day together, I thought I'd send you this now rather than waiting until 1 March.

I know it's not quite the same as the one I broke, but I hope you find it a fun way to remember our first (almost) year together.

xxx all my love, Hugh

I frowned. What was Hugh on about? What had he broken? The only thing I could think of was a coffee cup that he'd chipped on the tap a couple of weeks back. It wasn't even mine – it was just one I'd found and gotten into the habit of using when I moved in. Surely he hadn't bought me a coffee cup for Valentine's day? It was the sort of thing you bought someone you hardly knew when they embarrassingly invited you to their birthday party. I opened the box with a leaden feeling in my stomach.

It wasn't a coffee cup. It was something plastic – or like plastic – red and white in color. My hopes faded even further. It was only when I pulled out the old 1970s View Master that I understood Hugh's message – and the trouble he'd gone to in order to get me something really special. I'd had an early 1960s View Master that had belonged to my father. He'd given it to me, along with a whole bunch of Disney slide reels, when I was a kid, and I found it again when we were cleaning out the house after he died. It was one of the few possessions I decided to keep and take back to New York with me. One night when Hugh and I were fooling around, the View Master had gotten knocked onto the floor and Hugh stood on it and broke it. Although I told him it didn't matter, it was clear from the tears I tried unsuccessfully to suppress that it did. Everything linked to Daddy mattered at that time.

I brought the new View Master up to my eyes, expecting to see Donald Duck or Goofy. Instead, Hugh's face smiled back at me – along with my own. *What the ...?* I pressed the blue lever to change slides. The next one was of the two of us as well. I quickly flicked through all seven slides. They were all of Hugh and I – mostly snapshots and a couple of group wedding photos. I put the View Master down and pulled out the slide reel to examine it. There was a black and white picture of us in the center, with a big red heart drawn around it in permanent marker pen. Hugh's initials were on the left of the heart and mine were on the right. He must have had it specially made. No wonder he'd been so disappointed last night when I hadn't even mentioned it. Instead, I'd hung up on him and told him to watch porn. All because I couldn't wait for him to tell me something that probably wasn't important anyway. I felt like a prize bitch. I wished I could call him or text him or communicate with him *somehow*.

Since he didn't have his phone and I was too embarrassed to ring Madeleine to find out where he was staying, there was only one other option. Taking the View Master with me, I went upstairs to our bedroom and opened my iPad. I didn't usually email Hugh at work, but it was better than nothing. I was so used to texting that I hardly knew what to write, so I kept it short, hoping he would see it before the end of the day.

Darling H

I love my present. You are so kind and thoughtful and I feel rotten about last night. You were totally right when you said your suggestion would have made me feel better. Can we try again tonight? I'll be online @ 8 – wearing the present I got for you (which I promise to remove on demand).

I love you.

xxx G

I wasn't quite sure which of the outfits I'd bought in the lingerie store I would wear. It didn't matter. The main thing was to stop this silly arguing.

I closed the iPad again and rolled onto my back, grabbing the View Master so I could have a proper look at the slides. I recognized the first from Willa's Facebook page. It was the night Hugh and I met. If Willa hadn't invited him to that gay dance party, our paths would probably never have crossed. And if I'd encountered him in any other situation – if I hadn't assumed he was gay – I would never have been brave enough to talk to him, let alone accept his invitation the following week to be his date for a work dinner. And after that to lunch, coffee, movies, more dinner, trips to the flea markets, antique shopping, walks in the park ...

Thinking back, I was in love with him right from the start. I mean, what wasn't to love? He was the most beautiful specimen of a man I'd ever seen – laughing, cobalt blue eyes; dark, shiny hair just long and tousled enough to want to run your fingers through; strong, angular jaw sweeping up into high cheekbones surrounding a lush mouth, which was permanently arranged in a secret half-smile that implied he was thinking something a little bit naughty. And that was only his face. I'd been too shy to even think about his body until he swept me off my feet and into his bedroom the night of Macy's party.

The second slide, also from Willa's Facebook page, was from that night, nearly two months after our first meeting. Willa was staying at my place, like she usually did when she visited New York, and she'd smirked knowingly when Hugh told her not to wait up for me. Then, adding to my mortification, she'd snapped a photo of us with her phone, as if recording a virginal bride on her wedding night. It wasn't far from the truth, but I didn't want Hugh knowing that – then or now. I'd never even told Willa that I hadn't had an orgasm until I met Hugh. It seemed a shameful thing to admit to at the age of 28.

Now, I flicked back and forth between the second and third slides, studying them. The picture in the third was taken only a few weeks after the second, this time on Hugh's phone, after a particularly enjoyable Saturday spent entirely in his bed. In the picture from Macy's party, I looked startled, fearful almost. In the later one, there was a soft, lazy confidence to my expression that I knew had never been there before. Hugh, though, looked the same in both pictures. He smoldered with self-assurance – which was something I'd never understood. If he was so sure of himself, why had he waited for Willa to nudge him before he told me how he felt about me ... how much he wanted me?

I shook off the niggling discomfort that always came with those thoughts, reminding myself that we were together now and that was the important thing. I flicked to the fourth slide, taken by my father on the fourth of July. It was officially the day of our engagement, although Hugh had proposed to me two days earlier, on my birthday. He insisted on getting my father's approval when we went down for the holiday, and after Daddy congratulated us, he asked me to get out his camera for a 'proper' portrait. The three of us had walked together into the orchard to take the photo – the last time my father made it that far under his own steam. The verdant green leaves and ripe fruit on the trees were so at odds with my father's tenuous hold on life. The sky was a deep, azure blue, a shade lighter than Hugh's eyes, which glinted like the sapphires in the antique ring he'd given me. We had our arms around each other and the love between us was palpable. It was the same picture my mother had picked up off Daddy's bedside table the night before our wedding.

The fifth slide was the one of our wedding in Colorado – Hugh and I flanked by my parents on one side and Willa and Sera on the other. I knew why Hugh had included it. Getting married was an important event, after all – but I wished he hadn't. Unlike the joy and exhilaration in the previous picture, all I saw in this one was sadness, tension, fear and loss. My father had deteriorated rapidly since our engagement – just a couple of months away from death, he barely had the strength to stand for the photo. My only pleasure in seeing this image was that he'd lived to see the day at all. Our hasty preparations meant that Sera was the sole member of Hugh's family who'd been able to attend. She looked irritable and ill at ease – and I knew now it wasn't only because she didn't like the 1970s orange and pink bridesmaid's dresses that she and Willa were wearing. Even though Willa had agreed to be my maid of honor and helped me pick out the dresses from my favorite retro store on Lafayette, she'd seemed more alarmed than delighted when I told her I was marrying Hugh. Since I'd read her blog, I was beginning to understand why.

The only person in the photo who looked genuinely happy to be there was my mother. It was Hugh's idea to invite her, and I'd nearly canceled the wedding over it. It was the only time – apart from now – that we'd disagreed over anything more important than what to have for lunch. I was furious when he asked my father if we could invite her without discussing it with me first – I'd already told him I didn't want to cause Daddy any unnecessary distress. To my amazement, Daddy agreed wholeheartedly with the idea, so I felt obliged to go along with it.

It had been weird, seeing my parents together after all that time. I'd gone to my father's bedroom when Hugh and I arrived in Basalt the day before our wedding, and found my mother already sitting in the chair beside his bed. She was holding his hand and they were talking quietly. I could see her back reflected in the mirror of the dressing table opposite the bed, the slope of her shoulders eerily similar to my own. I froze in the doorway, then took a few steps backward into the hallway so I could compose myself before going in.

"I hope you've been happy," I heard my father say. "I hope Viktor's treating you well."

"Yes," said my mother. "We're happy. He's a good man, Rob. He's right for me."

A weight settled in my stomach, hearing her talk about Viktor. Then it knotted painfully.

"I could have been happy here, too," she sighed. "If only I'd talked to you. I'm sorry I didn't, for so long. I'm sorry I blamed you. I was just so young and ...," She trailed off helplessly, then started again. "I wish you could have forgiven me, Rob. I wish I'd been more forgivable. I would have tried again. I did love you. I know that now. I still do."

She'd walked out and left him. Us. And she'd never come back. *Now* she was telling him she still loved him? That she would have tried again? That it was somehow *his* fault they didn't? I took a step forward.

Daddy didn't have to put up with this. Not when he was dying. I felt Hugh's arm around my waist, holding me back. "Shh," he murmured into my hair. "Let them talk."

"I know," said my father. "It took me a long time to accept that I was just as responsible for what happened. I know now how unreasonable it was, the way I treated you. How impossible it made things for you – for both of us. I wish I'd been able to see that at the time. And Anna …"

He hesitated. I couldn't see him in the mirror, but I heard the bed creak, as if he was trying to sit up. "I'm sorry for the way things worked out, after you left. I'm sorry I couldn't be there for you."

My mother made a strange noise. She was sobbing. I felt like slapping her.

"I'm so sorry, Anna," my father said again. He was crying, too.

The bitter taste of fury filled my mouth. I wanted to go in there and tell my father to stop apologizing. Anna didn't deserve his forgiveness – then or now. And whatever had happened after she left, it wasn't his job to comfort her. Hugh squeezed me tighter, warning me again not to interrupt.

"Have you ... have you ever told Georgia?" asked my mother, still tearful.

There was a silence. Then I heard my father's voice. "There didn't seem any point. I thought it would only make everything worse. She was ... Well, you know how she was."

My mother started sobbing again. "God I've missed her, Rob. Missed her growing up." At the edge of the mirror, I saw her pick up the photo of Hugh and I off the bedside table and study it. It was only Hugh's arms, both around me now, that prevented me from marching into the room and snatching it out of her hands. "What's she like now?"

My father was silent again. "Quiet," he said at last. "After the incident with that ... boy, she kept to herself."

I suppressed a gasp. My mother knew about that? I was torn between staying, to hear what else she knew and leading Hugh away. He stood firm, forcing us to listen.

"In some ways it made it easier. I didn't have to worry about her sneaking out, or anything like that. She dressed in black, stayed in her room. She was like a little nun." I elbowed Hugh hard in the ribs as he stifled a chuckle.

"Except for the terrible music," My father continued, eliciting another shudder of mirth from Hugh. "Sometimes I thought she'd never get over it. I wondered about sending her to a therapist, but she seems to have worked her own way through it. The art helped."

He drifted off for a moment. When he spoke again, his voice was husky with emotion. "It was hell letting her go to New York, though," he said. "She was so ... fragile. I thought she might be sucked up. I thought I might never see her again."

I felt tears in my eyes. I remembered, too, how difficult it had been to leave him. How scared I'd been to go. If it hadn't been for Willa, I would never have done it.

My mother was looking at the photo again. "What about this fellow she's marrying?" she asked. "What do you know about him?"

"He seems great. Surprisingly normal," he said after a pause. "From Australia or thereabouts. She laughs more when he's around." He hesitated. "But they ... haven't known each other very long." He paused again, while his unspoken meaning sank in. I saw her glance up at him sharply. She put her hand to her chest.

"Oh, Rob," she sighed heavily. "She's not ..."

I knew what my mother was about to say, and this time I wanted to yell at them both. That I was 28 years old and I was marrying Hugh because I loved him – not because I'd been stupid enough to get pregnant without planning it.

Before I had a chance to say or do anything, Hugh tugged my hand and led me firmly, silently down the hallway and back to my own bedroom.

"I can't believe he apologized to her!" I hissed when Hugh had shut the door. "I don't know why you invited her."

Hugh pulled me onto the bed to sit beside him. I had expected him to agree with me – to tell me I'd been right not to want her around. That she was manipulating and insincere. He didn't. "You could take a leaf from your Dad's book, you know," he said somberly, touching my nose.

"What?" I glared at him. "Apologize? What do I have to apologize for?"

Hugh shrugged. "Fifteen years is a long time not to speak to your mother."

"God, Hugh," I said, wanting to slap him too now. "She left. She abandoned me. And him. I've got nothing to say to her."

"Georgia, you don't know what really happened," he said. "I know it hurt you, but you were just a kid. You're an adult now, and soon ...," he chose his words carefully, "she'll be the only family you have."

"I'll have you," I said stubbornly.

Hugh kissed me. A soft, sweet kiss that melted my pain for a moment. "Yeah," he sighed. "You will. I'm glad about that. But ... it's always good to have family." He was quiet for a moment, and I wondered if he was regretting the absence of his own family at our wedding. His parents were in England, awaiting the birth of his brother Duncan's second child. His other two brothers hadn't been able to rearrange their work schedules at such short notice.

"Are you having second thoughts?" I asked, worried about his faraway expression. "About the wedding?"

"No," he hugged me reassuringly. "I want to marry you. But … think about it, will you? Try and be a bit forgiving. It might make it easier on your Dad. If he thought you were speaking to your Mum again. Before he … goes."

It was the last thing he said that got to me. I knew Daddy had been worried about leaving me alone. I thought the knowledge that I was marrying Hugh would have been of some comfort to him. Deep down though, I knew Hugh was right. Daddy wanted to know I had family to turn to. So for his sake, I tried.

Even though I let Hugh do most of the talking, I sat in the same room as Anna that night and had dinner. I answered her questions. I let her kiss me on my wedding day.

After that, she started phoning me again and I didn't hang up any more. But the conversations were one sided. She talked. I listened. I never told her anything. I never asked her anything.

Fifteen

I didn't want to be thinking about Anna. I wanted to enjoy Hugh's present. I picked up the View Master again. The sixth slide was another group photo – this time of Hugh and me with his family. I hadn't known much about them when we arrived in Auckland. It was Fran herself who told me she was Hugh's stepmother – his biological mother, Catherine, died in a car accident when Hugh was only two years old and his brothers were five, six and eight. It was weird, though – as I'd gotten better acquainted with them, I couldn't help thinking Hugh seemed closer to Francesca than he did to his father. Hugh also hadn't told me his father was a judge, and I had no idea how wealthy and influential the family was until Fran asked me if I'd mind her organizing what she said was a 'small gathering' to celebrate our marriage.

I turned up to the Heritage Hotel with Hugh expecting dinner for thirty or forty close relatives and friends, and was shocked when he led me into the ballroom, where three or four hundred people were enjoying an exquisitely catered function in our honor, complete with a classical trio, formal toasts and a band afterward. It was only by concentrating on Hugh's crystal blue gaze and the movements of his perfectly sculpted lips that I managed to repeat my vows in front of all those strangers. Some of them, I realized, had been at my exhibition on Monday night. I hoped I hadn't offended anyone by not recognizing them. It was odd, I mused, that Xavier Bishop hadn't been among the guests at our wedding celebration, yet both Xavier and Hugh had told me they were old friends.

If I didn't want to be thinking about Anna, I wanted even less to be thinking about Xavier Bishop. As soon as I did, I noticed my grip on the View Master tighten and my pulse raced – whether from fear or arousal I wasn't quite sure. I quickly flicked to the last slide. I smiled at once. It was Hugh and me on our honeymoon in Piha. Hugh was standing behind me, smooching into my neck, laughing; one arm wrapped around my chest while he held out his phone with the other to take the picture. I was staring straight ahead, a strange expression of shock and rapture on my face. The sea and sky merged seamlessly at the horizon to form a shimmering blue backdrop; on one side of the picture a black slash in a wall of basalt rock indicated the entrance to a cave. I licked my lips and my gut clenched when I remembered the location of that photo and what we'd done there.

There had been a surfing competition at Piha, and Hugh was uncharacteristically grouchy about the crowds and noise on the beach in front of the house. When I suggested a little hiking expedition to find somewhere more private, his eyes lit up and he told me he knew the perfect spot. We headed South along the cliff tops and he led me into a tiny bay only accessible by scrambling down an almost sheer drop from the path above. He said he wanted to take me exploring in the caves at the Northern end of the beach, but we had to wait until the tide was further out. While we waited, we had a swim and lay down in the sun to dry off.

I had to agree with Hugh, it was nice to have some quiet and privacy after the bustle of the main beach. I basked on my back until my bikini top was dry, then I rolled over and closed my eyes. Hugh and I must have both dozed off – when I woke he was still on his back, hat over his face, snoozing peacefully. The tide had receded about six feet. I thought about waking him so we could go cave exploring, but I felt lazy and content and not much like moving. Instead, I lay there in a state of bliss, simply marveling at the loveliness of my husband. I watched his chest rise and fall gently under the mat of dark silky hair that covered his pectoral muscles and admired the tight raspberry of his nipple just visible through the fine thatch, resisting the temptation to lean across and suck it.

Rather than disturb him with such a blatant invasion, I reached out my hand, lightly exploring his palm and wrist with a touch so soft I thought he wouldn't notice it. I shut my eyes. I loved how smooth the skin on his inner arm was; how his pulse throbbed through the thick arterial cords that ran close to the surface. After a few minutes, his arm tensed slightly and I heard his sharp intake of breath. "Georgie," he murmured. "You might need to stop that." I squinted lazily over at him. He nodded pointedly at his groin, where a sizable bulge twitched beneath the thin, stretchy fabric of his swimming trunks.

I don't know what made me do it. Even though there was nobody there, we were right in the middle of the beach, fully visible to anyone walking on the cliff-top path above – or anyone who made the descent down to the bay. But the husky strain of his voice and the idea that my fingers had caused that sudden swelling of his body sent a thrill of excitement and daring through me. Instead of stopping, I slid my fingers further up his arm, licking my lips slowly and deliberately as I traced a circle in the crook of his elbow. "Impressive," I grinned, skimming my fingernails back along his forearm to his hand. "I'm not sure I want to stop, though. It might spoil my view."

I should have known better. If there was one thing I'd learned about Hugh in the few months we'd known each other, it was that teasing him usually backfired on me. Big time. But I only remembered that when I heard the distant voices from the track at the top of the cliff. It was about the same time that Hugh rolled towards me, flinging a thigh across my legs just under my buttocks and biting down on my shoulder, effectively trapping me and capturing my hand between us. "Fine by me, baby," he murmured into my neck. "Don't stop, then."

I gasped. A hot, heavy lycra-clad mass filled my hand, beating fiercely against my palm with a will of its own, trying to escape the confines of the swimwear that bound it so uncomfortably. With a deft flick of his hand, Hugh pulled the front of his trunks away from his body and the thick stem sprang free, leaping at my wrist in a blind frenzy. "Take it," he growled, pulling my hand inside the fabric and thrusting into my palm, squeezing my fingers around him.

I twisted my head in panic to look at him. "I thought I heard voices," I protested. I tried to move my hand, but it was so thoroughly wedged between us I couldn't shift it at all.

Hugh flashed me one of his naughtiest smiles. "So did I," he smirked. "So you'd better tighten those fingers ... unless you want whoever it is to come down the hill and find me lying on top of you, with my cock in your pussy." Before I had a chance to protest further, he swept his arm across my back, yanking quickly on the bows securing my bikini top and pants. "Just in case you were thinking of making a run for it," he grinned when he saw my eyes widen in alarm at the realization that I was now effectively naked beside him. He moved closer, as if to mount me. I tightened my grip in shock as much as anything else, and he chuckled. "Good girl," he whispered, nibbling my earlobe as he plunged more forcefully in and out of the sheath formed by my fingers. He rubbed his hand around my bare buttocks, cupping the sun-warmed flesh, sliding his fingers slowly into the groove between them.

"Hugh, stop," I whispered urgently. "I think they're coming down here."

Hugh's hand continued to explore the tight, secret space between my thighs, pulling his own leg down and back a little so that his knee rested between mine and forced my legs apart. "I thought you didn't want to stop," he teased. He dipped a finger lazily in and out of me a couple of times and lifted it to his face. He inhaled deeply, then sucked the finger speculatively, smacking his lips as if he were tasting a particularly delicious dessert. "*That* suggests you're enjoying yourself," he murmured. He trailed his hand back to my behind and slid the longest of his fingers inside me, deeper this time, using another to gently nudge the tiny bud that now ached fiercely for his touch. "So does that," he purred in delight as I unconsciously spread my legs further and tightened my muscles around his finger.

The voices drew nearer. They were obviously on the beach now, but I was too afraid to lift my head and look. My heart hammered madly in my chest, unrelentingly feeding the frenzied pulse between my thighs no matter how much I willed it to stop. I whimpered. "Shhh," whispered Hugh, withdrawing his fingers and slinging his arm casually across my back. He rested his hand lightly on my hip, holding my bikini pants carefully in place and strategically concealing the fact that they were undone. He nuzzled his face into my neck. "Close your eyes," he instructed. "Relax."

As the group of four or five people approached us, their laughter and chatter abated momentarily. They had obviously caught sight of us. A woman giggled and I froze, praying they wouldn't notice Hugh's glazed fingers or study too closely the angle at which my arm disappeared under his body. Somebody else said something I didn't catch and the woman giggled again. Then, to my immense relief, I heard a man's voice say 'Shh, they're sleeping.' There was a scuffling of feet as they circled around us and their conversation resumed, then faded again as they continued up the beach to the caves.

To my amazement, Hugh had remained hard as the group passed, even swelling a little while they were stopped and looking at us. As soon as their voices dwindled to a series of distant cadences, he resumed his slow gyration against my hand and slid his finger back inside me. To my equal astonishment, the pulse between my legs had intensified. I squirmed fiercely against Hugh's hand. I lifted my hips and spread my legs still wider, not caring any more who was walking along the beach or what anyone could see from above.

Hugh needed no further encouragement. His fingers slammed into me while his palm slapped against my buttocks, bringing me to the brink of orgasm in a shamefully short time. I groaned and whimpered, gripping his cock harder as I tensed, then started shaking, coming in dizzying waves against the unyielding beat of his frigging. His breath was hot and ragged against my neck. His thigh muscle tensed over my leg. "Hold me tighter baby ... tighter," he demanded, thrusting more and more frantically into my hand until he finally released a stream of hot, thick fluid against my wrist with a low, shuddering growl that send a shiver down my spine as I collapsed in the final throes of my own sweet release.

"I can't believe we just did that," I murmured when I finally recovered the strength to open my eyes. Hugh's pupils glinted at me through half closed lids and his lips curved back at me in a secret, drowsy smile that had me melting all over again.

"It was a little ... unexpected," he drawled. "I guess I should be more careful what I wish for."

My eyes opened wider. "What do you mean?" I asked. "Did you plan this?"

He chuckled softly and nipped my shoulder. "No. I had intended to be a little more discreet. I was going to take you into the caves and find a dark corner so I could give you a proper fucking."

I recalled the heat surging again between my thighs when he said that, and, as I lay on the bed, I was wet and throbbing with the memory of that day.

Hugh had made good on his promise to take me into the caves, and it was when we left that he'd taken the photo. His laughter and the look of consternation on my face were both the result of us nearly walking into another couple who were entering the cave as we emerged – and their raised eyebrows as they took in the very short slip dress I was wearing and my bikini pants in Hugh's hand.

I put the View Master down on the bed and idly ran my hands over my breasts, pinching my nipples.

They puckered instantly into tight knots of need and desire and further down, a third knot formed with a jolt that shook me. I shoved a trembling hand into my panties and squeezed the little nub that palpitated so desperately there. God, I wished Hugh was with me. I hoped he'd got my message and would Skype me tonight. If only I could phone him or text him now …

Sixteen

As if in answer to my prayers, my phone rang. It was a number I couldn't identify and my heart leaped. Maybe Hugh was calling me from his hotel. Maybe he was coming home early. I answered the call.

"Hello?" I said eagerly, my hand still down my pants.

"Hello, Georgia," said a woman's voice that I couldn't place immediately. She was American. I was tempted to hang up, telling her she had the wrong number. But she'd said my name, so she obviously recognized my voice.

"Georgia?" said the voice. "It's Anna. Your mother," she added when I didn't respond.

"Oh," I said at last. "Um ..." I still didn't know what to say to my mother – even when I wasn't on the verge of an orgasm.

"I wanted to congratulate you. About your exhibition. I saw the paintings on Willa's website. They look wonderful."

At her mention of Willa's website, I sat up in alarm. Had my mother been reading Willa's blog? Then I realized she was referring to the WVK Gallery website. "Oh, yeah. It was great," I responded, confusion flooding my thoughts. When I recalled the opening, the first things that came to mind were Xavier Bishop's hand on my thigh; his malted honey scent; his low, rich purr in my ear. I hastily pulled my hand out of my pants and stood up.

"Georgia? Are you still there? Is everything alright?"

Something had been bothering me since Monday night. Part of me said leave it be – don't go there.

Another part of me was opening my mouth and saying, "Can I ask you a question?"

"Of course. Anything." My mother sounded delighted. After fifteen years, I finally had a question for her.

"When you met Viktor. When you left. How did it happen? I mean, had you known him a long time, or ...?"

The silence was too long. I already knew it was a mistake to ask. Her answer was only going to make things worse.

"Don't worry," I said hastily. "It doesn't matter."

"No," she interrupted. "I hadn't known him long. But I knew ... I knew him enough. And I knew myself by then. I knew what I needed."

She sounded so dispassionate. It was all about her. What *she* needed.

"I met him at the opening soiree of the summer music school," Anna continued. "It was my job to check people off the guest list and hand out name tags. He was older than most of the other students; closer to my own age. There was an instant connection between us.

Once everyone had arrived, I stepped outside to take a breath of air and he appeared beside me. Then ..."

"What?" I demanded, despite the anger simmering in my gut.

"We talked for a few minutes. He touched my hair." My mother sighed uncomfortably.

An unwelcome image of Xavier Bishop standing behind me, his finger on my hair, hot breath on my neck, sprang to mind. I pushed it away. This was about her, not me.

"And then?" I didn't want to be having this conversation, but I could hear the discomfort creeping into her voice. It must be hurting her more than it was hurting me, to tell me what a slut she'd been. I'd suffered for fifteen years as a result of her actions; it was about time she did, too.

"We kissed," she replied at last, then corrected herself. "He kissed me. I didn't resist. I suppose you could say I let it happen."

Fifteen years' worth of rage bubbled in my throat. "You *let* it happen?" I hissed, the accusation burning my mouth like acid. "How could you *let* it happen? You were married. You had a husband and a child. You had no right to *let* anything happen."

"Georgia, it wasn't that simple." Her voice shook. "I was lonely. I was starving. I had been for a long time. *Something* had to happen."

I knew what she meant. But I forced her to spell it out. "What do you mean, starving?"

Anna swallowed hard. "I was starved of love, Georgia. Your father and I hadn't been ... intimate for some time."

It was like I was a child again and somebody had told me there was no such thing as fairies. "But," I protested. "He loved you. I loved you. You did have love. You weren't starving." I knew my protests were those of that same child, begging to be allowed to believe in the fairy story just a little longer. My mother knew it too, and I could tell from her wistful tone that she regretted being the one to disillusion me.

"There are different kinds of love, Georgia," she explained patiently. "I imagine you understand that, now you are married. The love of a child is a wonderful gift, as is the love of a friend, which your father never stopped being to me. Maybe for some people they are enough, but for me ... I needed more."

Her prudish skirting around the issue made me more determined than ever to unsettle her. "So, when did you fuck him, then?" I asked, keeping my voice icy cool.

"Georgia," she protested. "Is that really ..."

"Just tell me Anna." I persisted. "You said I could ask you anything. When did you first do it?" I was hitting way below the belt, but I couldn't stop myself.

There was a tiny click of exasperation. Then she let me have it. "About an hour after we first kissed."

The surge of power I'd felt over my mother when I was the one asking the questions, controlling the answers, was obliterated. My thoughts reeled in ... what? Disgust? Admiration? Fear? The sound of Sera's voice calling Hugh's name; the image of him whirling in the doorway; the empty chill on my thigh as Xavier removed his hand – all rose through my mother's words like a cold mist. It was as if I'd been looking through a window and the mist had darkened the air behind it, transforming the glass instead into a mirror – a mirror of what could have been if my mother had been interrupted; a mirror of what could have been if I had not.

I shook my head. I couldn't let this happen. I couldn't let her manipulate me into somehow thinking it wasn't her fault. People made their own decisions and they had to live with the consequences. She'd decided to sleep with a random stranger. To leave me and my father for him. And I would always hate her for that.

"So," I said sarcastically. "Good to know you thought about it carefully. Before you tore our family apart."

"Oh, Georgia," she sighed. "That's how it started. But the reason I left was about so much more. I could envisage a real life with Viktor – a chance to make a fresh start ..." She trailed off as she realized what she was saying.

"It's OK," I said harshly, trying not to let her hear the lump in my throat. "I get it. You never wanted to be stuck in Basalt with an office job and a kid. We cramped your style."

I remembered how she'd come alive every summer when the town filled with musicians attending the summer festival and school. How, in an effort to inspire me to practice, she'd tell me stories about this or that young violinist moving forward to an exciting career in a big city somewhere. Now I saw with the absolute clarity of hindsight that all along she had wanted to be one of those musicians – and eventually that longing had become more powerful than her love for me or my father. So powerful that she'd been prepared to destroy our family in order to fulfill it.

As if she was reading my thoughts, Anna spoke up. "Georgia, darling. It wasn't because of you that I felt stuck. Being a parent didn't always come naturally to me, it's true. And yes, I *had* had other ambitions. But I was happy enough. I was making it work. Then, long before I met Viktor, something happened. I did something, and Rob couldn't forgive me. He couldn't— didn't want me any more – *physically*. If only we hadn't lost that intimacy, we might have found a way to heal the other wounds. If I'd thought there was any hope of that, I would have stayed." Her tone was genuinely sad. I almost felt sorry for her.

She carried on, a sense of urgency creeping in to her voice. "If there's any advice I can give you in your marriage, Georgia, it's to never neglect that part of it. And don't use it as a weapon. In the end, you'll both lose ..."

My anger resurfaced. I didn't want to hear her motherly advice about sex. And I didn't like her implying it was my father's fault she'd left. "Actually, Anna," I snapped. "I don't need your advice about sex. Hugh and I are just fine, thanks. In fact, he's here right now, waiting for me to get off the phone so we can *fuck.*"

I spat the last word at her and hung up without waiting for her to reply. I flung the phone onto the bed and stomped up to my studio. I couldn't focus on my work. I walked up to the convenience store to buy fruit, milk and cereal. I took a shower. I ate. I threw myself into the task of taking my clothes out of the trunks and suitcases that littered our dressing room floor and arranging them on the shelves and hangers. I played Ministry and Nirvana, turning up the volume so I wouldn't have to think.

Even so, her words tumbled around in my head, like a song that you can't stop humming, despite not even liking the tune. How could she have slept with Viktor an hour after they met? What did she mean by using sex as a weapon? Did my refusal to undress for Hugh the night before count? The questions continued to plague me well into the evening, along with a gnawing need to fuck my husband, like I'd told her I was doing.

By 7:30, there was no email from Hugh. I put on the satin slip and a pair of stockings and hung around online anyway. I googled View Master and discovered the one Hugh had given me was a rare collector's model, released in 1976 to celebrate the United States Bicentennial. After an hour, I'd checked a week's worth of Facebook posts from my friends in New York and he still hadn't contacted me. I wondered if he simply hadn't read my message or if he was deliberately ignoring me because he was mad with me for hanging up on him. I was so horny and agitated, I contemplated starting without him, but I convinced myself he would still call. He *had* to call. I stared at my iPad, trying to think of something to distract me. Without questioning the wisdom of the idea, I typed willowyblonde.com into my browser bar.

There was a new post, dated last night.

A weird thing happens when I stop at an all-night gas station as I'm heading North into the back of beyond. It's a tiny little one-horse town and there's only one pump. When I go inside to pay, there seems to be no-one around. I'm about to leave a note with my number on it when I hear a noise coming from the office. When I check it out I find this gorgeous young Maori guy of about 18 behind the desk – jerking off with a Penthouse in front of him.

Now it seems a bit mean to let him carry on making love to his Penthouse pet when I'm not in a great hurry to get where I'm going, and I could do with some entertainment, so I flick open a couple of buttons on my top and ask him if he'd like a taste of the real thing. I just love how a hot young guy's cock dances of its own volition with the slightest provocation and, to be fair, my provocation is more than slight, so his cock is fairly boogieing on down.

I let him suck my tits while I stroke him with my hand – I tell him he's just my size and if he'll kiss me a little lower down for a while I'll let him fuck me. He's pretty good for a novice – so good he's about to make me come, when suddenly another guy shows up. He's taller, older and bigger than the boy – he says he's his uncle although I wouldn't put him much past my age. The amazing thing about him is he's tattooed all over as far as I can see – not trashy home-made tats or gang stuff, but genuine Maori moko, even covering his face and lips. He looks like a god.

At first it's a bit disconcerting, then I want to kiss those black tattooed lips, and see how far the ink goes down the rest of his body. I'm trying to figure out how you ask a god if you can suck his cock when he eyeballs me and says, "You look hungry." ...

I stared at the screen in astonishment. I couldn't believe Willa had written this. *Done* this. As I read on, my hand drifted into my pants, where I found the slick pool of sticky heat from the afternoon had reformed. I spread it along the tingling crease between my thighs, feeding the tiny, demanding pulse that throbbed more and more urgently there as I imagined myself at the mercy of the tattooed god and his young apprentice. I used my own hands to simulate the feel of their fingers and tongues on my most sensitive parts. I twisted my nipples until I gasped in a kind of sweet torture. I rammed two, then three fingers deep inside myself. I pressed my palm against my swollen mound and whipped my fingers back and forth across my clit until I was coming violently in powerful convulsions that racked my body again and again, for long minutes that seemed like hours before I was finally still.

When I had partly recovered from my state of euphoric bliss, a wave of shame washed over me. How could I have taken such pleasure from Willa's story when I'd denied my own husband that same pleasure the night before? It wasn't the first time I'd made myself come with my fingers, but it was the first time I'd done it without Hugh watching – or at least being at the end of a webcam or phone. It seemed like a gross infidelity – much worse, somehow, than letting Xavier Bishop explore my neck and thigh in the dark corridor of Willa's gallery. I crawled under the covers in despair, my mind even more agitated than it had been the night before.

As I slept restlessly, images came crowding into my mind. I was traveling with my mother in a car. She was driving. It was late. We stopped to get gas and I went in to pay, leaving her outside. In the office, I found Hugh, watching porn and wanking. Before I could speak, a tattooed hand covered my mouth and I heard a voice whisper in my ear, 'Do you like that, Mrs Fraser?' I recognized the voice as Xavier's. His other hand slid under my dress and into my panties. I noticed his whole arm was covered in tattoos. I felt his erection pressing into me and it occurred to me that he was naked behind me. I tried to twist around, wanting to kiss him – kiss his black tattooed lips, but he pushed me forward into the room, bending me over the desk and indicating I should take Hugh in my mouth. However the desk was too wide and I couldn't reach him. The more I tried, the further away Hugh seemed to be.

Xavier pushed my dress up around my waist and pulled down my panties. He was touching me, fingering me. He teased me with his cock, sliding against my wet opening, nudging my clitoris. It was thick and heavy. I wanted him. I wanted Hugh. The desk stretched in front of me like a banquet table – I couldn't make out Hugh's face, he was so far away now. I realized with a shock there was another person in the room, right beside the table, watching us. At first I thought it was Willa; then I saw it was my mother. I wanted to run, to hide in shame, but Xavier was whispering in my ear, 'I'm going to fuck you now, Mrs Fraser,' and I stayed still. I wanted him, so badly. Hugh was no more than a speck at the end of the table. My mother had disappeared. Then I heard the revving of a car engine and Xavier turned away, swearing.

I was alone at the edge of the forecourt – the car was gone; my mother with it. Hugh and Xavier were nowhere to be seen. My dress was still around my waist – I couldn't seem to pull it down. My panties had disappeared. I stepped into the road. The asphalt melted into black, swirling water. Too late, my feet lost contact with the sand as the water got suddenly deep and the waves crashed over my head, forcing me under. Stinging salt water flooded my eyes, my nose, my mouth. My legs and arms were tangled in something – wide straps of seaweed, binding me, preventing me from swimming to the surface ...

I woke in a cold sweat; the sheet wrapped around my legs, pinning my arms to my body. It was pitch dark. I cried as I struggled to disentangle myself, fumbling for the light switch. My chest ached as I breathed in lungfuls of air. I felt weak and nauseous. There was a salty taste in my mouth. I half expected to cough up sea water, but the salt was my own tears. I sat for a long time, hugging my knees to my chest, adjusting to the light and waiting for my breathing to return to normal. Eventually, I got out of bed and headed shakily for the shower. Even after washing away the sweat, the fear remained. I couldn't go back to my bed, with its twisted sheet lying like a snake in the middle of it. I dragged my duvet and a pillow up to my studio and huddled on the couch, whimpering like a wounded animal until I fell into another anxious sleep.

Seventeen

When I woke in my studio on Friday morning, the sun was already streaming in the windows. For a moment, I wondered where I was. Then I remembered the dream. I crept quietly down to my bedroom, half expecting to find Hugh or Xavier or my mother there, waiting for me. To my relief, all I saw was the familiar room and the bed where Hugh and I had made love hundreds of times. I opened one of his drawers and pulled out a T-shirt. It was clean, but it still smelled of him – fresh, with hints of citrus and sandalwood. I held it to my face and inhaled deeply. *Tonight*, I thought. Tonight I would see him and his presence would chase away the demons that had haunted me ever since the stupid misunderstanding with Xavier Bishop.

In the meantime, there was the issue of Willa and the blog. I'd organized to go into the gallery at lunchtime to finalize arrangements for my visit with Hugh that evening, and while I showered and dressed, I considered my options. I could continue reading it, without telling Willa. Then I'd never know if it was her writing it. And I'd never know if it were true. The second option – trying to erase it from my memory – presented the same problems. I knew I couldn't do it in any case. The third and most obvious course of action was to ask her about it. But what if she *was* having some sort of affair with Hugh? I'd lose my husband and my best friend in one fell swoop. The possibility sat like a lead weight in the pit of my stomach.

I knew I was procrastinating in order to delay my conversation with Willa as long as possible. I prepared and ate breakfast slowly, had a second cup of coffee and paid uncharacteristic attention to tidying the kitchen. I checked my email, finished putting my clothes away in the dressing room, checked my email again and chose to walk the long way into the city rather than catch the bus that was waiting at the stop.

When I finally got to the gallery, it was well after midday. Willa was in the storeroom pulling out paintings and prints ready for hanging later that evening, when my work came down. I tensed when she came over to hug and kiss me in her customary greeting. She stepped back and studied me in the gloom.

"Are you OK, babe? You look like you haven't slept in a week."

When I didn't answer immediately, she tried again. "Have you talked to Hugh? Since Tuesday morning? Is everything alright?"

I nodded. "I talked to him."

"But it's ... not alright?" guessed Willa. "What did he tell you?"

"No, it's all cool – really," I reassured her. I couldn't face another inquisition. I was already dreading the conversation I knew I had to have with her about the blog. Hugh had told me he wasn't having an affair with Willa, and that should have been enough. But I'd known Willa a lot longer than I'd known Hugh.

If I could count on anyone for a straight answer, it was her. I only hoped her story was the same as his. "Willa, I ..."

My mouth dried up. The storeroom, which was normally the coolest part of the gallery, felt stifling. A wave of dizziness swept over me. For a moment I thought I was going to pass out. "Um, can we go and sit in your office, please?" I said weakly.

"Sure." Looking worried, Willa took off her cotton gloves and ushered me towards the light.

When we were seated in her air-conditioned office with the door shut, I took a deep breath. I forced the question out of my mouth before I lost my nerve again. "Willa, have you ever ... slept with Hugh?" It was as if I'd strapped 20 sticks of dynamite to my middle and given her the remote control that could detonate them. The second hand on the clock ticked over. I couldn't breathe.

Willa's jaw dropped. "What? No, of course not." She was genuinely surprised. Outraged, even. My heart slowed from a stampede to a gallop. I opened my mouth to drag in some much needed air. I couldn't believe it had been that easy. Then it occurred to me that perhaps I hadn't asked her the right question.

"What about ... other stuff? Have you ever given him a blow job, for instance?" I tried to keep my tone cool, neutral. But my insides churned, dread and hope fighting for supremacy like rocks and water tumbling over each other in a concrete mixer.

A look of horrified revelation replaced her expression of innocent shock. My heart doubled its speed again, then stopped beating altogether. It seemed like my worst fears were about to be realized. Silence hung between us like a sheet of glass, the ticking of the clock slowly chipping away at it. I could feel myself cracking.

"It's you, isn't it?" I whispered. "W-Willowy Blonde?"

I'd expected her to be ashamed. But she seemed more annoyed than anything. "How on earth ...?" she began. I cut her off.

"That's irrelevant," I snapped, my heart disintegrating like sugar glass. "How could you?"

"I could ask you the same question," she countered, her voice taut, defensive. "Just because you found it, you didn't have to read it. Anyway," she continued haughtily, "there's no need to get on your high horse about it. It's only a bit of fun."

"*Fun*?" I retorted, bile burning my throat. "Hugh is my husband, Willa. And you're supposed to be my friend. Maybe sucking him off was fun for you, but ..."

Willa almost leapt out of her seat. "Jesus, Georgia – you're not serious? You don't really think I *did* that with Hugh?" She leaned forward to take my hand. I flinched away. My mouth moved open and shut several times before any words came out.

"But, why? All that stuff about him ... me ... both of us," I stammered. "Jimmy's bar ... India ..."

"They're just stories," she insisted, although her normally smooth voice shook a little. "Think about it. You know nothing happened between us in Colorado, right?" Willa was blushing. She never blushed. I nodded. I was sure my face was about twice as red as hers. "Well, the thing about Hugh is the same. It's just ... fantasy."

I studied her expression. Willa and I had been friends for nearly ten years – since we were teenagers. She'd introduced me to Hugh. I'd never known her to tell so much as a tiny white lie. "Why, though?" I asked her again. "Why write it? Why put it on the internet?" '*Why fantasize about Hugh?*' I wanted to add, but I was too afraid of what she might reply.

Willa frowned and thought for a moment. "I get a thrill, I suppose, from sharing my ... experiences. But I know not everyone approves of the way I choose to live. I've learned to be careful who I trust. With the blog, everything I say and do remains anonymous. It allows me to explore all sorts of things in a way that doesn't harm anyone."

"So some of it *is* true, then?" I asked, thinking about her detailed description of Hugh and I making love on the sofa while she spied on us from the balcony.

As if reading my thoughts, Willa gave me a wry grin. "I think you know the answer to that. Some of it's a hundred percent true, some of it's complete fantasy. Some of it's a bit of both."

"What about the thing on Wednesday night?" I asked, suddenly curious. "In the gas station?"

Willa's grin faded. She clicked her tongue and sighed irritably. "The blog's purpose is to explore ideas *without* exposing myself to judgment. It doesn't matter whether it really happened or whether I imagined it."

It was on the tip of my tongue to ask her if that applied likewise to her story about what she did to Hugh in our bathroom. It certainly mattered to me whether it had really happened or not. Although the idea of her imagining it was equally disturbing. Strangely, what she'd written about Hugh upset me more than what she'd written about me. Heat crept into my cheeks as I thought about it.

Willa misinterpreted the reason for my embarrassment. "Oh my God, Georgia," she teased. "You totally got off on it, didn't you?" She leaned back in her office chair and smirked at me, challenging me to deny it.

My blush turned to scarlet. Why was I squirming like I was the one with all the depraved thoughts? "Is it true, though?" I pressed, trying desperately to avoid her question.

Willa shook her head, a note of warning entering her voice. "Listen, Georgia, I keep the blog for my pleasure. I don't normally share it with friends. I still haven't decided what to do about the fact that you've read it. But don't be asking me every five minutes if this or that is true, OK? Like I said, it's irrelevant."

"Sorry," I said, even though I thought it was a bit rich, her telling me off. I thought it was very relevant that she was having sexual fantasies about my husband. I thought I had a right to ask her about it.

Instead, I kept the peace. I forced myself to keep talking about the gas station post. "I just ... couldn't imagine it. Either doing it or making it up." Even as I said it I knew I wasn't being entirely honest. But I wasn't about to admit that to Willa. I wasn't telling anyone about the dreams I'd had since meeting Xavier Bishop. And I was going to paint over those terrible canvases as soon as I got home.

"Sometimes necessity is the mother of invention," Willa muttered cryptically. When I raised my eyebrows in confusion she sighed. "Not everyone marries Prince Charming and rides off into the sunset, Georgia. Some of us have to be a bit more creative when it comes to getting off."

I gaped at her. She'd just assured me there was nothing between her and Hugh. And on her blog she'd made a big thing about his 'bad-boy reputation', as if he were some kind of sleazeball. "Prince Charming?" I asked. "I thought you didn't like Hugh."

Willa shrugged, making no attempt to confirm or deny it. "It doesn't really matter what I think of him, does it?" she replied briskly. "You're the one he married."

What? It almost sounded as if she *did* have feelings for him. Or had, at some stage – and they weren't reciprocated. Before I had a chance to process this unexpected bombshell, she stood up and grabbed her bag. "Come on," she said, clearly wanting to end our conversation. "Let's get some lunch. I'm starving."

As we walked, my thoughts whirred. If Willa really was in love with Hugh, it would explain a lot. For a start, her reluctance to set me up with him like she had every other eligible guy she knew. Her horrified reaction when I told her we were getting married. And the fact that she fantasized about him on her blog. Yet she'd also done things to encourage our relationship. Telling Hugh I wasn't gay, for a start. Agreeing to be my maid of honor. I imagined how difficult that must have been for her, and it struck me what a true friend she really was. If I'd had even an inkling that she liked Hugh as more than a friend, I would never have gone out with him. But she'd stepped aside without a murmur and now it was too late. I was in love with Hugh. I'd married him. And, even though the thought of it made my skin crawl, I couldn't ask her to stop daydreaming about him or writing stories about him on her blog. It was all she had. The only thing I could do was pretend – like she was obviously doing – that she wasn't particularly fond of Hugh. Anything else would be too humiliating for her.

Willa picked up on my pensive mood over lunch. "Hey," she said finally when I didn't answer her for the third time. "Stop fretting about the blog. We're still friends, right? I feel like I've seen less of you since you moved here than I did when you lived in New York. Why don't we go shopping this afternoon and get you something to wear for your hot date tonight? My treat."

I forced myself to smile and focus on our conversation. I didn't deserve a friend like her. Whether it be men or clothes, she seemed to know exactly what I needed before I was even aware of it myself. I thought about how I'd felt going into Hugh's office yesterday. Scruffy. Unkempt. Underdressed. It was true, I could use some more upmarket clothing. And going shopping would solve the dilemma of what to do all afternoon while I waited for Hugh to get back. I agreed, on condition that Willa promised to deduct whatever she spent on me from my check when she paid me at the end of the month.

By five thirty, I'd managed to push my guilt and worries to the back of my mind and we were giggling like a couple of teenagers. Together we had amassed half a dozen carry bags containing the sort of clothes

I'd seen people on High Street wearing on Valentine's day. My floppy velvet skirt, ripped mesh top and Doc Martens were stuffed into one of the bags, and I was wearing a floaty silk chiffon tunic dress in vivid teal and turquoise, with matching strappy sandals. After a trip to Willa's beauty salon, my toenails gleamed a pale frosted aqua and my normally paint stained fingernails were smooth and buffed. My hair had been freshly washed and styled into a graceful chignon, which swept smoothly off my face into a coil at the base of my neck. My lips were full and pouty under their coating of chocolate gloss, and a smudge of Kohl around my eyes gave my face the sensuous glow of a 1920s starlet.

Willa offered to drop me home once we had everything organized at the gallery. She helped me arrange the food on a series of small, high tables scattered throughout the space, and teased me again about my intentions as we dragged the couch out of her office and positioned it in front of the Erangi triptych.

Sitting in the traffic, I became more and more anxious about Hugh. I still hadn't heard from him since Wednesday night. He didn't know about my plan for tonight. What if he were still mad at me – or still trying to avoid telling me about Xavier Bishop? What if he decided not to come straight home? What if he went out drinking – like he had on Monday night? It wasn't as if he made a habit of doing that, but then, we didn't make a habit of arguing like we had either. I turned to Willa.

"Um, Wills, can I ask you a favor?"

"Ask away," she said.

"Could you take me to the airport? So I can meet Hugh there?"

She flashed me a lascivious grin. "What, planning an extra special welcome?"

I could just imagine what was going through her mind. She probably thought I was intending to drag him into a bathroom at the airport or get dirty with him in the taxi on the way home. I remembered reading stories about both on her blog. If I hadn't already told her everything was fine between Hugh and me, I would have confided in her that I was worried he'd go AWOL again. Instead, I tried to smirk back. "Something like that," I muttered shyly.

Willa agreed to take a detour to the airport and drop my purchases off at the house over the weekend, but she was uncharacteristically quiet for the rest of the journey. I began to wish I hadn't asked her. When we pulled up outside the domestic terminal, she turned to me. "Georgia, I need to ask you something."

"Uh, sure," I responded, wondering if she knew I'd guessed her secret. She looked so serious all of a sudden.

"I know I told you earlier not to worry about it, but I need to know. How did you find out about the blog?"

Shit. I'd forgotten we hadn't discussed that. When I told her I'd used her laptop while she was busy in the gallery, I thought she'd be angry, but she seemed more relieved than anything.

"So Hugh doesn't know about it?" she asked.

"No," I replied, all my worries about her and Hugh resurfacing. Willa's anxiety seemed to confirm them.

"Georgia, I need you to promise me you won't tell him about it. Don't tell anyone else either, but especially not Hugh. Don't show him the site. Don't leave it open on your iPad. In fact, have you got your iPad with you?" When I nodded in surprise, she held out her hand. "Pass it here, so I can clear your browsing history."

At first I misunderstood her concern. "I think you can trust Hugh not to tell anyone about it, Wills," I said. "I mean, he's a lawyer. He's used to keeping secrets."

"Only those he's legally bound to keep," she retorted sharply, still holding out her hand for my iPad. "I'm OK with you knowing about the blog, Georgia, but I need to be sure that's as far as it will go – otherwise I'll shut it down. If you don't think you can do it, I'd rather you tell me now."

Her lips were drawn in a thin, tense line. I hated the idea of keeping secrets from Hugh, and I resented her for asking me to. Then I clicked. I'd managed to conceal the fact that I'd guessed her secret. But how humiliating for her if Hugh knew she'd been fantasizing about him – was in love with him. She was right. It was better to keep it between the two of us. "It's OK," I reassured her, pulling my iPad out of my satchel and giving it to her. "I won't tell him."

Eighteen

Our tiff over not telling Hugh about the blog put a tiny damper on my fun afternoon with Willa, but nothing could dampen my spirits when I saw Hugh walk through the arrival doors inside the airport terminal. He didn't notice me waiting and I took a moment to admire his tall, lean figure as he loped towards the gaggle of cab drivers waiting near the door. His navy-blue pin striped suit, pale blue shirt and silvery blue tie all highlighted the brilliance of his eyes, and I was unable to contain the huge grin on my face as I headed towards him. To my disappointment, he made to step around me, his attention focused on the uniformed cab driver who was holding up a sign board reading 'Dr Fraser' in white letters. I moved into his path again, forcing a collision. He apologized distractedly and was about to sidestep me a second time when I slipped my hand around his arm, finally gaining his attention.

"Georgia," he said, his irritation turning to confusion as he glanced at my face, recognizing me at last. "What are you doing here?"

"Surprise!" I announced, still grinning madly. I jiggled excitedly in front of him like a kid at Christmas.

Hugh looked more panicked than surprised. "Uh, yeah," he muttered. "It is." He frowned. "Nothing's wrong is it?"

"No," I said, my smile fading a little. "Just wanted to make up for the other night. Didn't you get my email?"

Hugh looked at me blankly. "Email? I've had my email forwarding to Madeleine all week."

"Oh," I replied, my excitement deflating like a balloon. So Madeleine had received my email, promising to undress for Hugh on Thursday evening.

Great. But that wasn't the only thing wrong. I was still standing in front of him, holding his arm, yet he had made no move to hug me or ...

"Um, do I get a kiss?" I asked, tugging his sleeve hopefully.

"Huh?" Hugh was still a million miles away – looking through me as if I was a mirage. "Ah, yeah, sure," he said, planting a brief kiss on my cheek and starting towards the cab driver again, towing me along with him.

Humiliation was rapidly replacing my excitement. I heard my mother's voice, saying '*I was starving*'. I stood where I was, holding him back. "Hugh," I pleaded. "What's wrong? Aren't you pleased to see me?"

Hugh stopped and turned to face me. He gave an exasperated sigh. "Look Georgia, I said I'd talk to you when I got home. Surely you can see that it's not appropriate to start telling you everything here?"

Suddenly I saw things from his point of view. The last conversation he'd had with me, I told him information was the only thing that was going to make me happy. Then I told him to fuck off and watch porn. Now I was standing here in front of him, all goofy faced and grinning. I supposed it could seem a bit like an ambush.

I bit my lip and took his hand. "Hugh, I didn't come here to talk," I said. "I came here to do this." I reached my arms up around his neck and pulled his face towards mine. For a moment, he resisted, taken by surprise, then I felt his briefcase thud to the floor beside us and he was kissing me back – the way he was supposed to do all along. He sucked my lower lip and caressed my mouth with his tongue, melting me in seconds, making me open to him like a morning glory flower opens to the sun. With one arm circling my shoulders, he snaked the other down around my waist, pulling my body tight in against his, so I could feel the heat radiating off him; the hardness gathering in his groin.

I was vaguely aware of people having to walk around us, and of the cab driver's eyes upon us, but I didn't care. I twined my arms around him, pulling him closer still, inhaling his scent, melding against him. He squeezed my behind – his hand burning through the thin chiffon layers of my dress. I moaned, wondering if I should take a leaf from Willa's blog and drag him off into the nearest bathroom. It wasn't until someone walking past us muttered 'For God's sake, get a room why don't you?' that he pulled his face away from mine, leaving us both gasping for breath. Still keeping me pressed against him, he kissed my nose and gave me a wry, slightly foolish grin. He smoothed the hem of my dress, which had ridden dangerously close to the line of my panties. "You're amazing," he murmured. "And I'm an idiot. Now let's get out of here before I get arrested for doing something very indecent to you in a public place."

"Ditto," I giggled, allowing him to lead me at last to the patiently waiting cab driver.

It was only when we were sitting in the cab heading home that Hugh looked at me properly. "What's with the outfit?" he asked, his lips twitching curiously as he took in my elegant hairstyle, floaty dress and strappy sandals.

When I told him about my plan to take him to the gallery, he raised his eyebrows dubiously. "What?" I asked.

"I promised we'd talk when I got home," he said. "Now after all the fuss on Wednesday night, you want to take me out?"

I studied his suddenly serious expression. He was offering to tell me what I'd been agonizing about all week. It should have been my highest priority. But now he was here, holding my hand, I wanted that feeling to last forever. My mother's voice rang in my ears – *'Never neglect that.'* And Hugh's on Wednesday night, before I'd hung up on him – *'Might make us both feel better.'*

"We do need to talk," I said finally. "But ..." I ran my thumb inside his shirt sleeve, brushing the spot on his wrist that I knew drove him wild, "other things are important, too. Let's go to the gallery first and ... deal with everything else later."

"You sure about that?" he said.

I nodded. "Kiss me," I whispered. "Before I change my mind."

Hugh's expression changed from doubtful to carnal in a split second. After a quick look at the cab driver, whose eyes remained resolutely on the road, he leaned swiftly over me, crushing my mouth with another heart-stopping, thigh-melting kiss that bordered on indecent. "I love you," he whispered fiercely as he worked his fingers into my hair, tugging me towards him with an intensity that was almost frightening.

By the time the cab driver gave a little cough to announce we had arrived outside our house, my carefully styled hair had been completely unraveled and half of Hugh's shirt buttons were undone. Anticipation was fizzing through my veins, making me light headed and light hearted, like nothing could possibly come between us.

Ten minutes later, I was gazing out at the sun setting over the harbor when Hugh came into the bedroom freshly showered. I turned around as I heard him go into the dressing room and grinned when I saw him stop dead at the sight of all my clothes put away neatly on the racks and shelves opposite his.

"So you've decided to move in at last," he teased, glancing over his shoulder at me as he gathered up clothes to put on.

"Yeah," I replied, making no secret of the fact that I was checking out his naked body. "The house needs work, but it's got great views. Especially the ones inside."

He gave me a sly grin. I knew how much he liked me watching him – and he knew how much I liked doing it, too. He had a runner's body – all long legs and sinewy muscle – the sort of body that was perfect for anatomical life drawing studies. He'd posed for me a few times, but somehow I'd always ended up undressing not long after he did, and not much drawing had gotten done. Now, watching him dress for me was almost as exciting. I licked my lips as he sauntered out of the dressing room and laid a pile of clothes on the bed, then frowned slightly when I noticed he had selected a pair of jeans and a casual shirt to wear.

"What?" he asked, noticing my tiny pout.

"Suit?" I pleaded hopefully. That was another thing Hugh knew I liked. He was gorgeous in pretty much anything, but there was something about the way he looked in a suit that *really* turned me on.

Hugh stepped over to me and pulled me against him like he had at the airport – only this time he slipped his hands under the hem of my short dress and slid them inside my panties so he was gripping my bare buttocks. Without the barrier of his clothing, his semi erect state was glaringly obvious. "Suck?" he teased, grinding his lower body into me so I could feel the burgeoning thickness of his cock unfurling against me.

I was tempted to agree to his suggestion. It was only the fact that Willa was waiting at the gallery that made me pull away. I'd never hear the end of it if we didn't show up. I took his lovely hard cock in my hand and stroked it a couple of times, then bent to kiss its velvety tip before forcing myself to retreat to the middle of the sofa by the window. "Later," I promised, sucking a finger teasingly as I eyed his groin. "Suit?" I asked again, pulling my knees up to my chin, deliberately giving him a glimpse of my panties.

Hugh pursed his lips and studied me for a moment. Then he picked up his clothes off the bed and went back to the closet, returning a few moments later with a pin-striped Armani suit, crisp white linen shirt and the violet satin dress I'd worn at my exhibition opening on Monday night. He laid the suit and the shirt over one arm of the sofa and the dress over the other. He leaned in to murmur in my ear, running his hand up between my bare thighs as he did so. "I'll wear the suit if you wear this," he indicated the dress. "No tie for me. And these ...," his fingers brushed the gusset of my lace panties ever so lightly as he issued the challenge, "... stay at home."

A burst of molten heat engulfed my thighs and lower abdomen at his fleeting, tantalizing touch. Once again, my attempt to tease Hugh appeared to be backfiring on me. I was disappointed that he'd asked me to change out of my new dress. But I was determined to see him in the suit.

"Fine," I said nonchalantly, standing up and stepping past him. I stopped in the doorway to the dressing room and stripped off my carefully chosen dress, along with my bra and panties. I smirked as I saw his cock leap out of the corner of my eye. I sashayed into the dressing room to find stockings and shoes, feeling Hugh's eyes burning into my bare behind as I rummaged through my newly filled shelves and drawers. I returned to the sofa to dress, knowing he could see my naked pussy as I bent strategically in front of him to pull on the stockings and lace the shoes. I turned to face him as I shrugged on the dress, leaving it open with my breasts and lower body exposed while I fidgeted unnecessarily with the sleeves and fixed my hair before finally, ever so slowly, doing up the hooks and eyes at the front. I did it all for him, and although his arousal was far more obvious than mine, he knew as well as I did that beneath my dress I was equally throbbing, swollen, every nerve and muscle in my groin coiled tight with desire for him.

Nineteen

Willa raised an eyebrow at my change of attire and hairstyle when we got to the gallery, making suggestive comments about what could have happened to necessitate such a change since she'd left me at the airport. I didn't bother to correct her risqué assumptions – I just wanted her to go so I could have Hugh to myself in the gallery. After what seemed like half an hour, but in reality was probably only a few minutes, she stopped teasing me and headed off for drinks with a friend, reminding us she would be back at ten with her two student assistants to pack down the exhibition.

"Wait here," I murmured to Hugh when we were alone, leaving him by the door while I went into Willa's office to adjust the lights and turn on the music. I switched off the overhead ceiling lamps, leaving only the wall lights on to illuminate the paintings. It made them vast, mysterious, like portals into another dimension – the white walls of the gallery disappearing into the gloom behind. I flicked another switch and the whole gallery twinkled with fairy lights, dripping like wisteria from the ceiling and around the tops of the high walls. Then I slotted my MP3 player into the dock of the stereo system and hit Play. The quiet strains of the theorbo music filled the room, transforming the stark modern space into an enchanted other-world. I felt transformed along with it, a tingle of promise and mystery trickling through my body as I returned to Hugh and held out my hand for him to walk with me.

For a moment, Hugh stood there, his eyes flicking between me and the magical scene around us. He'd seen some of my paintings finished; others he hadn't seen at all, although he knew the stories behind them. He'd told me some of them and others I'd read to him from books and websites. There were bits of our own story, too – of steep forest tracks, tall cliffs, dark caves and exposed beaches – love and dreams and hope. I hadn't quite understood it myself until that moment, but together, the paintings represented much more than just the stories and the images they were based on. Not only were they a huge shift for me in terms of the style and subject matter of my work; they were a visual expression of leaving behind my old life – Colorado, my father, New York, being single – and embracing a new one. Like the act of finally unpacking my clothes and putting them away, the exhibition announced that I had arrived here, in my new home, with Hugh – and that I belonged. Hugh seemed to grasp the enormity of this at the same instant I did, and he stepped forward to take my hand. Although our fingers barely touched, the connection between us was electric as he allowed me to lead him silently through the gallery.

I was glad I'd negotiated extra time with Willa as we walked around. It wasn't only stopping at each painting that prolonged our journey. When we reached the first table of food, containing a small bowl of cherry tomatoes, I popped one into my mouth and rolled it around, then pulled Hugh's face down to mine and kissed him, passing the fruit into his mouth as I did so. As we continued our viewing, I did the same with the almonds and strawberries. I deliberately trickled tiny drops of watermelon juice onto his chin so I could lick them off. I maintained steady eye contact with him as I slid the asparagus spears slowly between my lips before feeding him as well. I made a point of holding the chocolate for longer than was strictly necessary, so I would have to carefully lick my fingers clean while he watched. The bulge in his crotch became more and more conspicuous at every stop. No less obvious to me was the increasing wetness between my legs, which had spread from my naked center nearly to the tops of my stockings by the time we finished our circuit.

I'd planned our path carefully, so we would end up beside the couch, strategically placed in front of the Erangi triptych. Once we arrived there, though, my plan failed me. Taking the lead around the gallery and teasing Hugh with the food was one thing, but what now? I was so used to Hugh initiating things, inventing things, telling me what he wanted; that I seemed to have no instinct for what should happen next.

Sensing my dilemma, Hugh took over without a moment's hesitation. To my surprise, he led me away from the couch and towards Willa's office and the storeroom. As naturally as he took it, I followed his lead – allowing him to stand me in front of the mirror that remained in the corridor; watching him take his place behind me, kiss my neck, run his fingers lightly up and down my bare arms, move beside me, turn me towards him. He kneaded my breasts, pinching the nipples hard through the heavy satin before allowing his hands to stray lower until they were resting on my bottom underneath the fishtail train of my dress. "Nice ass, Mrs Fraser," he breathed into my ear as he squeezed my buttocks, pulling me against him so I could feel his erection through his trousers.

I gasped as I realized what he was doing, scenes from Monday night flashing alarmingly through my mind. I started to protest, but he nipped my ear fiercely, forcing me to turn my head towards the mirror, where I fully expected to see Xavier Bishop. To my surprise and relief, it was Hugh kissing me, sucking me, nibbling a line down my neck and grinding against me through our clothing. Undoing the top few hooks and eyes, he manipulated first one breast, then the other until my nipples were peeking above the top of my dress. He sucked deeply on them one after another, sending white-hot spasms of pleasure coursing through my body. I staggered backward a little until I was half leaning on a pile of felt blankets stacked up against the wall. Hugh moved with me, ensuring his groin maintained contact with my throbbing mound throughout the whole exercise.

In a quick, fluid motion, he shrugged off his jacket and tossed it onto the floor. He turned his head so our eyes met in the mirror. He loosened the bottom of my skirt, slipping his hand inside just as Xavier had done a few nights earlier. My entire body jolted at the sensation of his fingers on my bare thigh – and again as they made contact with the warm, moist and naked entrance to my pussy.

"Is this what he did?" murmured Hugh, holding my gaze as he slipped a finger inside me.

"No!" I responded, panicked. I tried to struggle free, but I was pinned firmly in place by Hugh's finger and the hand that maneuvered it.

"But you wanted it, didn't you?" Hugh squeezed my mound for emphasis, tugging my hair lightly to ensure I kept eye contact with him in the mirror.

I was about to deny it when I figured out the gleam in Hugh's eyes was not anger. He seemed to be enjoying this game of teasing ... fantasy. I thought about my conversation with Willa earlier – that it didn't matter if something was real or a fantasy. Perhaps Hugh wanted me to play along. "Yes," I whispered fiercely. A groan of pleasure from him confirmed my instinct had been right. He ground his hand into me.

"Did you like me watching?" Hugh released my hair. Even so, I remained immobilized by his hand – and the sight of him flicking the remaining hooks and eyes of my dress apart until it hung open at the front, giving him unrestricted access to my body. With the fingers of one hand still inside me, he smoothed the other over my hip and up to my breast, cupping it gently, then rolling my nipple firmly between his thumb and forefinger until it stood, taut and tingling, to his attention. With his mouth, he attended to my other breast, keeping his eyes on my face in the mirror the whole time, delighting in my reaction to his touch; waiting expectantly for my answer.

"Yes – No – I don't ..." I was torn between telling the truth and telling Hugh what I thought he wanted to hear. Then I realized I didn't know myself which was which. I'd been so shocked by what had happened with Xavier, I hadn't for a moment thought to question whether I liked it. If I had, was it wise to admit that to Hugh? And if I just said I did, was that the same thing? Things got even more complicated when Hugh continued, apparently unaware of my inner conflict.

"Did you want him to fuck you?" he challenged me dangerously, unbuttoning his shirt and grazing his bare chest against my torso in order to continue kissing my face and neck and breasts.

I hesitated again, so aroused and so afraid all at once. "I wanted *you* to fuck me," I said finally. "I wanted to fuck, but I wanted it to be you and I thought you were in Wellington and he was right there and ..."

Hugh mashed his lips against mine, preventing me from saying any more as his tongue entered my mouth. He undid his trousers, pulling away from me for a split second to allow them to fall to the floor. He pulled his fingers out of me and used them to guide his hot, hard cock into the space between my thighs, anointing it in the treacly crease of my vulva. "Oh, Baby G," he whispered, "You are sooo gonna get what you wanted." I was vaguely aware of a flash of white as his shirt joined his jacket on the floor, and in one swift move I was impaled by him. Grabbing my buttocks, he pushed into me so hard I was forced to wrap my legs around him to support myself.

"Look at yourself baby, you're so fucking hot," he breathed into my ear, making me turn my head again to watch the couple entwined in the mirror. His breathing was shallow and fast in my neck. His heart thudded madly against me as I ground back into him, clinging to him in a giddy haze. Slowly, impossibly slowly, he slid in and out of me, our movements against each other gaining momentum until we moved as a single being, with a single purpose to our actions. Wave after wave of fire stabbed my swollen clitoris as our copulation became faster and more intense until finally the sensation consumed me and everything disappeared into a blinding white void. My head was buried in Hugh's chest, so I felt, rather than saw, as he convulsed heavily into me, calling out my name, shooting his load deep into the heart of my flames.

While I was still breathless and dizzy from the force of our orgasm, Hugh managed to stagger, carrying me, into Willa's office. He sat on the chair at her desk, leaning back and pulling my legs tight around his waist to prevent himself slipping out of me. We stayed like that for some time – Hugh prone in the chair with me clinging to his front, still joined at the center by his semi-erect member. I snuggled into his neck, deeply inhaling his post-coital scent and tracing lines on his scalp through his hair as our breathing gradually calmed together. He ran his hands lightly under my dress and over my back, finally resting them on my buttocks, which he squeezed occasionally, bunting me gently from below at the same time to let me know he was still present.

When I squirmed ever so slightly back against Hugh, he shifted his position, pulling me more tightly against him and murmuring in my ear, "You asking for seconds, already, greedy girl?" I wriggled a little more vigorously in assent and Hugh pushed more insistently back against me. I sat up and put my hands on his shoulders, rocking purposefully now as I felt him hardening inside me. He groaned, pulling my upper body towards him so he could taste my nipples as they brushed near him each time I moved forward.

I was already well on my way to another orgasm when our state of bliss was interrupted by a sound in the hallway and the light flicking on above us. It was Willa, back as promised to pack down the exhibition.

"Shit, sorry guys," she said. "I thought you must have gone." I blinked at her over my shoulder and Hugh sat up in alarm. As he did so, I slipped off his lap exposing my own nakedness and Hugh's to Willa, who raised her eyebrows and stared at my breasts and Hugh's erection rather longer than I thought was polite. All three of us jumped when we heard voices in the gallery – the students. "Wait there guys, I'll be with you in a moment," called Willa over her shoulder. She grinned conspiratorially at Hugh and me, then whispered, "You've got five minutes." A few seconds later, Hugh's clothing was dropped discreetly onto the floor just inside the office, the lights went out and the door shut softly as Willa loudly directed the students to begin work at the far end of the gallery.

"Lean over the desk," said Hugh softly, standing up and indicating with a glance where he wanted me. I did as I was instructed, closing my eyes in blissful anticipation of what I knew was coming next. "Look up," he murmured into my ear as he grasped my hips and entered me from behind, filling me so deeply I had to resist the urge to cry out. Moments later, when I opened my eyes, Hugh's hand over my mouth was the only thing that again prevented me from calling out – this time in alarm. As I was bending over the desk in anticipation, I discovered he had opened the blinds between the gallery and the office – providing Willa and the students a clear, albeit dim, view of the two of us should they chose to look in our direction.

"Shhh, Baby G," he whispered as he removed his hand from my mouth and trailed it down and under my body, stroking my clitoris as he leaned over me and fucked me from behind. I pushed my head down onto the desk, mortified. I was sure I would never be able to come knowing that we could be seen at any moment. Within seconds however, I was responding fiercely to Hugh's relentless pounding, his harsh breath in my ear, his fingers twitching against my clit. With his other hand between my shoulders and wrapped in my hair, I was pinned to the desk, completely at his mercy as he brought us both to a fast and silent orgasm.

Hugh grinned wickedly at me a minute later as he stood me up. "You naughty little slut," he whispered, turning me around, planting tender kisses on my exposed torso as he fastened the hooks and eyes of my dress one by one from the bottom up, ending at my cleavage and continuing the kisses up to my mouth. I barely had the strength to respond – my legs were still shaking and my entire body was weak from the assault of my orgasm. Hugh smirked at me as I leaned dizzily against the desk while he dressed himself in a way that I knew was intended to afford me maximum visual pleasure. Then, to my surprise, he produced a pair of my panties from his jacket pocket and waved them in front of me. "You are very wet, my darling," he murmured, kissing me again. "I thought you might need these."

I had just recovered my senses sufficiently to wonder why Hugh had chosen my oldest cotton underwear when he surprised me again. Crouching in front of me, he wriggled his head up inside my dress and suckled my moist, tender skin. I groaned and closed my eyes, my strength ebbing again in the wake of the delicious aftershocks that rippled through my body. I only opened them again when he began gently wiping me dry with the underwear, to find Willa standing in the doorway watching us.

Noticing my immediate tension, Hugh stood up and wrapped an arm around me. "Mmmmm," he murmured, winking lasciviously at Willa as he inhaled my scent from the panties and put them back in his pocket.

Willa shot him a not quite evil, not quite admiring glance as she stepped aside to let us pass, and I wondered what she was thinking as Hugh and I slipped out into the night unnoticed by the students.

Despite my indignation at being bent over and taken in full view of anyone who cared to look, I dissolved into a fit of giggles as soon as we were out of earshot of the gallery. "*You* are a bad, bad man," I gasped, punching Hugh's chest ineffectually as he pulled me into a doorway for a deep lingering kiss.

"And *you* are a sexy, sexy woman," said Hugh, abruptly serious, looking deep into my eyes. "I love you."

"I love you, too," I replied, suddenly wanting to be safe at home with him, the events of the past week erased as if they had never happened.

Silence settled on us during the drive home, tension building as we went through the familiar motions of undressing, showering and brushing our teeth. Questions hung in the air between us, thick and heavy as thunder clouds – questions that neither of us wanted to raise, for fear of destroying the perfect magic of the evening we'd shared. As we reached the bed, it would have been the easiest thing in the world to crawl into Hugh's arms and drift off to sleep. Hugh pulled back the covers, inviting me to do just that. But I sat cross legged, halfway down the bed, forcing him to sit up against the headboard opposite me. With my heart in my mouth, I stared into his perfect blue eyes.

"Tell me," I whispered. "I want you to tell me now."

Twenty

Hugh looked over at me, his expression grave. He grabbed a pillow and stuffed it behind his head, leaning back against the headboard. He exhaled deeply. "OK," he said at last. "Whatever you think about this, and no matter what happens between us as a result, I need you to promise that you won't talk to anyone about it. If any of this gets out ... There are reputations at stake. Careers. And not just mine."

It felt like a re-run of the conversation I'd had with Willa a few hours earlier, making me promise not to tell anyone about her blog. "Yeah, OK," I muttered impatiently.

My casual response wasn't enough for Hugh. He frowned at me. "This is serious, Georgia," he said. "I need you to swear."

I hated the look on his face. In the two days since our Skype call on Wednesday, I'd convinced myself that what he was going to explain would be nothing more than a silly misunderstanding – like the ones about his phone and Madeleine. Now, a chill crept up my spine as he talked about keeping secrets and putting reputations at risk. This wasn't the Hugh I knew and loved. "Alright, I swear," I said returning his solemn gaze. "Now, will you please tell me?"

"OK," he said, blowing out another deep breath. "Right." He closed his eyes momentarily, as if in prayer. Finally, he started.

"When I was younger, I was a bit ... I suppose you could say I was a bit of a player. I had a really high libido. I loved sex and I wanted it all the time ..."

I couldn't suppress a smirk. Hugh shot me a wry grimace. "No baby, I know you think I'm always up for it now, but back then ... I could hardly go more than a few hours without getting off. I usually had two or three girlfriends at once, and I pretty much took whatever else was on offer, too."

He paused, waiting for me to say something.

I shrugged. If it hadn't been for Willa's blog, I would have been more shocked. Reading it had confirmed what I'd known deep down all along. I'd been naive in the extreme to think Hugh was less experienced than me when we met – no matter what he'd told me. I'd already decided there was no point fretting about his 'bad-boy reputation'. Since I didn't know anyone who'd been hurt by it, and I was the lucky beneficiary of Hugh's years of experience, I told myself I should be grateful, rather than angry. As long as ...

"It *is* in the past, though?" I asked carefully, not wanting to revisit our argument from Wednesday night. "You haven't been like that since we ...?"

Hugh shook his head and smiled – a seriously bad-boy, heart melting smile. "Nah. Well, not the multiple girlfriends. I just want you all the time now." As if to demonstrate, he ran his hand up my arm, around my neck, under my hair and drew me closer to him, sinking a kiss so hot, so tender onto my lips that I forgot for a moment he was supposed to be divulging some terrible secret involving Xavier Bishop. He kept his arm around me when he resumed talking, pulling me against his chest as if he were telling me a bedtime story, lulling me with his calm, deep voice.

"When I started working at Angus MacTaggart, both Dad and my brother Aidan worked there too. Because we had the same surname, they both ended up fielding a few phone calls put through to them by mistake, from girls I'd promised to call back and never did. Dad had already had a go at me several times about it – telling me that sort of reputation could affect my career prospects. Then I made the mistake of getting involved with a couple of women from work ... kind of concurrently." Hugh lowered his eyes sheepishly. "It caused a bit of trouble when they found out about each other."

I bit my lip, reminded uncomfortably of Matt, the only 'proper' boyfriend I'd had before meeting Hugh. Well, I'd thought he was a proper boyfriend – until I discovered he was also seeing one of my classmates. I'd never told Hugh about him – I was too ashamed to admit how naive I'd been. Two years ahead of me at Art School, uber cool with his long black hair, leather jacket and tattoos, I'd been so stunned when Matt told me he was taking me back to his place after an exhibition opening one night that I went without question. He had no idea that I was a virgin – or that, as a result of his complete lack of sensitivity to my needs, I spent the next six years telling myself I must be one of those people who didn't like sex. Hugh had blown that theory apart in spectacular fashion, but the revelation that he'd treated other women the way Matt had treated me left a bitter taste in my mouth, like I'd swallowed a spoonful of salt when I thought it was sugar.

"I must have been working there for about a year when I did something really stupid," said Hugh, recapturing my attention. I wondered what could be more stupid than sleeping with two women you worked with at the same time – especially when your father was the boss.

"I was staying out at Piha with a few friends just after Christmas, and Aidan came out too with his wife, Colette. They'd been married about three years at the time. She was a bit of a model-type – not keen on too much time in the sea. Complained it was bad for her hair, you know? One morning it was a bit windy on the beach for her liking and she stayed back at the house while Aidan and I and the guys all went down for a surf. I forgot my surfboard wax and when I nipped back to grab it, I stopped to chat with her and she ..."

Hugh's grip tightened around my shoulder, his discomfort evident as he searched for the words. "Well, I told myself then that she seduced me, but if I'm honest, I was a pretty willing participant and I didn't take a lot of convincing. I guess I was flattered because she was a few years older than me, but what it came down to is, I'd been stuck in a house full of guys for three days and I couldn't stand the idea of another two weeks like that. I wanted some puss– ... I wanted a woman."

I inhaled sharply, twisting to look at Hugh. He was staring straight ahead, his face devoid of emotion, as if he was reading from a script. I tried to figure out how old he'd been, wondering if there was any possibility his behavior could be excused as youthful foolishness. But if he'd completed six years at University and was already working, he must have been at least 25 – more than old enough to know better. Barely noticing my reaction, Hugh continued, like a penitent confessing sins after many years without absolution.

"The worst thing is, we didn't do it just once. After that first morning, we found more excuses to be alone together. She spent less and less time on the beach and

I kept 'forgetting' things so I'd have an excuse to go back. Sometimes we'd disappear separately into the dunes and then hook up. I even took my car around to the next bay once and picked her up there after she told Aidan she was going for a walk. Eventually we got found out, of course – Aidan got a bit suspicious after a week or so. He followed me back from the beach and basically caught us in the act."

Hugh was obviously distressed by the memory, yet I couldn't feel much sympathy for him. All I could think of was my father – distraught, broken – after my mother left him for a younger lover. How much worse it must have been for Aidan, for his own brother to be the other party in his wife's infidelity. I remembered how Hugh had taken me into the dunes on our honeymoon. I thought of the caves and what we'd done in there. Had he done that with Colette, too? His grip on my shoulder felt heavy and uncomfortable as he continued the story.

"Aidan was pretty pissed off. We had a fight – a punch-up. He beat me up really badly. I probably would have ended up in hospital if my mates hadn't showed up and pulled him off me. When Dad found out, he was furious. He made it pretty clear he'd arrange it so I was stuck in a back office doing research for the rest of my law career if I so much as looked at a woman in a way he thought was inappropriate from then on."

I wriggled away from Hugh, leaning against the headboard beside him so I could look at him. He continued staring straight ahead, unable to meet my eyes. "I know, it was a bloody terrible thing to do," he muttered finally. "Don't think I haven't regretted it ... wished I could turn back the clock."

I didn't know what to say. Was it something that could ever be forgiven? None of Hugh's brothers had been able to make it to our wedding in Colorado, but Aidan, the eldest, hadn't come to the celebration in Auckland either. Now I understood why. I recalled Hugh telling me that he lived in Australia. "What happened to Aidan and Colette?" I asked.

Hugh winced, rubbing his face. "They separated a couple of months later. Aidan went to live in Sydney. I haven't spoken to him since. I don't know where Colette is. And Dad ..."

"... has never forgiven you," I finished, thinking I knew how the story ended. The somewhat cool interactions I'd observed between Hugh and his father suddenly made sense.

"Dad should have kept out of it," snapped Hugh, unexpectedly savage. "He was always trying to control us. The first time he caught me sneaking a girl into my room, he gave me this huge lecture on morality and setting an example for my sister. That's when I started spending a lot more time here, with Uncle Don. Don gave me my own room and a key and let me bring whoever I wanted home. I was living here permanently by the time I finished high school."

I sat there in stunned silence. From the little Hugh had told me, I'd imagined Uncle Don as a kind, generous man who'd mentored and guided Hugh – not someone who'd encouraged him into a hedonistic, womanizing lifestyle which had resulted in him breaking up his brother's marriage. No wonder the family never talked about him.

But what did all of this have to do with Xavier Bishop? When I asked him, Hugh sighed. "I quit my job of course. I left home because I didn't want my father telling me how to live my life. There was no way I was putting up with it at work. That's when I went to work for Bishop, Underwood and Nash."

Twenty-One

So Willa was right. Hugh had worked for Xavier. But it wasn't until I prompted him again that he told me what happened while he was there and why he'd ended up back at Angus MacTaggart.

"I didn't completely learn my lesson from the whole fiasco with Aidan and Colette," he admitted ruefully. "When I started at Xavier's firm, I was a bit more careful about dating women I worked with. But there was a woman who worked at another firm in the same building. I'd seen her several times in the lift and she always smiled at me. Her hair was an amazing color – sort of dark copper. One day, I saw her waiting in our reception area, so I went over and started chatting to her. She was really friendly, like she was interested, and I was about to suggest we meet up later when Xavier came out and they went off somewhere together. He was kind of ... formal to her, so I assumed it was some sort of business meeting they were going to. I only found out who she was the next week, when he called me into his office and told me ..."

Hugh drifted off, recalling their conversation.

"What?" I asked impatiently, when he hadn't resumed after a moment. "What did he tell you?"

"It's weird," he replied, still lost in the past. "I never thought about it before, but he kind of said the same thing to me as Dad did. About that sort of behavior affecting my career prospects. Except it didn't feel ... like a criticism, or like he was trying to control me. Which is really ironic," he muttered, more to himself than to me.

"Hugh, what did he say?" I prompted him again after another long silence. "Who was the woman?"

"Huh?" he replied, as if he'd forgotten I was there. "Oh, yeah. Diana. She was his wife."

I winced. "You hit on your boss's wife?" Was this really Hugh I was talking to, I wondered? A small smile played on his lips. I stared at him, unable to comprehend how he could be smiling at a memory like that.

He looked at me sheepishly. "Yeah, I felt pretty stupid when he told me. To be fair, though, I didn't know who she was. And Xavier wasn't strictly my boss. He's a divorce lawyer. I worked for his partner, Simon Nash." He grinned again.

Why was Hugh still smiling? "B-but ...," I stammered. "Even so. Wasn't he furious?"

"No," said Hugh, more seriously now. "I was surprised about that, too. He kind of laughed it off – although he did tell me not to do it again. Then he offered ..."

Hugh stopped again. This was maddening. Why couldn't he just tell me? Five minutes into our conversation about Xavier Bishop, I was still none the wiser. "What, Hugh?" I demanded. "What did he offer?"

"Well, basically ... um ... Xavier said ... Diana, um ... he offered ...," blundered Hugh. It was the first time I'd ever seen him tongue tied. "Fuck!" he hissed at himself, shaking his head sharply, then looking helplessly back at me.

"Oh my God," I whispered, horrified realization dawning on me. "He offered you his *wife*?" What had Xavier said to me on Monday night? *'What's the matter Mrs Fraser? Only fun when you have an audience?'* Is that what had happened? He'd watched Hugh with his wife? Is that what Monday night had been all about? Was he expecting Hugh to return the favor?

"No!" replied Hugh. Then, "Yes. Well, not exactly. He offered … to help me."

"Help you?" I squeaked. "What do you mean?"

"He said," Hugh paused, fidgeting uncomfortably. "He thought I had great potential … he recognized that I had a sharp and enquiring mind, but he was also aware of my reputation for – 'enquiring more enthusiastically than most' I think is how he put it – into 'pleasures of the flesh'. He told me he'd like to help me – before it affected my career. Him and Diana. If I was willing to be trained."

"*What?*" I said. This was getting more and more bizarre. "What do you mean, *trained*?" It sounded like they'd invited him to join some sort of circus act.

"This is the stuff you can't talk to anyone about," he said gruffly, waiting for me to acknowledge him before continuing. When I nodded, he picked up my hand and took a deep breath.

"You may have noticed Xavier has a somewhat ... dominant personality," he began. "He's also very voyeuristic. He likes to watch others in a sexual situation – especially Diana. You wouldn't think it when you meet her, but in that context she really enjoys being submissive. And she loves to be watched. Xavier's one of a group of people who run a club – Club Eros. We went there together. He arranged 'scenes' where he instructed others about what he wanted to see, and we would do as he said ..."

"Others?" I exclaimed. "You mean it wasn't just you and ... them?"

"No – not usually." Hugh tightened his grip on my hand, as to prevent me from running away. "The scenes were often quite elaborate. Sometimes there were fifty or more people at the club – men and women."

"Fifty! Did you all ... was it like an orgy?" Scenes from my paintings came flooding into my mind. Just as I'd wanted to paint over the unfamiliar images, I wanted Hugh to stop talking. I wanted to put all of his words back into his mouth. I tried to tug my hand away, but Hugh refused to let go, forcing me to remain beside him while he continued.

He looked over at me. "It's not ... it wasn't ... some sort of ... kinky thing," he said, defensively. "It was a mutually beneficial relationship and it did really help me. A lot of it was around teasing and being teased and being in control of ourselves – although Xavier had ultimate control over everyone. If anyone ... transgressed, he would punish them."

"Did he punish you?" I asked, curiosity winning out over the urge to put my hands over my ears and shout 'La-La-La-La-Laaa'.

"Sometimes," Hugh admitted. "More at first, until I learned to do as I was told."

"So, were you like ... a slave?" I asked doubtfully. An image of Hugh in a collar and chains flicked into my mind. I pushed it away.

"I guess," said Hugh slowly. "But it didn't feel like that. It wasn't ... humiliating or anything. He wasn't into that. It was more like an erotic ... dance, where Xavier was a very strict choreographer. I liked – like – being watched. You know that."

"You like watching too, though." I had a sudden insight into Hugh's requests to see me dress, undress and perform for him in specific ways. "And you've never behaved very slave-like around me." I was confused again, trying to figure out how someone could go from being a sex slave to the confident lover I thought I knew.

Hugh shook his head. "It was always Xavier's intention to train me to be dominant, like him. When I first started going to the club with them, I thought I was going to get lots of sex. But Xavier didn't allow me to do anything except watch – for a long time. It was very frustrating. Even when he finally gave me permission to participate, it was months before he let me anywhere near Diana. Eventually, once I'd learned to control myself, I became one of their preferred ... performers, I guess you could call it. Then Xavier began handing control of scenes over to me. He liked to watch that too – it was like a ... second layer of submission. It's odd, but we became quite close. It felt like we could read each other's thoughts sometimes."

"Did he ever touch you?" I wondered, trying to subdue images of the two of them engaged in some sort of naked confrontation.

"No – only with a whip or a cane." Hugh winced a little for effect and, despite my state of shock, I smiled weakly.

"Did you ever whip anyone?"

"Only if Xavier told me to. I prefer using whips in less violent ways."

I squirmed at his reply. The thought of Hugh tracing a whip along my exposed buttocks and down to the soft, secret space between them sent an unexpected burst of heat between my thighs. I peeked over at him curiously, wondering if his thoughts were running along similar lines to my own. "Um, have you ever wanted to do anything like that to me?" I asked.

"Yes," he said darkly.

"So, why didn't you?" I squeezed my thighs together, creating another shockwave at the point where they met.

His lips twitched in contemplation. "It was something I did when I was with Xavier and Diana. I didn't want to impose that on you. Plus ..." Hugh studied me carefully before continuing. "I actually do, quite often. You just don't realize it. You're naturally quite ... very ... submissive."

I stared at him in confusion, not sure whether to be flattered or insulted. I tried to figure out how and when I'd been submissive around him. And what did he mean, 'with' Xavier and Diana? Before I had a chance to ask, he picked up my hand and turned it over in his, tracing soothing lines on my palm and wrist. "There are many ways of being dominant, baby," he explained, reminding me uncomfortably of my mother, telling me there were different kinds of love. "I don't feel the need to create elaborate scenes or dish out punishment like Xavier. I find it very sexy when you just ... obey me."

I was dumbstruck. Did I really obey him? How could I not have noticed? I was only vaguely aware of his fingers, still stroking my hand as it lay passively in his, when he cleared his throat.

"The stuff at the club was just the start, Georgie," he said, looking at me cautiously. "One day, about eighteen months after I first went there with them, Xavier phoned me out of the blue and invited me to their home. He told me Diana wanted ..." He paused, searching for the right words. "... something more intimate. I ended up living with them."

"What?" My jaw dropped. "You ... slept with them both?"

"Yes."

"But I thought you said Xavier never touched you." I wondered if my instincts had been right after all, the image of them embracing like wild animals in a kind of savage lust floating once again into my mind.

Hugh gave me a brief smile. "Xavier was never interested in me in that way," he reassured me. "It was always all about Diana."

"What, so you shared her?"

He nodded. "Yes."

"Did your family know?"

Hugh shook his head. "No. My family thought I was still living here."

"What about people at work? Your friends?"

"I'd just started my PhD when I moved in with them, so I wasn't actually working in the office. And I didn't go out of my way to see my friends during the time I was with them. It was a very private arrangement. Nobody else knew about it."

"How long did it go on for?"

"We were together about two and a half years before it ended."

I almost leapt off the bed. "Two and a half *years*?" No wonder Xavier had been surprised when I didn't know who he was.

Hugh nodded regretfully, although I couldn't tell if it was because he lamented not telling me, or because he was sorry it was over.

"So, what happened? Why did it end?" I asked.

Hugh chewed his lip in contemplation before answering. "I slept with someone else," he said finally.

To my surprise, I leapt to his defense. "But surely they can't have expected you to abstain from proper relationships? That's completely unreas– "

"It *was* a proper relationship," he said abruptly, cutting me off. "We had an agreement and I broke it."

"Why did you agree to it, though?" I asked, still outraged. "Didn't you want a … normal relationship?"

"Georgia, I'd never had a 'normal' relationship. I didn't know what one was. Admittedly, I did find it hard to understand at first why Xavier wanted to watch his wife with other men. Then, as I spent more time at the club ... and with them, I realized that, for Xavier, Diana's pleasure was more important than his own. It kind of was his own, I guess. He loved her ... loves her so much that he derives pleasure from seeing her fulfilled. Being part of that with them was a great ... privilege." He stared up at the ceiling. "I learned a lot from them. I just wish it hadn't ended the way it did."

"Did Xavier have you fired?" I asked.

Hugh shook his head. "No. I was supposed to go back to work there once I finished my PhD, but when the relationship ended, I resigned. It would have been too hard, working in the same building and bumping into them all the time. Dad had left Angus MacTaggart by then to become a judge, so it was easy enough to go back there."

"That's why you didn't invite Xavier and Diana to our wedding," I said. So much was becoming clear.

"Pretty much," said Hugh. "I didn't see any point in raking everything up again. And I wasn't sure they'd want to see me anyway. Especially Diana." His voice shook.

I studied his bloodshot eyes and weary expression. "You were in love with her," I said, the realization hitting me like a punch in the stomach.

Hugh looked away, swallowing back tears. "Yeah. I didn't realize until it was too late. If I had, I would never ..."

The way he trailed off was like a second punch – like there was still something between them. "Do you still love her?" I asked.

Hugh looked at me uncertainly. "Once you've loved someone I'm not sure you ever stop," he replied. Before I could react, he grabbed my hand and spoke urgently. "I love *you*, Georgia. You know that?" I nodded, but all I could think of was that he loved Diana. A bitter taste crept into my mouth, as if I was being burnt up from the inside. He kept talking.

"I'm sorry I didn't tell you all this before, but ... by the time I knew you well enough, there didn't seem to be any point. We were so happy. I still am ... so happy with you. I didn't want to do anything to risk that. I want it to go on forever, I want to go to sleep with you and wake up with you and ... make babies with you and grow old with you and love you every day for the rest of my life. You know that, don't you baby? Nothing I've told you changes that."

I kept nodding. I let him wrap his arms around me and pull me down into the bed with him. I let him kiss me and make love to me again. I came for him and I let him come inside me. But I didn't feel any of it. All I felt was the sharp agony of knowing that Hugh loved someone else and he would never stop loving her. Long after he was asleep, the thought continued to plague me, keeping me awake for hours, like a mosquito attacking, retreating, attacking again, refusing to give in. Finally, I slid out of bed and crept up to my studio, hoping that some distance from him might dull the pain. It didn't, but I eventually fell asleep on the sofa, where I woke a couple of hours later from a terrible dream.

Hugh and I were trying to make love in the gallery in front of the mirror, but every time Hugh came near enough to touch me or kiss me, Xavier cracked a whip against him, forcing him to retreat. When I looked at the mirror, a crowd of people were watching us, as if through a window. A woman was lying spread-eagled on a table nearby, blindfolded and handcuffed to the corners. One by one, Xavier directed men and women from the crowd to perform various sexual acts on the woman – a man put his cock in her mouth; two women writhed on her handcuffed fingers while sucking her breasts; another straddled her face, forcing the bound woman to perform oral sex on her; a man knelt between her legs and licked her completely bald pussy.

A tattooed man tried to enter her, but Xavier whipped him fiercely until he backed away.

Finally, Xavier turned to Hugh and motioned for him to approach the woman. He instructed another woman from the crowd to suck Hugh's cock until he was hard. Then Xavier nodded at him. "Fuck her," he commanded, indicating the woman on the desk. Hugh obeyed, watching me quite calmly as he did so. I tried to go to him, call out to him, but Xavier, who was standing behind me now, restrained me, covering my mouth with one hand and putting two fingers of his other hand inside me, so that every time I moved to struggle free, the pressure of his hand against my mound increased, causing waves of desire to flood my veins, weakening me into submission. Pressure built in my womb and I knew I was close to coming.

Without warning, Xavier released me and walked over to the edge of the desk, watching Hugh and the woman intently. He removed his black shirt and jacket, so he was naked from the waist up, revealing intricate Japanese Yakuza-style tattooing over his entire upper body. I made to follow Xavier, discovering too late that I was tied to some sort of frame and couldn't move. Somebody gave me a baby, but they didn't seem to notice that my arms were bound and I couldn't hold it.

The baby fell and it disappeared – everything disappeared and I was back at the beach again.

Mercifully, I woke before I entered the water this time. I needed to pee. Returning from the bathroom, I stole into our bedroom and sat on the edge of the bed, listening to Hugh's slow, regular breathing. It was as if all the turmoil of his past had been transferred from his mind into mine, leaving him floating blissfully free while I drowned in confusion. If he still loved Diana, what was he doing with me? And why had he allowed Xavier to touch me? Was he planning some kind of wife swapping arrangement that would allow him to resume his relationship with Diana? Was I expected to be obedient and submissive and go off with Xavier?

Exhausted, I lay down and tried to go back to sleep, but Hugh's presence beside me was like static – keeping me awake even as it obliterated all rational thought. I padded out into the hallway and back up the ladder to my studio, feeling more alone than I had the whole time he'd been away in Wellington.

Twenty-Two

On Saturday morning, I was woken by the sound of Hugh roaming the house, frantically calling my name. I sat up, but I didn't answer him. When he found me, huddled at one end of the sofa in my studio, he squatted in front of me and tried to take my hand. I kept my arms wrapped stubbornly around my knees, feeling an irrational urge to protect myself from him. He sighed and went to sit at the other end of the sofa, facing me. "Ask me anything," he said quietly. "I'll tell you the truth."

I turned my head sideways to look at him. "Why didn't you stop Xavier on Monday night when he followed me?"

Hugh shrugged. "I was … curious, I suppose."

"Curious?" I lifted my head and glared at him. "What were you hoping to see?"

He shrugged again. "I don't know. I just wanted to see what would happen."

"But what did you *want* to happen?" I thought of what he'd suggested in the gallery as we stood in front of the mirror, replaying the scene Xavier had created with me just a few nights earlier. "Did you want him to … actually …?" I couldn't say it. Just thinking about it created a tingling sensation in my groin.

Hugh chuckled. "He would never have gone that far."

"If he had, though?" I demanded. "Is that what you wanted?"

"Baby, he wouldn't have. Trust me."

"Trust you?" I exploded. "How can I trust you? You stood there and watched him put his hand up my dress and you did nothing about it. You slept with his wife.

For two and a half years. You're still in love with her – a tiny little fact you didn't think to mention before you married me. And now you want me to trust you?"

Hugh sighed. "Georgia, I told you, it's in the past. You're the person I want to be with now. I'm sorry about the thing on Monday night. It was totally my fault. It won't happen again."

"What do you mean, your fault?" I snapped. Earlier in the week he'd told me the whole thing had been initiated by Xavier.

"When I saw the two of you talking, I ... gave him a signal. I didn't mean to, it was just habit, really. By the time I thought about it, he was already following you and, like I said, I was curious. I've already talked to him about it."

"What?" I said, my chest tightening. "When did you talk to him?"

"I phoned him on Thursday," said Hugh. "To set the record straight, and to apologize for misleading him. Like I said, it won't happen again."

"What did he say?" I asked anxiously.

"He said I was a bloody fool. For letting things get out of hand. But he was OK about it."

"He didn't ask to see you … us?" I remembered that he'd invited himself to dinner the night I met him.

Hugh shook his head. "We agreed it was better to leave things in the past."

"What about Diana?" I asked. "Don't you want to see her?"

Hugh shook his head again, more slowly. "It's over, Georgie. Just leave it be."

I didn't know if I was relieved or disappointed. I should have been pleased that they didn't want to see us, and that my wife swapping theory had proved to be false. But now all the demons had been let loose, I couldn't just let them be. I sometimes wonder if we'd still be together, and what sort of relationship we'd have, if I'd done what he asked. I didn't, of course. I dropped one hot potato and picked up another.

"OK," I said, turning to face him, "Tell me something else, then. Why did you tell me, the night we first slept together, that you were a virgin?"

"What?" he replied, thrown by my sudden change of tack, looking at me as if I'd lost my mind. "I never told you that."

"You did," I retorted. "You said 'I've never done this before.' Then you told me you loved me and it wasn't a one-night stand."

Hugh frowned, trying to remember. Finally, he rolled his eyes and grinned shyly at me. "I'd never told anyone I loved them before," he said. "That's what I meant."

My frostiness melted a little. I bit my lip. "Not even Diana?" I asked.

Hugh shook his head. I felt a small surge of triumph. Maybe his feelings for her were in the past, after all. So why was he looking over at me all anxiously?

"Did you really think I'd never ...?" he began. "I mean, as far as first nights go I thought it went pretty well ..."

I had to giggle when I realized why he was so worried. "Relax," I said, straightening one leg and nudging him playfully with my foot. "Your reputation as the world's greatest lover is safe. Nobody in their right mind could have thought you didn't know what you were doing that night."

He grabbed my foot and brought it up to his mouth, sliding his tongue rudely between my toes, his usual cockiness returned. "Oh, baby, I knew exactly what to do with you … from the night I first met you." His eyes scorched me with a meaningful gaze as he ran his hands up my calf, stroking the sensitive skin behind my knee, exploring my thigh with feather light strokes. For the first time that morning, I relaxed, allowing myself to soak up the heat of his touch, tiny shocks throbbing their way up to the center of my body as he continued sucking and nibbling my toes without breaking eye contact. He was right. He *so* knew what to do with me. My brain turned to jelly along with my thighs. I stretched out my other leg, sighing and leaning back against the arm of the sofa as he repeated his ministrations.

"So why didn't you?" I asked, not especially interested in the answer, just making idle conversation now. "Do what you wanted … the night we met?"

Hugh paused, removing my foot from his mouth, holding it against his chest and continuing to stroke it as he spoke. "Apart from the fact that I thought you were gay?" he said, tweaking my toes. "I really liked you. I held off because I didn't want to fuck things up. I decided to try and do things properly for once."

I opened my eyes, which were half closed in bliss. He really did love me the most, then. I thought about the two months we'd hung out together as friends before we became lovers. It hadn't been that difficult for me, because at the time I'd never known any different. It wasn't as if I was used to 'getting off' every few hours like Hugh. But, thinking of the two weeks I'd recently spent without him, it occurred to me that those first two months must have been torture for him. "I guess it was kinda hard for you." I gave him a sympathetic smile. "Going without sex for two months."

As soon as I said it, I saw the expression on his face flicker. I sat bolt upright, snatching my foot out of his grasp. "God," I whispered. "You didn't, did you? You were seeing other women during that time."

"No!" protested Hugh, leaning towards me, reaching for my foot again. I leapt up and away from him. He stood, too. "Georgia, I didn't. I ..."

"What?" I snarled. "What did you do?" I couldn't believe I had been so stupid as to think a man with his record had overnight become a model of restraint and celibacy. Except, of course, I hadn't known about his record then. His explanation for why he hadn't made a move on me earlier suddenly seemed a lot less romantic.

Hugh gave me a sulky look. "I watched a shitload of porn," he growled. "And did a hell of a lot of jerking off."

I returned his sullen gaze, knowing that he was holding back. I was starting to recognize the signs. "And?" I demanded. "You promised me the truth. The whole truth." *So help me, God*, I added silently as I stared at him in agony.

"I didn't ... date other women," he sighed. "But I did ... pay for it sometimes."

I sank back down onto the couch, black spots blurring my vision like a cloud of insects. The pain in my chest was unbearable. I was barely conscious of Hugh sitting down again beside me. But when he touched my hand, I recoiled as if from a venomous snake, shrinking back into my corner. "Don't touch me," I hissed.

"Baby," he pleaded. "Don't be like this. It was just sex ..."

"Just sex?" I raged. "Is that supposed to make me feel better?"

Hugh looked genuinely perplexed. "Uh, yeah. I mean, it wasn't like I was *involved* with any of them."

I glared at him. "No," I snapped. "I thought you were involved with me. I obviously got that wrong."

"I was very involved with you," he retorted. "In fact, I thought I was going crazy. I'd never felt like that before. It was very ... confusing for me, thinking I was in love with a lesbian. If anything, it made me want sex even more than usual. I thought paying for it was more ... honest."

"*Honest?*" I countered. "I don't think you know what the word means." I was still sitting in the corner of the sofa. When he moved towards me a fraction, I folded my arms, glaring at him, warning him not to come near.

He sighed, running his hand helplessly through his hair. "Georgia, I didn't set out to deceive you," he remonstrated. "You've got to remember, I was used to living a life of secrets. The whole thing with Xavier and Diana and the club and ..." He trailed off, the regret clear again on his face. "For years I'd been operating on a need to know basis – with my family, friends, people I worked with. Moving to New York provided an opportunity for me to ... reinvent myself a little. It wasn't an instant transformation. But what good would it have done for me to tell you – any of this?"

"I would have had a choice," I spat back at him. "I could have made a decision based on the facts, not on some ... façade created in order to trick me."

"I didn't do it in order to trick you," he protested. "I did it because I loved you. I didn't want you to base your opinion of me on my past. I wanted you to see me as the person I thought I could be – the person I thought you deserved. I worked hard to become that person, Georgia, and I thought I'd succeeded." He lowered his voice seductively. "Just like you've become the person I wanted you to be."

For a second, I was lulled by his hypnotic tone. Then a flash of indignation erupted inside of me. Who did he think he was, taking credit for transforming me? "Who I am has nothing to do with what you wanted!" I said fiercely. "I could be packed and on a plane back to the US this afternoon and there's nothing you could do to stop me."

Hugh's face closed over, his jaw set in a grim expression. "You're right, baby, there is nothing I could do about that." The continued steadiness of his voice belied the strain behind his eyes. "But that's not who I want you to be. I don't want you to be a person who gives up at the first hurdle. I don't want you to reject those who love you because of silly assumptions. Remember the night before our wedding, when we talked about forgiveness? Well, what I'd like is for you to accept that what's past is past and forgive me for whatever ... harm you think I've caused you by my omissions. I want us to forget about all this and move forward."

He stood up and headed for the trap door and the pull-down staircase. "Think about it," he said quietly. "I'll be back tonight. Text me if you want me home sooner." Then he added, before his head disappeared from view, "I love you, Georgia."

My aching heart wanted to call him back. But my brain – full of the rules of love, what was right and wrong, forgivable and unforgivable – froze my mouth, preventing my lips from moving. I sat mutely, tears burning the back of my throat as the sound of his footsteps faded down the attic stairs. A few minutes later, I heard him descend the main staircase. The front door opened and closed behind him. The Audi rumbled for a moment in the garage and driveway, and then there was silence. I was alone. Free to leave. Free to stay. Or trapped. Which was it?

Twenty-Three

I stood up and paced the room. If I sat down again, I would cry and never stop. I needed something to stem the hurt, like a tourniquet. My eyes fell on the six canvases under their sheet. I yanked the sheet off and, ignoring my initial urge to paint over them, dragged the two unfinished works into the middle of the floor.

Hours later, they were filled with more bound and gagged people being subjected to various types of sexual pleasure and pain. A woman was strapped to the edge of one canvas, where a winding column of men, all with large, erect penises lined up to service her. A man on the opposite edge flung a river of hundred-dollar bills at them as large-breasted women in tall boots performed fellatio on him. In the middle was a circus ringmaster, brandishing a many tailed whip in one hand and a medieval spiked club in the other. More terrifying, though, were the babies – with dreadful, distorted, crying faces; playing with macabre toys – knives, mincers, instruments of torture; some missing eyes and limbs, gouged out or ripped off by their companions; one beheaded by its playmate as it hugged a teddy bear, a maniacal grin on its face.

When I looked at the decapitated child, I dropped my pen and flung myself face down on the sofa, the tourniquet falling away, tears coming anyway. Great heaving sobs racked my body, rendering me incapable of speech, thought or movement and I gave myself up to the grief, letting it flow from me like blood from an open wound until there was nothing left in me to vent. Hugh had been my Prince Charming. But instead of rescuing me from a high tower, here I was trapped in one, unwittingly submitting to his every wish.

I wiped my eyes and dragged myself to my feet. Picking up my pens again, I signed the two paintings on the floor, then pulled out the other four and did the same. I stood all six of them up in a semi-circle around the sofa, sat down and scrutinized them.

They were good. Really good. I was glad I hadn't painted over them. They were also terrible. I had to get rid of them. I hardly dared show them to Willa, for fear of what she might think of me. But she would know where to sell them – somewhere far away, where nobody knew me. I picked up my iPad and photographed each one carefully, emailing them off to her with *FOR YOUR EYES ONLY* in the subject line. Then I cleaned up my pens and headed downstairs to our bedroom. There was nothing keeping me here now.

In the dressing room, I looked at my clothes, all neatly hung and folded on the racks. I dragged my antique traveling trunk and four suitcases out from where I'd stacked them in the corner and began putting everything back into them. As I did so, I realized how many of the items Hugh had bought for me. Most of the choices had been made when we were out shopping together, but there were also some cute surprises he'd come home with, like the butterfly choker and the matching butterfly Doc Martens I'd been wearing on Wednesday when I saw Xavier Bishop. I almost had a pair of Docs from Hugh for every month we'd been together. In addition to the butterfly ones, there were five more pairs of standard boots – one in shocking pink patent leather, two floral prints, a Jackson Pollock-like paint splatter pattern and a crimson velvet pair with cherry blossoms embossed on the sides. There were also the black Mary Janes, some classic 20-hole red leather knee-highs and my latest treasures, which he'd given me for Christmas – soft indigo leather biker-style Docs with tiny floral patterned lining and violet satin ribbon laces.

The colors of my wardrobe had altered, too, in the time I'd known Hugh. When we met, nearly everything I owned was black. At first, pale shades of lavender, washed out blues and peachy creams had crept in amongst the dark colors, delicate as the dawn sky. Now, glimpses of shocking pink, orange, indigo, teal and scarlet permeated the collection as well, blooming like flowers in a tropical forest. Hugh's words – 'You've become the person I wanted you to be' – replayed in my mind as I fingered each item. I wondered how I had allowed myself to become so influenced by him without even realizing it – not just submissive in bed, but in every part of my life. I let him choose my clothes; drive me places; support me financially. He did all the grocery shopping and cooking. Since we'd moved to New Zealand, I didn't have any friends of my own apart from Willa. She would never let herself be kept by a man. It was time to take a leaf from her book and stand on my own two feet.

Even as I made the decision, a sick feeling came over me. I wandered into the bedroom, checking under the sofa and on the bedside tables for any more of my possessions so I could pack them. I had no idea how to stand on my own two feet. Where was I going to go when I left here? Run to Willa? Take a cab to the airport? And then where? What would I do? I'd never had a job, apart from the one at Jimmy's bar, and I'd never had to survive on the income from it. I was still living at home with my father back then. I thought of Jessica at Rakinos, struggling to pay the rent.

I picked up the View Master from my bedside table and sat on the bed with it, flicking through the slides. Hugh told me he'd lied to me, or at least avoided telling me certain things, because he loved me. Was that so different to me not telling him about Matt, or Ryan McGregor? He'd tried to conceal his promiscuity, his bizarre relationship with the Bishops, because he didn't think I'd want a man with a history like that. But hadn't I equally avoided disclosing my lack of experience, my foolish, fearful naivety, because I thought he'd find me uninteresting? He said he'd reinvented himself, worked hard to be the person he thought I deserved. Shouldn't I be honored by that?

And what about me? Despite my earlier indignation, I had to admit he was right. I was the person he wanted me to be. Like my wardrobe, my whole life had transformed from dull monochrome to glorious technicolor when I met him – a bit like Dorothy arriving in the land of Oz. Unlike Dorothy, though, I didn't want to go home. I didn't feel at all dominated by him. If anything, he inspired me. I was an artist and he was my muse. The idea of going back to being the timid, lonely creature hiding behind the scary black facade filled me with dread. I liked having a husband, and I liked being a wife. Hugh was the only man I could imagine being married to. Despite his bad-boy past, he really was my Prince Charming, just like Willa said. I was hardly likely to find another, even if I wanted to. I had to forgive him.

I put the View Master down on the bed and went back into the dressing room, rummaging through the suitcases for something to wear. I needed to get out of the house, so I could think clearly. Was I capable of that sort of forgiveness? I pulled on a Dr Seuss T-shirt and a short denim skirt upcycled from an old pair of jeans. It wasn't the fact that he'd slept with other women, even prostitutes, that bothered me most. It was the fact that he'd loved one of them – maybe still did. And that, somehow, she'd given him something I couldn't. That was the thing I was going to find the most difficult to let go of.

I dug out the pink patent leather Docs and shoved my feet into them. Even supposing I could forgive him, I still needed to figure out what I wanted. If I was going to stay, both of us deserved to know why. Once I'd done up my laces, I looked around the dressing room. Garments and shoes had erupted everywhere. Hugh had been so pleased on Friday night to see I'd finally put all my clothing away. I knew he'd be disappointed if he came home and found it all in a mess again, so I shoved everything back in the cases and stacked them behind the door. If I was going for a walk, I had to get moving. A few tiny clouds were gathering on the horizon, signaling rain later. It was still a few hours away, but I didn't want to get soaked like I had the other day. I could put my clothes back where they belonged when I got home again.

Twenty-Four

After my mother left my father, I spent my time in one of two ways – holed up in my room with the stereo on full blast, drawing; or walking the streets around Basalt, trying to make sense of things. I kept telling myself that, when I got home and opened the front door, I'd discover I had been stuck in some sort of altered reality and everything would be back to normal. Now, as I stepped outside, I told myself the same thing. When I came back, Hugh would be home; we'd make up and move on. All I had to do was walk.

As soon as I got to the street, the heat rising from the asphalt hit me like a blast from a jet engine. Even though the tide was out and it was muddy at the edge of the harbor, I decided to head down a nearby walkway towards the sea, where there was a cooling breeze. I stayed as near to the coastline as possible, seeking out hidden alleyways and unfamiliar streets in order to do so as I loped along, thinking deeply. After an hour, I'd reached the end of the beach at Point Chevalier. I was hot and sweaty and my legs ached, but I was no closer to figuring out what I wanted or how to move forward.

I wandered into the park at the end of the Point and flopped down under the trees. The nearby playground was overrun with what seemed like hundreds of children at the tail end of a birthday party. Their shrieks and squeals, coupled with the repeated calls of their weary parents rounding them up only contributed to the chaos in my head, and I sat up again immediately, deciding to look for a more tranquil spot to do my thinking. Before I could get to my feet, a little girl of about three or four stood in front of me. She regarded me with piercing blue eyes and twisted a stumpy blonde plait uncertainly.

"What's *your* name?" she demanded.

"Uh, Georgia," I answered, unsure of the protocol for speaking to unknown children who accosted me in public places.

"George?" she giggled. "That's my brother's name. He's still in my Mummy's tummy." She pointed at a woman who was standing by a park bench, packing a plastic lunch box and drink bottle away in a small pink and purple backpack. She retrieved a pink gingham sunhat from behind the swings and strolled towards us. She had the same bright blue eyes as the little girl; her hair was a rich, coppery chestnut, sculpted into a long bob which curved elegantly in under her chin. Her legs and arms and face were slim, but from the voluptuous curve of her breasts and the swelling around her abdomen it was obvious that she was pregnant. Her face flushed apologetically at me as she took the little girl's hand. "Nina! What have I told you about bothering people?" she scolded gently. Then, to me, "I'm so sorry, she's always doing this ..."

I stared at the little girl and at her mother's swollen belly. Hardly hearing what she said, I was suddenly consumed by an overwhelming desire to be that woman. To have a little girl like that, or a little boy like George and to be filled with the potency of new life, waiting to bloom. Dizzying in its power, the feeling robbed me of speech for a moment. I gulped and waved my hand to indicate there was no need to apologize. By the time I had recovered, they were already walking away and I could hear the girl saying, "I knew she was friendly, Mummy. She had pink boots ..."

I was in a state of shock. Was that really what I wanted? A baby? It wasn't something Hugh and I had ever discussed. Now, it glittered like a perfect jewel on a beach of black sand, flicked up beyond the tide line for me to discover when everything else had been sucked away in the swirl. A baby was something I could give him that Diana couldn't. And it was what he wanted. He'd said so on Friday night – *'I want to make babies with you'*. I wanted it too. The idea of him burying himself in me, giving me his seed not just for our mutual pleasure, but for the purpose of creating a child, embedded itself in my mind, multiplying like cells until it bubbled through my entire consciousness – joyous, unrelenting, alive.

In the same instant, images of the screaming, maimed babies from my paintings tugged at my elation like a dangerous undertow. I heard my mother's voice – *'being a parent didn't come naturally to me'*. I thought of the way I'd submitted to Xavier Bishop on Monday night. And of my mother, saying '*I let it happen*'. What if I turned out to be the same sort of mother my own had been? One who let things happen, abandoning her child, leaving it to wither like a severed limb? And what of Hugh? Did he really want to make babies with me, or was that just a throwaway comment, to convince me he wasn't still in love with Diana? There was no way I wanted any child of mine to suffer the way I had because one of my parents loved someone else. How could I be sure I could trust him? How could I trust myself?

I stayed under the tree for hours, until all the children had gone home and the color had faded from the sky, trying to work out what to do. No matter how many times I thought it through, I always came back to the same unpleasant conclusion. I was going to have to ask Hugh for something that would be incredibly difficult – for both of us. Something I didn't know if our relationship would survive. With a heavy heart, I hauled myself to my feet and headed for home.

I don't know if it was my preoccupied mind, or the fact that I'd taken such a roundabout way to get to the park, but I must have taken a wrong turning on my way home. I ended up beside the entrance to a freeway, which was not the one I could see a glimpse of from our house. I walked up the arterial road that fed into the freeway, hoping to find a familiar street name or landmark that would help me get my bearings. But I was in a part of town I'd never been before. The houses all looked the same, albeit newer than the ones in my street. All the road signs pointed to more unknown suburbs. When I reached a small block of shops, I tried asking directions at a Chinese takeaway. Although the staff were sympathetic after I finally managed to communicate that I was lost, they all shrugged helplessly when I told them my address; no more familiar with the geography of the city than I was. Back on the street, everything else was closed. The only feature of the landscape I recognized in the growing darkness were the lights of the Sky Tower in the center of the city, several miles away. Reluctantly, I trudged in their direction, figuring that, even if there was probably a faster route, once I located Hugh's office or the gallery, which were both near the tower, I could find my way home from there.

As I plodded away from the smell of the takeaways, my stomach growled, protesting its lack of sustenance for the past 24 hours. If I'd thought to bring some money, I could at least have eaten something, but all I had was my keys and my phone. Even my water bottle was empty. The sun had bled well down below the horizon and it was now completely dark. To top it all off, as I left the shelter of the shop canopies, I felt the pressure plummet and the first drops of rain splattered onto my arms.

I was soaked to the skin by the time I finally reached a service station on the edge of the city. My relief on finding someone who spoke English and could tell me where I was was short lived, however, when I pulled out my cellphone to call Hugh and discovered the battery was flat. Despite my tears, the attendant was firm on their policy of not allowing anyone to use the phone unless they paid for it or made a minimum $20 purchase, offering instead to drive me home when his shift finished at midnight. I took one look at his thinning, greasy hair and leering grin and stumbled back into the rain.

By the time I got home two hours later, I was freezing cold and shaking, dizzy with hunger and fatigue. The house was in darkness, although when I peeked into the garage, I was comforted to see Hugh's car parked inside it. Assuming he was already in bed and asleep, I let myself in quietly. Without going upstairs, I stripped off my wet clothes and wrapped myself in Hugh's puffer jacket which was hanging near the door. Then I headed into the kitchen for something to eat. To my delight, the refrigerator and pantry had been fully re-stocked in my absence, and I skipped upstairs with the feeling that everything *was* going to be OK. I'd left that altered universe outside in the rain, and Hugh was in bed, waiting for me.

Except he wasn't. When I crept into our bedroom, the bed was still made and there was no sign of him. Confused, I walked back into the hallway. The attic stairs to my studio had been pulled up. I looked around for the hooked stick I used to pull them down, but it was nowhere to be found. A growing sense of panic spread through me as I hunted around for something I could use instead, finally succeeding in opening the trap with a wire coat hanger that I taped to the end of a broom handle.

There was an eerie silence as I climbed into my studio. The rain had stopped and a wide crescent moon had emerged from behind the clouds. The six paintings looked like oversized tombstones in the dim glow coming in through the windows. Hugh was lying on his back on the sofa, one arm folded behind his head, the other holding the View Master, which rested on his stomach. He was wearing board shorts and a T-shirt; an old cotton blanket lay on the floor beside him. He was so quiet that a cold fear gripped my heart as I approached him, only dissipating when I saw the View Master shift slightly with his soft, even breathing.

I stood at the end of the couch, studying him. Normally, he looked beautiful when he was asleep – younger than his 33 years, and peaceful. But tonight, his unshaved face and worried expression reminded me of a hobo sleeping on a park bench in New York. I noticed a few specks of gray had crept into his beard. I didn't care. All I cared about was making up with him and telling him what I wanted. I only hoped he would agree.

Silently, I unzipped the puffer jacket and let it drop to the floor. I moved closer, gently removing the View Master from Hugh's hand and putting it down beside the sofa. I lowered my naked body gradually onto him as he slumbered, pulling his free hand up until it rested around my waist, holding me. I snuggled my head into his neck. He smelled salty, like the sea – he must have been out at Piha. I stroked his hair softly, adjusting my breathing to match his, waiting for him to wake up.

He moaned and shifted slightly, tightening his grip on my waist, making my pulse race a little. I tugged his hair more firmly and nibbled his earlobe, wriggling meaningfully against him. His body tensed beneath me and his head lifted slightly. "Stop it," he muttered. I giggled, and moved my mouth from his ear to his face, slowly edging my kisses towards his lips. "Don't." Hugh turned his head away sharply, scratching my cheek with his stubble.

"Ow!" I said playfully. "That hurt!" I shifted my weight so I could slip my hand under his T-shirt to tickle him in retaliation, but he sat up abruptly, almost throwing me to the floor.

"Get off me," he said angrily, retreating to the far end of the couch, glaring at me with bleary eyes.

"Hugh? What's wrong? It's just me," I said, sitting up in shock. "I'm back."

"You think it's funny, do you?" he growled, standing up as I slid towards him. "Well it's fucking not."

"Hugh, what do you mean? I have no idea what you're talking about ..."

"Don't toy with me, Georgia." I shivered at the menace in his voice. "What was I supposed to think, when I came home to find all your clothes gone and this on the bed?" He flicked the View Master with his foot, sending it skittering across the floor.

"But Hugh ..."

"And this," he gestured at the paintings arranged around the room. "What the fuck is this? Some sort of ... final offering? Was that supposed to make me feel better?"

"Hugh, I can explain ..."

"There's nothing to explain, Georgia. I can see now that you decided to make it look like you'd left and it would teach me a lesson and then we'd be even and it would all be OK again. God! Do you have any idea how ...?" The hurt I felt at every word was reflected in his face, but every time I opened my mouth to protest at his unfair accusations, he lashed out again, making me powerless to do or say anything to calm his rage.

"You have some fucking nerve to accuse *me* of being dishonest," he continued. "And then you come home and expect me to fuck you! Is that all I am to you, Georgia? A good fuck? Because if that's all you want from me you can ... you can just ... fuck yourself!"

I cringed as he stormed past me and headed for the trap door, clambering noisily down the steps and across the landing to our bedroom. My first instinct was to go after him and try again to explain to him, but I was too afraid. Not of any physical harm, but of more hurtful words between us. Even more, I was afraid of telling him what I wanted. Afraid that I'd got it completely wrong. Afraid it would only make things worse between us. Perhaps I should have left, after all.

I stayed on the sofa, naked, with my knees pulled up under my chin and my arms wrapped around my legs until I was numb with cold and fatigue. Pulling Hugh's abandoned blanket around myself, I finally lay down and shut my eyes. I was nearly asleep when I remembered it was Francesca's birthday the next day and we were expected at Hugh's parents' place for a family lunch. I'd never dreaded the dawn more.

Twenty-Five

The sun was high in the sky and the house was silent when I woke up the next morning. I felt like an intruder as I crept quietly down from my studio to our bedroom. The bed was made and there was no sign of Hugh. Then I saw the note on my bedside table – '*Gone 4 a run*'. No love, no x's, no smiley face. I left it where it was and drifted into the dressing room with a heavy heart.

I looked at the suitcases still behind the door, wondering how Hugh could have missed them there when he got home yesterday. I opened the first one, a battered old leather thing that used to belong to my father, and started putting T-shirts back on the shelves and hanging skirts and dresses on the empty rails with a sense of déjà vu. I was onto the third case, placing shoes neatly in pairs when Hugh came back from his run. His face was impassive as he stood in the doorway. "What are you doing?" he asked.

"I'm staying," I said. "I was always staying." I was about to continue, but when I looked up again he'd gone. A moment later, I heard the shower running and sighed, still none the wiser as to his mood. I'd just finished arranging the last of my Doc Martens back in their rows when Francesca rang, asking if we could pick up some fresh cream and strawberries on our way over for lunch. While I sat on the bed talking to her, Hugh came back from the shower and went into the dressing room, emerging a couple of minutes later dressed in faded jeans and a white V-necked T-shirt. He left the room and went downstairs without looking at me.

Shoving the empty cases into the corner, I headed for the shower myself, washing away layers of hurt, exhaustion and confusion from yesterday – and sex from the night before. It seemed so long ago. Once I was dressed, I padded downstairs to get some breakfast and found Hugh standing at the kitchen table, car keys in hand.

"Where are you going?" I asked.

"Mum and Dad's," he muttered.

"So, were you planning to take me?" I enquired in surprise.

Hugh shrugged. "I didn't think you'd want to come."

"Well, I do," I snapped. "So would you mind waiting until I've had something to eat?"

Hugh normally made an excuse to be in the kitchen with me, stealing kisses and fondling my behind as he made coffee or stacked the dishes. Today, he sat at the table with the newspaper, drumming his fingers impatiently while I nervously sliced fruit and poured muesli and yoghurt into a bowl. All thumbs, I spilt the coffee twice, then cut myself slicing a nectarine. I racked my brains for a way of getting him out of my space for a few minutes. "Do you want to, um, grab a couple of bottles of wine for your Mom?" I asked, noticing the absence of a gift as I smeared nectarine juice and blood and coffee all over the bench in a futile effort to clean up after myself.

Hugh got up wordlessly and went to the small wine cellar under the stairs, returning a few minutes later with a red and a white, which he stuffed into a gift bag recycled from a drawer in the kitchen, then resumed his former activities. I flung my dirty dishes into the sink and left them there, unwashed, ignoring Hugh's critical glance as I ran upstairs to grab my bag and shoes so we could head off.

The atmosphere in the car was no better – Hugh docked his iPod and turned up the volume on the car stereo as soon as we were out on the road. I couldn't help feeling he'd deliberately chosen the irritating jazz fusion to further test my already jarred nerves. Finally, I could stand it no longer. As we approached a small group of shops where I knew there was a fruit and vegetable store, I reached over to the stereo and pushed the Off button.

"We need strawberries and cream," I announced. "And when I get back, we need to talk." He glowered at me as he pulled over beside the shop, but he didn't turn the music back on.

When I returned to the car, I twisted in my seat to face Hugh. To my annoyance, he continued looking straight ahead at the windshield, his hands still on the steering wheel. I took a deep breath and spoke anyway. "What you found last night, when you got home ...," I began. "It's not what you thought. As soon as I put everything in the suitcases I knew I didn't want to go. It's just ... I needed to think about what I did want. I decided to go for a walk before it got too late and I know how you hate me leaving things in a mess, so I just stuffed everything back in the cases, planning to put it all away later. Then I walked much further than I intended and I got lost on the way home and ...," I swallowed hard to stop the tears that seemed to be constantly at risk of overflowing my eyes this morning.

I touched Hugh's arm and when he didn't move it away, I continued, softly, "Hugh, I had fully intended to be back long before you came home and have everything put away. I would never have done that deliberately to hurt you. I am so sorry ..."

Finally, he looked at me, but it wasn't a kind or forgiving look. It was the sort of look you give a stranger who stops you in the street and asks you to take a survey. "Have you finished?" he asked.

"Um, I guess. For the moment. Unless there's something you want to ..."

"Nope. Can't think of anything just now," he replied gruffly, eyes on the road again. He put the car in gear and squealed the tires slightly as we pulled away from the curb.

He didn't speak again during the journey, and my throat and chest felt tight with anger and uncertainty by the time we reached his parents' house. "Hugh?" I said quietly as he turned off the ignition when we were parked outside.

"What?"

"Two more things. Silly assumptions and forgiveness. Don't be a bloody fool," I whispered finally, using Xavier's words on him as he opened the driver's door.

Twenty-Six

Hugh barely had time to wish his mother a happy birthday before he was assaulted by his brother Lachlan's sons, aged seven and nine, jostling each other and calling excitedly, 'Uncle Hugh, we've been waiting AAAges for you.' They grabbed his arms and dragged him through the house to join them and Lachlan in a game of soccer on the back lawn, leaving me standing awkwardly in front of Fran with the wine, strawberries, cream and a bunch of flowers. I suddenly wished I'd been five minutes later going downstairs that morning and Hugh had left me behind after all.

"Er, Happy Birthday," I said to my mother-in-law, trying not to drop everything as I exchanged tentative hugs with her and John.

I followed Francesca into the kitchen, where full-scale preparations for lunch were in progress. Sera was washing salad greens freshly picked from the garden and tossing them into a bowl along with cherry tomatoes, chunks of cucumber, olives and crumbly Feta cheese. Lachlan's wife Marnie had just put a dish of chicken drumsticks into the refrigerator to marinate and was making burger patties for the barbecue. Fran put a pasta salad on the table just outside the open window, then deftly emptied the cream into a small metal bowl. In a couple of minutes she had whipped it, washed and sliced the strawberries and was busy layering them with the cream into a pair of freshly made sponge cakes which had been cooling on the bench.

I stood at the kitchen window, watching Hugh and his brother playing with the boys. The sea shimmered at the edge of the lawn, which extended right down to the harbor's edge. Hugh was laughing, carefree, feigning despair one minute as he 'accidentally' let nine year old Tom kick the ball past him into the makeshift goal; then hoisting little Harry triumphantly onto his shoulders to do a victory lap of the garden as their team evened the score. He and Lachlan shoved each other good naturedly, trying to take the ball off each other, and when the younger boys ran to their father's defense, dragging Hugh to the ground, he rolled around on the grass tickling them until they begged for mercy. For a moment, I thought he was smiling at me as he glanced over to the window, laughing, but my heart sank when I realized his joyful expression was directed at Harry, who was now asking him to chase him around the garden 'like a dinosaur'.

As I moved aside to let Marnie open a drawer full of herbs and spices all in neatly labeled glass jars, I knew I should offer to lend a hand in the kitchen rather than just standing there. However, I'd learned from previous experience that I was generally more of a nuisance than a help in food preparation activities at the Frasers. I didn't know what half the utensils were for; it took me forever to find ingredients in Francesca's expansive pantry; and the others seemed to be able to chop, slice, spread and peel so much more quickly and expertly than I could. Besides, just at that moment, I was afraid I would burst into tears if I opened my mouth to ask anything at all.

Marnie gave me a curious glance as she retrieved a jar of nutmeg from the drawer, but, to my relief, didn't say anything. Marnie was my favorite member of the Fraser family. A midwife and naturopath, she'd made a real effort to include me when I first arrived in New Zealand with Hugh, and as a result I often sought refuge with her at family gatherings. A few minutes later, she was back at my side with a stainless-steel tray full of burger mix, neatly formed into flat rounds. "Georgia, could you take these out to the barbecue so John and Duncan can start cooking them for the kids?" she asked me. Then, more quietly, "We're all OK in here, so no need to come back if you need a little space."

I nodded gratefully and took the tray of meat out onto the deck, where John and Duncan were standing by the barbecue discussing the neighbors' renovations. Duncan was an architect, three years older than Hugh and the third of the four brothers. He'd recently returned from England with his Polish wife, Ula and their two children. Rebecca, aged four, was galloping excitedly around in circles with her five-year-old cousin Grace, Lachlan and Marnie's youngest child. They both had ancient hobby horses, rediscovered in the 'treasure room' full of old toys that Fran kept especially for her grandchildren when they came to visit.

Duncan and Ula's baby, Reuben, had been born three days after our wedding and was now nearly seven months old. He chortled loudly from his blanket under a nearby tree as his mother chattered to him and held out toys for him to play with. Once I'd delivered the burger patties and said a brief Hello to Duncan and Ula, I turned and walked quietly back into the house, past the kitchen and into the formal lounge, where it was cool and quiet and I could be alone. On the heavy antique sideboard were dozens of family photos in pewter and silver frames. I picked up one of Lachlan and Marnie, with their four laughing children; then another of Duncan and Ula with Rebecca and Reuben, just after Reuben was born. There was none of Aidan and Colette; or of Hugh and me. I wondered why. Maybe you only counted in this family if you produced children and could cook, I thought bitterly. I put the photo down and went to lie on the couch, closing my eyes.

"Auntie Georgia?" I became aware of a young hand patting me on the arm. I sat up, blinking. It was Olivia, the eldest of Lachlan and Marnie's children. "Mum says you're good at drawing. Will you play Pictionary with me?"

"Uh, sure," I replied, still half asleep.

"Great!" she said enthusiastically. "We can play in here – the little kids can be so *annoying*," she added conspiratorially. "I'll just go and get everything." Moments later she returned with the Pictionary box, paper and pens, explaining the rules and generously allowing me the first turn of the game. Soon, we were sitting on the floor, giggling and chatting like old friends. I discovered that she shared not only my love of drawing, but also my aversion to noisy crowds and my taste for chunky boots.

We were laughing hysterically at my pathetic attempt to guess Olivia's depiction of 'wind' in under sixty seconds when I realized Hugh was standing in the doorway, watching us pensively.

"Oh, Hi Uncle Hugh," grinned Olivia. "Do you want to play too?"

Hugh smiled faintly. "No thanks, Liv – I'm the world's worst artist. But I was hoping you could spare Georgia for a minute."

Olivia looked disappointed to have her game interrupted. "Only if you promise it will really only be a minute," she grumbled. "I know what you grown-ups are like."

"How about three?" he bartered, coming into the room.

Olivia sighed. "I guess so." Then she brightened. "I know," she said. "I'll set the timer, so you don't cheat. I'll turn it over three times for three minutes."

Hugh chuckled and ruffled her hair as he offered me his hand, tugging me to my feet. "Alright," he agreed. "You're going to make a great negotiator when you grow up, Livvy."

"Your time starts now," she called after us as Hugh lead me halfway up the stairs, stopping to sit on the landing and pulling me down beside him. He wrapped his arm around my waist and kissed the top of my head tenderly.

"I'm sorry about last night and this morning," he murmured into my hair. "You're right, I probably did jump to the wrong conclusion."

I eyed him warily, wondering what had caused his abrupt change of mood. "Yeah, you did," I muttered when I finally felt able to speak. Then, a sudden wave of relief sweeping over me, I poked him hard in the ribs, making him jump. "Monster," I accused, trying out a weak smile on him.

"Grrr," he replied, playfully growling into my neck and wrapping both arms around me in a bear hug.

As soon as he pulled me against him, I lost the battle against my tears. With a giant sob, I buried my head in his chest, taking in large, shaking gulps of his warm, male scent, slightly grassy from rolling on the lawn. "Don't ... ever ...," I whimpered, ineffectively thumping his back and clinging to him all at once, not knowing whether to be happy or angry.

"Hey ... Hey," he whispered reassuringly, stroking my hair and taking hold of my hands, gently preventing my mock assault from continuing.

It was only when I heard Olivia calling, "Two minutes to go," from the lounge that I sat up and stopped crying enough for Hugh to continue talking.

"Hey," he said again, bringing a hand up to stroke away my tears and brush the hair back off my face. "I'm sorry. Really." He tilted my chin up, compelling me to look at him. "So, is there another conclusion I should have come to – instead of ...?" I stared back at him blankly.

"Because it would be OK, in fact more than OK with me ..."

"What do you mean?" I asked, struggling to sit up properly, completely baffled.

He kissed me slowly, sweetly. Despite my bewilderment, I found myself kissing him back, leaning again into his warm, strong embrace, then somehow climbing awkwardly into his lap, straddling him and wrapping my arms around his neck so I could pull his soft, sexy mouth down to me, sucking urgently on it. I writhed against the bulge in his jeans, wondering madly if it would be possible to sneak up into one of the bedrooms for a couple of minutes without being missed.

"One minute left," chimed Olivia, as if in answer to my thoughts.

Hugh groaned and, with a huge effort, disentangled himself from my embrace. "Jesus, Georgia," he panted. "Maybe Marnie was right."

"What did Marnie say?" I smiled more definitely this time, wriggling in his lap, trying to kiss him again.

The lust in Hugh's expression was unmistakable, but he carefully avoided my smooching. "She said it sometimes makes women ... extremely horny," he said, his eyes misting.

"What does?" I frowned, wondering why the way he was looking at me had gone so unexpectedly from sexy to ... mushy.

"Pregnancy," whispered Hugh, triumphantly. "Are you ...?"

A void of panic abruptly replaced my hunger for Hugh's kisses. "No!" I said, slithering off his lap in alarm. "God, no. That's the last thing I'd want right now ..."

The gentle mist suddenly cleared from Hugh's eyes and I could see the thunder clouds of the morning threatening to return. "I ... I didn't mean it like that," I backpedaled, trying frantically to reignite the spark that had flared so deliciously when we'd kissed moments ago.

"Time's up. You have to send Aunty Georgia back now Uncle Hugh." Olivia was standing at the bottom of the stairs, hands on her hips, staring up at us.

"Be there in a minute Olivia," I called. Then quietly, sidling back to Hugh, "I just mean there are ... other things we need to deal with first." I squeezed his arm, desperately. "I'm not saying never ... Can we talk about it properly, later?"

"Aunty *George*-a. I'm *way*-ting."

Marnie appeared beside Olivia at the base of the stairs. She whispered something to her daughter and Olivia stomped off back to the lounge. "Sorry about that, guys," called Marnie from around the corner. "Take your time."

I looked forlornly at Hugh. "Hugh? This doesn't change what you said before, does it? You didn't say it just because ..."

Hugh looked miserably back at me. "I don't know," he sighed. "I feel like I don't know anything anymore." We sat there a while longer, each waiting for the other to speak until we heard Olivia, humming loudly and deliberately from the lounge, where she had obviously been instructed to wait quietly by her mother. Hugh pulled his arm away and patted my behind. "You'd better go," he said, indicating the direction Olivia's voice was coming from.

We'd been playing again for about fifteen minutes when Olivia looked quizzically up at me. "Aunty Georgia?" she said.

"Uh huh?" I replied, still distracted by my conversation with Hugh.

"Did you have a fight with Uncle Hugh?"

I forced myself to focus properly on Olivia. "Not exactly. Why?"

"Well, it's just, you're not very good at drawing any more. And your eyes are kind of ... red."

"Oh."

Before I could think of a way to explain my change of mood to her without lying – or telling her the truth, Olivia shuffled over to me and put her arms around my waist, resting her head against my breast. "Mum says sometimes a cuddle helps, even if you don't want to talk about it," she announced sagely.

"Thanks Olivia," I whispered. I hugged her back, thinking how comforting it was to be loved so simply and innocently by this child. But it wasn't enough, I realized, recalling my mother's words. I also craved the love of my husband. Complex, adult, carnal.

"Aunty Georgia?" said Olivia again.

"Yes?" I replied absently, stroking her flaxen hair.

"Boys can be really mean, can't they?"

I was surprised by my gut reaction. "I don't think they intend to be mean," I said slowly. "But I guess they make mistakes sometimes." I looked down at her, wondering if, at eleven, she was old enough to be having trouble with boys, and if she was looking for advice. I didn't dare ask her – I was the least qualified person on the planet to be giving out relationship advice – even to a child. Luckily, Francesca popped her head in the door at that moment to tell us it was time for lunch. I stood up quickly and headed to the bathroom to wash my hands.

Twenty-Seven

I loitered in the bathroom, preparing myself mentally for the lunchtime noise and chatter. By the time I emerged, most of the family were already seated at the long table on the deck. There were only two empty chairs remaining – both on Hugh's right. I was heading for the one beside him when Sera darted in from nowhere and sat down on it.

Hugh turned, then frowned when he realized it was Sera, not me who was sitting beside him. He looked at me, standing uncertainly behind her chair. I felt a rush of gratitude when he spoke up. "Move over, Sera." he said, nudging her gently. "Let Georgia sit there."

Sera looked up at me with a glimmer in her eye that I'd learned to dread. "No," she smirked, tossing her golden ringlets. "I want to sit next to my Big Huge Brother." I recognized the pet name Hugh told me she'd given him when she was three years old.

"Move over please, Sera," he said more firmly. "I want to sit with Georgia."

"Oh, don't be so mean, Hugey," she chastised. "I haven't seen you for ages. Georgia gets to see you all the time."

"Sera, *move*," he said, loudly and angrily now. There was a sudden silence at the table as everyone turned to see why normally fun, laughing Hugh was shouting at his sister.

"Hugh," said Francesca soothingly. "Just ..."

"Mum, I want to sit with my fucking *wife*!" he said, banging his fist on the table. "Is there a problem with that?"

"Hugh! That's quite enough." John stood up, glaring at him. Fran gasped. The other adults sat in awkward silence, carefully avoiding eye contact while Tom and Harry nudged each other, unsuccessfully trying to suppress giggles. The girls gaped, open mouthed, at their uncle. Reuben started to cry.

Sera turned again to face me, still standing, stalled, beside the remaining free chair. "Let's ask Georgia," she said brightly, smiling at me expectantly.

I froze as all eyes turned to me. I glanced at Hugh. Even with his face like thunder, I wanted to be near him more than anything. Ula, on the other side of the vacant chair, with her heavy eye shadow, stiletto heels and dripping gold jewelry, was nervously trying to shush the baby. He had thankfully stopped bawling, but was now babbling loudly, oblivious to the tense silence around him. I wondered if Sera's behavior towards Ula was anything like the treatment I received. If it was, she needed Sera beside her even less than Hugh or I did. Carefully avoiding Hugh's wounded stare, I slid quietly into the empty seat between my two sisters in law.

"Thank you, Georgia," said Francesca primly, glaring again at Hugh, who fixed his gaze sullenly on his plate while John said grace.

Despite my good intentions, I hardly had a chance to speak to Ula as she was constantly preoccupied with Reuben. The baby spent most of the meal time gleefully flinging cutlery onto the ground and rubbing food into his hair, much to the delight of Tom and Harry, who were sitting opposite. Hugh and I both picked glumly at our food while Sera tried to engage her brother in bubbly chatter; studiously ignoring me at the same time. By the time we'd finished the strawberry sponge cake, however, Sera had barely managed to elicit more than two syllables from Hugh, and it was with obvious relief that she leapt up to help her mother clear away the dishes at the end of the meal.

After lunch, I headed down to the water's edge to help keep an eye on Tom and Harry, who wanted to play with the remote-control boats they'd been given for Christmas. Reuben's fretful grizzling was starting to grate on me and I was hoping Hugh would follow me so we would have a chance to talk. To my disappointment, he disappeared into the house with the baby and it was Lachlan who ambled down beside me.

In complete contrast to Hugh's rangy, athletic frame, Lachlan, like Duncan and Aidan, had their father's stocky build. Unlike their father, all the brothers shared the same vivid blue eyes as their late mother. Lachlan was the second in the family – four years older than Hugh and two years behind Aidan. He had a firm, gentle manner which I imagined would be appreciated by the patients of his medical practice.

Once he'd helped his young sons launch their boats and ensured that Harry in particular was clear on the rules around not going into the water above his knees, Lachlan joined me as I sat on the low hanging bough of an ancient Pohutukawa tree, staring out over the water.

"That was very awkward earlier," he said quietly. "I'm sorry you ended up getting stuck in the middle of one of Hugh and Sera's little displays."

I glanced curiously at Lachlan. "Is it something that happens often?" I asked.

"I must say, it's a while since I've seen them behave quite that badly – especially Hugh," he said, "But when they were children ... Sera, being the youngest and the only girl, is used to having things her way. And Hugh doesn't like to lose. Sometimes it's a bad combination."

I sighed. "I just thought she didn't like me." I was relieved to be able to talk about it to someone who didn't seem to be wearing Hugh's rose-colored spectacles. "She's never been very nice to me – even at our wedding."

Lachlan gave me a surprised glance. "That's curious. I would have thought the two of you would have enough in common – I mean, you're the same age and ... both in creative jobs."

"That's what I thought, too," I replied. "From what Hugh told me in New York, I was really looking forward to meeting her. But she doesn't seem to want me around. I know Hugh meets her for lunch quite a bit, but she never comes over to the house or invites us to her place – well she doesn't invite me, anyway. I just don't know what I've done to offend her."

Lachlan contemplated my words for a moment. "Married her favorite brother, perhaps?" he suggested.

I looked up at him in surprise, raising my eyebrows.

"Despite their quarrels, Sera and Hugh have always been extremely close," he expanded. "She may be having trouble adjusting to the fact that she's no longer the most important woman in his life."

I bit my lip at the irony of his remark. If Sera was jealous of me, imagine what she would have thought of Hugh's involvement with Diana. I wished I could tell her how little she really knew her 'Big Huge Brother'. It might wipe that smug little smile off her face and make her appreciate me a little more.

Just then, there was a loud splash from the water, followed by Tom calling out, "Da-ad, Harry's fallen in." Both of us looked up in alarm, then smiled at each other at the sight of Harry, already pulling himself out of the water, sopping wet and beginning to wail because he'd momentarily lost sight of his boat.

Lachlan stood up calmly, patting me on the shoulder as he headed for the water to retrieve his son and the boat. "I'll have a word with Sera," he said. "I'm sure we can work it out."

I offered to stay down at the water with Tom for another five minutes while Lachlan took the loudly protesting Harry up to the house to get him changed. When we got back, Marnie and Lachlan were preparing to head home – gathering up stray clothing, toys and books whilst simultaneously managing to prevent any of their four children from vanishing or re-scattering their collected belongings. Things went better once Fran sat the children down in the family room, giving them ice blocks and putting on a DVD to keep them all in one place.

As I finished helping Marnie pack up the Pictionary in the lounge, I asked her if she knew where Hugh was. After the incident at lunchtime, I half expected her to tell me he'd gone home, but she smiled and led me to one of the bedrooms upstairs, standing with me in the doorway. Hugh was sprawled, fast asleep on the bed, his arms wrapped protectively around Reuben, who was snoozing peacefully on his chest. "He walked him around for an hour before he fell asleep," whispered Marnie. "He's so great with kids. He'll be a wonderful father."

My chest constricted painfully. Like it had in the park the day before, hope and joy surged through me, immediately turned to stone by uncertainty and fear. Seeing Hugh and the baby lying there together so blissfully made me realize it was more important than ever that my plan worked. But, given the tension between us, the possibility of Hugh agreeing to the idea seemed more remote than ever, too. Conflicting emotions welled inside me until they erupted together in the form of a thick, choking sob. I turned and rushed away from the bedroom as the single sob multiplied rapidly until I was shaking violently with unexplained grief.

I only got halfway down the stairs before I sank to the floor in the same place I'd sat with Hugh only a couple of hours earlier. Marnie was sitting beside me in a moment, rubbing my shoulders comfortingly until my tears abated. "Georgia, I'm sorry if I put my foot in it earlier with what I suggested to Hugh. I didn't realize it was such a sensitive subject. I know how upsetting it can be if you're trying and nothing seems to be ..."

"We're not ... *trying* anything," I snapped. "It's not a sensitive subject, it's not even a *subject* ... we've ever discussed."

"Oh," said Marnie, embarrassed. "Well, then I really have put my foot in it, haven't I?"

I immediately regretted my abrupt tone. "Don't worry," I said quickly, then, trying to direct the conversation away from myself, "Olivia's lovely, by the way."

"Yes. It was good that she got to spend time with you. Being the eldest, she often draws the short straw when it comes to one on one attention." Marnie paused, deliberating whether to continue our previous conversation. "Georgia, if you and Hugh ever do decide to ... discuss the subject, you know you won't be alone, don't you? I mean, I know you don't have any family of your own here, but if there are things you are worried about, we'll all be here to support you. It's not something you have to do on your own."

"Thanks," I sniffed just as Lachlan popped his head up the stairs to let Marnie know the children were all in the car. After they had left, I sneaked back upstairs to lie on the bed beside Hugh and Reuben, studying them thoughtfully until Hugh opened his eyes.

"Hey," he said, looking around, surprised at his unfamiliar surroundings.

"Hey," I said softly, hopefully. "Are you ready to go home now?"

To my great relief, he smiled – a lazy, sexy smile, full of promise. "Sure," he whispered, sitting up carefully so as not to wake Reuben. "I'll just give this baby back to its owners."

Twenty-Eight

Hugh was still quiet in the car driving home, but he took my hand and pulled it over to rest on his thigh. Although the silence between us was no longer the tense, hostile standoff it had been in the morning, it was still an unwelcome intruder in place of the things that needed to be said. It wasn't until we were home and in our bedroom that I had the courage to tackle them. I led him to the sofa by the window and sat down cross-legged at one end, with my back against the armrest. "We need to talk," I said nervously.

Hugh gave me a wary look as he sat down opposite me, mirroring my pose. "Yeah," he sighed. "I guess we do." He chewed his lower lip thoughtfully, waiting for me to begin.

"Promise you won't get mad with me?" I asked.

He nodded.

I uncrossed my legs and stretched them out in front of me, then bent my knees, tugging the long skirt of my dress apprehensively down over my legs. It was only now that I fully appreciated how difficult it had been for Hugh on Friday night when I'd asked him to tell me everything. I didn't know where to start either. In the end, he rescued me.

"Baby, you know you really are the only woman I'm interested in now, don't you?"

"What do you mean?" I asked, hoping he would say something, anything to reassure me once and for all about Diana. Then I wouldn't have to ask him to do this.

He swallowed uncomfortably. "Well, I do occasionally look at a woman and think she's hot, but I … I don't have any desire to act on it. And I haven't … paid for sex since the night we were first together."

I studied his earnest expression. "Not even when you're away?" I asked. "All the times you were in Wellington?"

He shook his head and nudged my foot with his, grinning. "No. You've completely ruined me, baby." I smiled hesitantly in response. "I do still watch a bit of porn," he admitted cautiously. "Especially when I can't Skype you or ..."

"I hang up on you?" I finished, remembering my mulish behavior on Wednesday night. I lowered my eyes, feeling foolish. "I am sorry about that," I muttered.

"Don't worry about it," he said good-naturedly. "You don't mind, though?" An edge of concern returned to his voice. "About the porn? I can stop that too if you want me to."

I shook my head, giving him a wry smile. "I've been watching it, too," I confessed. "And ... reading some ... stuff." I could tell him that much at least about Willa's blog without breaking my promise to her.

Hugh raised his eyebrows and smirked. "Really?" His seductive murmur made my pulse race suddenly. "What have you been reading? Did you make yourself come?"

I hid my face in my knees, my cheeks turning pink as I recalled what I'd done after reading Willa's story about the gas station. I wondered if he'd mind. I peeked out at him through my fingers. "What you said last night about me ... expecting you to ... fuck me. Well, you're right. I do. I have been wanting ... expecting that. All the time. The thing is," I looked up at him, watching his face carefully. "Does that ...? Is that really how you feel? Am I too demanding? Do you find it a burden? Would you rather I did it myself?"

Hugh closed his eyes. A look of intense pain crossed his face and he sighed deeply. "God, you have no idea how much I regret saying that," he muttered when he met my gaze again. "I was just angry, OK? I wanted to hurt you. So bloody stupid." He shook his head. "One of the things I love most about you and I have to go and throw it in your face." He leaned forward and took my hands, pulling them onto his knees, rubbing them softly. "You are not too demanding, baby. I would happily fuck you every hour on the hour if ...." He flashed me a dreamy smile. "Piha was magic," he continued. "But it wasn't real. I mean, I have a job, responsibilities."

He was right. Piha had been magic. Even after a month, I hadn't tired of being with him day and night.

But our life in New York had been better than what we had now. At least in New York he hadn't been sent away to work in another city for weeks at a time. I lifted my head. "I really don't like you being away overnight, Hugh. I can't help thinking the whole thing with Xavier would never have happened if I hadn't been missing you so much." I sighed. "Is there any way you can ... not go, or maybe I can come with you next time?"

Hugh frowned. "They're kind of old fashioned at work about taking wives and partners on business trips. And, the more interesting cases often do involve travel. I'll try to be around more, though," he said when he saw my disappointed expression. "Maybe I can come home for a mid-week nookie break if I'm away longer than a couple of days." He squeezed my hands, giving me a sly grin. "You didn't answer my question," he reminded me.

"What question?" I asked, still dreaming about what it would be like if we could stay in Piha forever and life was one long nookie break.

"Did you make yourself come?" He licked his lips salaciously.

I couldn't help smiling as I nodded. He was totally getting off on this. "Just once," I admitted self-consciously. "But I wish it had been you. Don't get mad, but you really are a good … fuck, you know."

"Hmmm," Hugh's lips curved into a meaningful smirk and his eyes glittered. "Is that an invitation?" He brought my hands to his mouth and kissed them softly, leaving tingling smudges on my knuckles where his lips had been. I succumbed to the thrill of his touch for a few moments before forcing myself to pull my hands away.

"Almost," I murmured, returning reluctantly to our conversation. "There's something else I need to talk to you about first." Hugh raised his eyebrows briefly, inviting me to continue, although by the secret smile playing on his lips and the way he sprawled back against the sofa, making the bulge in his jeans brazenly obvious, I knew he was humoring me. He was already imagining what we were going to do once our deep and meaningful chat was over.

"The … club," I said, observing his reaction carefully. "I want you to take me there." This was the thing I had to get right. So much depended on him not only agreeing, but remaining unaware of my real reasons for wanting to go. To my dismay, his smile fell away and tension crept into his pose. "I know you said it's in the past," I continued quickly. "But this isn't about the past. It's about you and me. I feel I don't know you any more. There's a whole part of you I know nothing about. And ..." This was my trump card. "Maybe there's a whole part of me I know nothing about. When you said you think I'm ... submissive, it was a bit of a revelation. I'd never thought about it. Maybe it's something we can explore together – properly."

Hugh was silent for a moment. Then he swiveled slowly, putting both feet on the floor and resting his elbows on his knees, his chin in his hands. He took a deep breath and twisted his head to face to me. "I'm not sure that's a great idea," he said at last.

"Why not?" I pouted. "What's the worst thing that could happen?"

He sucked in another deep breath. "Xavier ... doesn't tolerate disobedience well."

"Would I have to obey him?" I had an unexpected flashback of myself standing in front of Xavier in the gallery, my hand trapped helplessly in his. A current sizzled through me, like a subliminal message, saying *'Don't Go.'*

"Yes," said Hugh soberly. "You would have to obey him."

I ignored the warning. "But you said on Friday you liked me being obedient," I cajoled.

"I said I like it when you obey *me*. Xavier's style of dominance isn't really for beginners."

"You could teach me what to do," I countered. "Then I wouldn't be a beginner."

Hugh sighed. "Is this really what you want, Georgia?"

"Yes," I said urgently. "I want to understand you. I want to make ... informed decisions about our life together. How can I do that if I don't know what it is I'm deciding about?"

Hugh swallowed audibly, misunderstanding what I meant by 'our life together'. "You're ... you're still thinking of leaving?" he asked. His voice was calm, but I saw the hurt in his eyes.

"No," I protested, desperate not to start another argument. I needed him to believe me. "I love you, Hugh, but ... everything you told me. I can't stop thinking about it. If we go there together and try it out, it really will be in the past. Or it will become part of our future. Either way, I need to know for sure."

It wasn't a complete lie. It was more an error of omission. I *was* mildly curious about the club, and about the whole dominance and submission thing. But what I really needed to know was, did Hugh still have feelings for Diana? And it was only by observing them together, without either of them being aware I was looking for signs, that I'd know for sure he was over her. Only then would I feel comfortable raising the subject of children with Hugh.

Hugh was silent for a long time, staring moodily at the doorway opposite us. "I still think it's a bad idea," he insisted. My heart sank until he added, "But I'll think about it." He got up distractedly. "I'll just go take a shower, OK?"

I stared bleakly after him. Maybe he did have my interests at heart when he said he didn't want to go to the club. Maybe he really did think Xavier was a danger to me. Or maybe I was right. Maybe he didn't want me to see him with Diana. Either way, I was more determined than ever to convince him when he came out of the shower. I was perfectly capable of making my own decisions about Xavier Bishop.

I flopped over to lie on my back, idly flapping my dress against my legs to cool off. I wondered whether I should take Hugh up on the offer he'd made earlier. It was Sunday evening, and we'd wasted most of our weekend in pointless arguments and foolish sulking. I was desperate for his touch. To my annoyance, though, every time I tried to picture him coming out of the shower, dropping his towel and sliding on top of me, Xavier Bishop's wolfish grin appeared before my closed eyes.

Twenty-Nine

When Hugh came back into the bedroom, I was relieved to see his mood had lifted and the sparkle had returned to his eyes. He sat beside me and ran his hands seductively up my shins, pushing my dress up with them. A faint, delicious whiff of citrus emanated from his damp, silky chest He kissed my bare knees and leaned forward to whisper in my ear. "Do you want to try something?"

"Like what?" I sat up, my senses instantly on high alert.

"You'll see," he grinned wickedly. Tugging my hands, he sat me up in the middle of the sofa and pushed my knees up under my chin. Then, to my disappointment, he pulled the hem of my dress down over my legs, leaving only my frosty blue toenails peeping out.

"What are you doing?" I asked. I'd expected him to be pulling my clothing off, not putting it back on again.

"Submission 101," he informed me casually as he stood back to admire me.

I gulped, my eyes wide. I hugged my arms defensively around my legs. "What?" I asked in a panic, thinking of the bound and gagged women in the dreams I'd had about Xavier. I searched his hands for ropes, whips, chains, handcuffs, relaxing only slightly when I saw they were empty.

Hugh raised an eyebrow. "I thought you wanted to try it out?" he challenged. Then without waiting for me to respond, he gently unwrapped my arms and laid them along the back of the sofa. "Now," he murmured, leaning over me, his palms resting just below each of my wrists, his fingers gripping them. "All you have to do is keep your hands up here. No touching – me or yourself – you just have to keep your hands here until I give you permission to move them."

"You're not going to ... tie me up?" I asked, confused.

"Not unless you think it's necessary," he replied smoothly, cocking his head provocatively to one side. "Do you?"

"Um, what are you going to do to me?" I asked. Images of Xavier brandishing a whip sprang to mind. In which case it would definitely be necessary to tie me up, I decided.

"I won't hurt you, if that's what you're worried about," he smiled with the air of a stranger offering sweets to a child. "But as to what I *am* going to do – the whole point of submission is trust. Either you do," he traced a line from my wrists to my neck with his fingers. He wrapped his hands loosely around my throat and kissed me lightly on the lips, increasing the pressure of his grip ever so briefly before lifting his hands away from me with a flourish. "Or you don't. Trust me. Which is it, baby?" He took a step back and folded his arms, daring me to accept his challenge.

I touched my neck where his hands had been. His eyes shone with anticipation and his lips were curved in a sultry, predatory grin that reminded me dangerously of Xavier Bishop. I shivered. Could I trust him? After everything he'd told me, I didn't know any more. But I wanted to. I wanted him to think I did, too. And not only because I wanted him to take me to the club. "I do," I whispered, a chill of anxiety trickling down my spine.

"Good," he murmured approvingly, reminding me again of Xavier. "Veery good." A rush of hot, liquid desire bubbled between my legs, transforming the chill into a warm, heavy syrup that pooled low in my abdomen as he sat on the floor in front of me.

It seemed odd, to be sitting on the sofa with Hugh on the floor below me when I was supposed to be being the submissive one. But he wouldn't enter into any discussion with me about it – he just reiterated his first requirement – I was not to move my hands off the back of the sofa without permission – and added a second – I was not to speak unless spoken to.

He started by softly kissing my exposed toes. With his tongue, he gently explored the gaps between each one before sucking them greedily two or three at a time. I sighed blissfully. I could feel the syrup spreading from my belly down my thighs, making my knees suddenly weak, fluid. So far, being submissive seemed very easy and pleasant.

When Hugh had thoroughly explored both my feet with his mouth, he casually undid the lowest button on my dress. Watching my face intently, he ran his hand up my foot and around my ankle, gently rubbing the flesh that had been newly revealed by his action. Then he traced the movement of his hand with his lips and tongue, sending a volley of unexpected charges in the direction of my heart. "Oh!" I gasped.

"What's that, Baby G? Did you say something?" Hugh murmured, undoing the next button.

"No," I breathed remembering my promise to be silent.

"Good," he said, adjusting my dress to see more of my legs, then pausing to admire his new arrangement. As before, I felt him exploring the freshly exposed area of skin with his hands, quickly followed by his mouth. Then, as he moved up my legs, his naked torso grazed the previously kissed areas like a thousand silken butterfly wings gently fluttering against me. Before he'd undone half the buttons, I was shaking involuntarily. I ached to touch him, but I kept my hands where he had put them along the back of the sofa.

"Aaah," he exclaimed in whispered joy as he reached the button that allowed him a first glimpse of my pink floral hipster briefs. He ran both hands excruciatingly slowly up my shins to my knees. Swiftly, he pushed them apart, spreading me wide open. For such an aggressive move, it was surprisingly gentle, for he met no resistance. He pressed his face against the damp cotton of my underwear, inhaling deeply. I trembled and felt him tremble too. He stayed there a long time before he returned to his original task. From then on, after he popped each button open and explored the newly exposed portion of my legs, he returned his mouth to my panties, gently biting me through them, pulling at the lace edges with his teeth, slipping his tongue fleetingly under the edge to taste the sweetness seeping from me. Tiny tremors buzzed through me every time I felt his mouth seeking, then finding, its desired object.

When Hugh ran his hand up to undo the top button of my dress, I unconsciously reached down to stroke his hair. Without thinking, I pulled my hand against the back of his head, trying to increase the pressure of his mouth on the spot that throbbed so deliciously under his touch. I realized my mistake immediately when he tensed and pulled away from me. Leaving the final button in place, he came to sit beside me on the couch, gently returning my arm to the back of it. "Disobedience," he murmured, "will be punished by the withdrawal of favors."

Rather than returning to the floor, he stayed sitting beside me. With the lightest touch of just one finger, he traced a line from my hand to my shoulder, then from my shoulder to my collarbone before heading down in a straight line as if towards my nipple. But his fingers turned at the last moment to connect the line to the shallow groove between my breasts, where the button sat. He stroked the area thoughtfully, letting his fingers drift just under the button, toying with it as if unable to decide whether he should open it.

"Hugh ... please ..." I blurted out. I was desperate for more contact – aching for him to return to his position on the floor, to nestle his head between my legs again, to take my breast in his hand, suck me, kiss me – anything but this slow, teasing, torment.

Hugh raised his eyebrows and frowned. He lifted his hand away from me. "Georgia," he purred. "You've already broken both of the agreements you made with me. Now tell me, are you going to be obedient or do we need to stop ...?" His hand hovered tantalizingly close –

so close I could feel its warmth pulling at the pulse between my breasts.

"No," I gasped, gripping the back of the sofa, knuckles white in an effort to keep from ripping the dress open myself and pushing his head down to connect his mouth with my shivering nipples. "I'll ... obey."

He smiled languidly at me and slowly, so slowly, crossed his tracing finger to the other side of my body and back up to the opposite shoulder, challenging me to disobey him again. When I didn't, he rewarded me by dropping soft, tiny kisses on the square of skin between the top of my dress and my neck, allowing his hand to drift across my bare abdomen as he did so.

I shut my eyes, stifling a moan as Hugh continued the trail of kisses up my neck to my ear. When his mouth was close enough, he murmured, "That's better. Now tell me. How does this feel ...?" He slid his hand down inside the front of my briefs and his fingers made fleeting contact with my aching clitoris as he dipped them in me. My eyes flew open and I gasped as my entire body jolted against him. He removed his hand immediately and studied his wet fingertips, then looked quizzically at me as if he was genuinely curious as to how they got that way. His eyes never left mine as he put his fingers in his mouth and sucked them, then licked his lips appreciatively. "Hmm?" He reminded me he was still waiting for my answer.

"G-good," I stammered, suddenly finding it difficult to breathe, let alone speak.

"Would you like me to touch you there again?" he enquired conversationally.

"Y-yes ... please," I gulped.

"And would you like me to use my fingers or my tongue?"

I blushed. Hugh knew I was shy about asking for certain things. And I was also pretty sure he already knew what I wanted. "T-tongue," I whispered, only just managing to cling to the back of the sofa.

"Excellent choice, Madam," he smirked as he returned to his position on the floor. He closed my legs for a moment so he could remove my panties, then spread them apart again.

He rested his cheek lightly against one thigh, gazing intently up at me. He trickled his hand delicately up the inside of the other leg until his fingers again brushed against my tiny throbbing bud. I convulsed in shock and pleasure. Hugh smiled lazily, almost to himself, as he observed this. He repeated the move several more times as if to confirm its effect before nuzzling right into the apex of my thighs and tasting me. At first he continued to watch my reaction as he flicked his tongue lightly between my swollen labia – teasing, waiting for me to lift a hand off the sofa. When I didn't, he sighed in mock disappointment. Then he licked his lips lasciviously and gave himself over completely to our mutual pleasure, closing his eyes blissfully and sucking my pulsing mound as if he were sucking the juice from a late summer peach.

After a few minutes I felt his fingers enter me, pressing faintly, then more insistently up against my most sensitive spot. "God, Hugh," I muttered, so quietly I thought he wouldn't hear me. To my consternation, he released the pressure of his fingers, paused and looked up at me as he spoke.

"What is it, baby? Do you want me to stop?" There was a provocative glint in his eyes.

"No ..." I groaned, then "Oh ..." The second was a more of a guttural moan of relief than a formed word as he took pity on me and continued, beating an increasingly rapid tattoo with his fingers in perfect time with his tongue on my clitoris, which felt like it was about to burst. "Oh …" I cried again, and again he stopped.

"Did you say Stop?" His eyes were a deep, crystal blue. His fingers were poised, maintaining an agonizingly sweet pressure on my G spot. I could feel his breath against my throbbing button.

"No. Don't. Stop," I cried, squirming against his hand, my blood on fire.

He lapped once, twice – slowly – and nudged his fingers equally idly inside me. He was holding me right on the edge and he knew it. "Are you sure you don't want me to stop?" he whispered in delight, continuing to torment me.

"God. No," I gulped, finally releasing the back of the couch and bringing both hands around to grip his head. "Don't. Stop," I panted when he paused again, realizing what I had done. "Please," I begged, staring at him with wide, pleading eyes.

For a moment I thought he was going to stand up and walk away, so I almost cried when he not only resumed the pace of his thrumming, but increased it. He didn't even push my hand away – he thrust his fingers deeply into me, allowing me to dictate the exact pressure of his mouth on me by pulling his head against my burning center. The room started spinning and everything turned black for a second before my eyes filled with stars. I convulsed for what seemed an eternity, writhing against his hand and his mouth until my entire body exploded in a scorching rush, completely oblivious to the fact that I was nearly suffocating Hugh with my fierce grip.

When I recovered my senses what seemed like hours later, Hugh was still gently probing me with his fingers and nuzzling my vulva, casually flicking his tongue out every now and then to deliver another delightful aftershock to my melted limbs. With a great effort, I managed to make the hand that floated on the end of my rubbery arm curl itself around his head and stroke his soft, damp hair. "Mmmm." I had intended to say something more articulate, but that was the only sound I seemed yet capable of making.

"Mmmm, indeed." Hugh looked up at me, his eyes glazed, his chin glistening with my juices. "Delicious, but hardly obedient," he remarked pointedly, running his tongue along my warm wet slit, sucking up the taste and smell of my nectar.

"It … wasn't what I was expecting," I confessed, suddenly ashamed at how easily I had lost control.

"What were you expecting, baby?" he asked. Hugh pulled me off the couch and into his lap, nibbling my earlobe as he spoke. I could smell my own sweet, salty scent on his face.

I shrugged, feeling foolish and naive. "I guess I thought you were going to ... whip me or ... tie me up or something."

Hugh looked serious. "That can happen, too," he said, and I knew he was talking about the club.

"Show me," I whispered.

He didn't answer. He just held my gaze with eyes that glittered like sapphires – I wasn't sure whether from anger or arousal. He fiddled with the last button on my dress as if trying to decide what to do – or whether to do anything at all. Then he slipped it undone and slid the dress off my shoulders. He twisted it around my arms, pinning them temporarily behind me. I could feel his erection pressing insistently against me as he pulled my buttocks towards him and leaned forward to suck deeply on my taut, tender nipples. I arched back against the couch, delivering myself up to him, drunk with the pleasure of his touch. Once again, at that moment, I thought submission seemed pleasant and easy.

But then, still pinning my arms behind my back with my dress, Hugh got to his feet and in one swift move carried me over to the bed. He pushed me onto it face down and spread himself on top of me. Most of his weight was distributed on his knees and elbows, yet he felt heavy, powerful, easily capable of crushing me. He wrapped his hand around my hair and tugged it hard, forcing me to twist my neck at an awkward angle to look at him.

"How about this, baby?" he muttered, all at once savage. "Is this more what you had in mind?" His cock pulsed thick and heavy between my buttocks and his mouth was hot on my ear. "Or what about licking a woman's pussy …? Fingering her ….? Letting her finger you …? Being spanked until your ass is bright red and throbbing …? Having your body criss-crossed with whip lines …? Sucking another man's cock…? Letting him fuck you…? Being bound and gagged and blindfolded …? Knowing that five, six, seven men are lining up to fuck you…? What about doing that with 20 people watching…?" Each time he spoke, he pulled my hair a little harder and lowered himself more heavily onto me.

"Stop!" I cried, my panic muffled by the bedding as I tried to struggle free. My hands fluttered uselessly against his stomach and I could hardly breathe. To my immense relief, Hugh slid off me and rolled onto his side. I turned to look at him, gasping, trying ineffectively to disentangle myself from the dress. "Is that what you want?" I whispered, shocked not only by what he had said, but the menace with which he'd said it; the feeling that I was, truly, utterly at his mercy. He could have killed me if he'd wanted to.

"It won't be up to me, baby," he replied, still grave, but gentle again. He edged closer and put an arm around me, helping me to untwist the dress and free my hands. "It's Xavier's playground. If you want to go, you have to play by his rules."

"Would he really ... do all that?"

"I've seen him tease people for hours without letting them come. I've seen someone come for hours under his control. I've seen every variation and extreme of pleasure and pain there – everything I just told you and more." He flung my dress onto the floor and returned his arm to my waist, stroking the small of my back and my hip.

"But there must be ... I don't know ... an out?" I said. I was suddenly grateful to Hugh for not prolonging the sweet torture he'd subjected me to earlier, even though I had disobeyed him. "If you don't like what's going on?"

Hugh nodded. "There is. There are safe words you can use if you're involved in something and you want it to stop. But they're used very rarely. People go there with the expectation of having their boundaries pushed. It would be a bit pointless if everyone piked out the minute that happened."

"Is that why you think we shouldn't go? Do you think I'll pike out?"

He studied my face, running his hand absently around my buttocks. "I don't know what you'll do, Georgia. To tell you the truth, I haven't given it a lot of thought. I mean, if there are things you want to explore at home, I'm happy to do that." He flashed me a sly, sexy smile and squeezed my butt cheek. "I don't mind tying you up, for example. And what we did before was ... well, I liked that." He looked uncertain. "But other stuff, well, obviously some of it requires other people. And I'm not sure I'd want to do anything that would hurt you – spanking, whipping, that kind of thing." He took a deep breath, as if the thought of even watching 'that kind of thing' made him feel ill. "So if that's what you're interested in, then we'll have to go to the club."

Hugh's hand was warm on my behind, but I felt cold. He believed my reasons for wanting to go. He trusted me. Why couldn't I just trust him? Why did I need to subject the two of us to every variation and extreme of pleasure and pain, just to prove a point? What if my plan backfired?

I'm not sure whether Hugh interpreted my silence as stubborn insistence on having my way or shy reluctance to disclose what I was really 'interested in', but when I didn't answer straight away, he sighed. "OK baby. I'll talk to Xavier," he said, kissing my forehead and pulling me close.

The silk of his chest brushed seductively against my bare breasts. Instinctively, I sought his lips. His cock pulsed between us and I writhed against it, coaxing it to further attention. It was done. I couldn't back out. All I needed to ask him now was ...

"Fuck me," I whispered.

Hugh groaned, rolling onto his back, pulling me with him. His erection pressed into my mound, deliciously familiar. I ground against it, then lifted my hips for a second to let it slip into the groove between my thighs. Whimpering in anticipation, I slid up and down, coating his shaft with my own sweet glaze before I ...

"Georgia," panted Hugh, his voice rough and uneven. He grabbed my buttocks, stilling me, preventing me from completing the move. "Baby, there's something else I need to tell you."

"Shhh," I whispered, putting a finger to his lips. "You're right, honey. What's past is past. Let's make this about now." I twisted my hips out of his grasp and sank onto him, all thoughts driven from my mind as his full length filled my hot, slick core.

The BUTTERFLY Series

Georgia's story unfolds over the course of four novels – this is Book 1 of the series.

To receive a notification when the next book in the BUTTERFLY series is released:

Subscribe to new release emails for Violet Gregory on Amazon.com

Like **Violet Gregory Author** on Facebook

Visit www.violetgregory.com and subscribe to the news group

If you enjoyed this book, please leave stars and tell other readers what you love about BUTTERFLY in a review on Amazon or Goodreads.

For more information and books by Violet Gregory, visit www.violetgregory.com